Daughter of the Stars

Books by Phyllis A. Whitney

DAUGHTER OF THE STARS
STAR FLIGHT
THE EBONY SWAN
WOMAN WITHOUT A PAST
THE SINGING STONES
RAINBOW IN THE MIST
FEATHER ON THE MOON
SILVERSWORD
FLAMING TREE
DREAM OF ORCHIDS
RAINSONG
EMERALD
VERMILION
POINCIANA
DOMINO
THE GLASS FLAME
THE STONE BULL
THE GOLDEN UNICORN
SPINDRIFT
THE TURQUOISE MASK
SNOWFIRE
LISTEN FOR THE WHISPERER
LOST ISLAND
THE WINTER PEOPLE
HUNTER'S GREEN
SILVERHILL
COLUMBELLA
SEA JADE
BLACK AMBER
SEVEN TEARS FOR APOLLO
WINDOW ON THE SQUARE
BLUE FIRE
THUNDER HEIGHTS
THE MOONFLOWER
SKYE CAMERON
THE TREMBLING HILLS
THE QUICKSILVER POOL
THE RED CARNELIAN

Daughter of the Stars

PHYLLIS A. WHITNEY

CROWN PUBLISHERS, INC.
NEW YORK

For Georgia,
my daughter, my best friend,
always my first editor.

Through the gloom of the night, Sunday, October 16, 1859, a small band of men tramped silently behind a horse-drawn wagon down a winding Maryland road leading to Harper's Ferry, Virginia.

From the shoulder of each man hung loosely a Sharps rifle, hidden by long gray shawls that protected the ghostly figures against the chilling air of approaching winter. A slight drizzle of rain veiled the towering Blue Ridge Mountains with an eerie mist. Not a sound broke the stillness, save the tramping feet and the creaking wagon.

—From *John Brown's Raid,*
based on National Park Service reports
by William C. Everhart and Arthur L. Sullivan

Foreword

BEFORE I FINISH work on a current novel, I am alert for the setting and opening situation for my next book. However, with my novel *Star Flight* winding toward its climactic scene, I had no idea where to turn next. These days I limit myself to settings that are not too far away from where I live, so I don't have the whole country to choose from. By chance, Madeline Delgado, a friend of my daughter, suggested Harpers Ferry, which is only a two-hour drive away. I wasn't especially interested. To me, Harpers Ferry was only a dot on a map made famous by John Brown, and his story had already been told many times. But Madeline's enthusiasm for the beauty of the place (apparently shared by Thomas Jefferson) caught my attention. So we set up the trip and my daughter drove me north through the Shenandoah Valley.

The redbuds and dogwood were in bright bloom, though they had already had their day in Charlottesville. The anticipation of a new "adventure" was strong, and I wasn't disappointed. Before I had spent an hour in Harpers Ferry, I knew how much I had to learn about John Brown, and how exciting the details of his story are in the place where it all happened. I explored the small area—unlike any setting I had written about—and came home with armloads of books, maps, and pictures. I still had no idea where any of this was going to take me, but then something happened that has never happened to me before.

I dreamed the opening for *Daughter of the Stars.* The details were vivid and the dream stayed with me. I had no idea what the strange scene in the dream meant, but I knew it would be central to my story. I've written this into my opening paragraphs under the heading of "History." The novel takes place more than a hundred years later.

As always, strangers who became friends helped me find my way. Linda Rago was in charge of the Historical Society's bookstore on the day when we walked in from Shenandoah Street. She filled a shopping bag for me with books and pamphlets, maps and pictures; she invited us to visit her beautiful house, which had survived the fighting and still stands as it has since before the Civil War. Linda's delightful book, *Dooryard Herbs,* gave me the inspiration for the herb garden in the story.

It was Linda who arranged for us to visit Philip Stryker and Pierre Dostert in their remarkable, early-twentieth-century house.

Thank you, Phil and Pierre, for your hospitality and interest, and for not minding when I gave away your house to a character in my novel.

Nancy Manuel, Director of the Bolivar–Harpers Ferry Public Library, became a constant source of information after I came home and began to find out how much I didn't know. She even talked to the Park Rangers for me, and walked about Virginius Island to find answers to my questions. I wish I could have used that charming library for a scene, but this didn't work out. The town of Bolivar received its new name (it had been called Mudfort) about fifty years after the American Revolution. Simon Bolívar was popular in America and the press called him the George Washington of South America. This was the first town in the United States to be named Bolivar, and a handsome bust of the hero stands outside the library.

I want to thank Paul R. Lee II for his lively and informative guide to Virginius Island. When he wrote of the legend of the Shenandoah, he gave me the title for my book.

My special thanks to Megaly N. Green for her enthusiastic welcome when we walked into the Interpretative Design Building of the National Park Service. She introduced us to Nancy Haack, whose beautiful maps, drawn for the Park Service, suggested an avocation for my heroine. Megaly also sent us to the Division of Conservation, again part of the Park Service, where artifacts are expertly repaired for Park displays all over the country. There I discovered an old Civil War drum—which, of course, really belongs to a character in my story.

Every visitor to Harpers Ferry is impressed by the work done by the National Park Service in preserving and presenting the treasures of Harpers Ferry. While I strive to be historically and geographically accurate, I would like to add my apologies for any liberties I may have taken as a fiction writer.

In my memory I can still smell the exotic scents of the Herb Lady's enchanting shop. I have borrowed it for my story.

A good editor is priceless. I have found such an editor in Shaye Areheart. Long ago I learned to listen and my gratitude runs deep.

Daughter of
the Stars

HISTORY

THE TWO MEN in Union blue stood back to back in pale, early-dawn light. A thin mist floated around them, mingling with smoke rising from rifles recently fired.

The old man was tall and thin, almost to the point of emaciation. His face wore an inner glow of exaltation because of what he had just accomplished. The younger man, his son, seemed undistinguished in appearance, with the blank, uncomprehending expression of an ordinary man who had committed an extraordinary deed. True, he had killed before in battle. Even in hand-to-hand fighting. But this had been an execution.

Beyond the aura of thinning mist and the more quickly dissipated gunsmoke lay the bodies of the three men they had slain. The dead men also wore blue.

Morning scents rose fresh and sweet around the living, contrasting sharply with the scene of death. Just after midnight a storm had thundered through the Gap where two great rivers met and became one, and the younger man breathed deeply of rain-swept air, trying to steady himself. Once more he longed for the peace and safety of his boyhood and an end to all the killing.

Early-dawn stillness waited for the sun. The town that lay along the tongue of the peninsula below these heights had hardly stirred in its sleep, too long accustomed to the sounds of gunfire to give heed.

Easing his rifle into the crook of an arm, the old man walked across stubbled grass, where tents had been pitched only a week or so before. Now the fields lay empty, except for three sprawled bodies.

"It is done. Finished," the old man said. He went to check for himself, to make sure that no life remained. His son watched bleakly, and when his father was satisfied, the two set off to rejoin their regiment.

But it was not done. It was not finished. The ending still lay far in the future. The reverberations of what had transpired here would echo through time to touch a generation that would not be born for a hundred years.

One of the fallen men regained consciousness and moaned in pain. A small boy of ten, hidden behind the trunk of an oak tree, came fearfully into the open. For a moment he bent over the wounded man, and then ran down a path that cut steeply toward the town and the place where the rivers met. There in Harper's Ferry he could find help.

WEST VIRGINIA —
THE PRESENT

THE WOMAN sat near the herb garden she loved to tend. A nearby redbud tree, about to burst into spring color, shaded her from the morning sun. On her crossed knees rested a notepad upon which her pen moved slowly, her fingers uncertain.

It was hard to write to a niece whom she had once loved so dearly and had not seen in thirty years—through no fault of her own. She'd loved the little girl, too—her niece's child, Lacey, who was now a grown woman. Perhaps it had been right for Amelia to take away the child after the terrible events that had disrupted all their lives.

Now everything had changed and she could not deal with this new fear and worry. She set down the words in a hand that wavered a little, and when she had finished, she read the letter aloud to herself.

Dear Amelia:
   This morning I have been remembering the time when your mother died so tragically. You were twenty-nine and I was your very young aunt. I loved you and I know you loved me. I have always been sad that everything changed when you married.
   Poor Ida. Your mother was always fearful. Perhaps her own nature helped to create what happened. When you

took your little daughter and left us after Ida's death, we all had a hard time dealing with the aftermath. Lacey was only four, so she couldn't have understood much of what happened.

I don't write these words reproachfully. I understood that you did what you thought was best. Perhaps Lacey has been able to grow up without these horrors of the past affecting her life.

But now, Amelia, it is time for you to come home. *He* has returned to town and I am frightened. Why should he return after all these years? What does he want?

I can remember when you were the strong one who stood up to him. Come back to us, Amelia. I am feeling old and I have no courage left. There is no one here I can turn to.

She signed the letter "Aunt Vinnie," the name by which Amelia had called her in the long-ago time before the dying began.

★
ONE

WHEN I PICKED up the mail at the post office, I found one first-class envelope in with the usual junk. It was addressed to my mother, and I drove home in an unsettled frame of mind.

I recognized the neat handwriting; I had seen it every year of my life, though only at Christmas. That a letter from this person should arrive in April seemed to indicate an urgency my mother might not be able to deal with in her present condition.

The postmark had always been Washington, D.C., with no return address—impossible to trace. There was still no address in the upper left corner, but this time the postmark was Harpers Ferry, West Virginia. Somehow this hinted at urgency too.

When I reached the porch steps of our house, I could hear a voice from an upstairs window. Mother's nurse was reading aloud to her. I caught familiar phrases from *A Tale of Two Cities,* an old favorite.

My mother's bout with breast cancer had frightened me, though her doctors were pleased with her recovery from the operation, and the future seemed hopeful. If only she would make more of an effort to get well. She was listless about therapy, listless about everything.

Now this letter had come and I was faced with a dilemma. What if its contents were so upsetting that they caused a setback in her condition? On the other hand, I could never open it without her permission. She had a right to her secrets, though as I grew up I'd become increasingly resentful of them. I'd never been able to convince her that all the things she held back also concerned me.

I climbed steps to the porch and sat down in the old swing that dated from my childhood. From here I could look out toward the distant mountains that rimmed Charlottesville. I had grown up here, and I had an affection for this lovely old Virginia city, with its winding, tree-shaded streets and abundant flowers.

With April's arrival, banks of azaleas were just coming into full bloom. I could hear the muffled sounds of traffic from arteries that snaked across the valley floor, but our house had always seemed remote from city life. I couldn't see Monticello from here, but I'd grown up with Virginia history as part of my life, even though I'd never been sure whether or not I was Virginia-born.

Down there in the older part of town stood the buildings of Thomas Jefferson's university, forever lending a special distinction to Charlottesville. I'd gone to school in this city, and my memories were both pleasant and disturbing. I'd liked my studies and done well in them, but even as a child I'd recognized that my mother and I were not like other families. Other girls had fathers as well as mothers. Or at least they knew something about their fathers. Most had grandmothers and grandfathers, some kind of extended family. I had only my mother and no explanation for our lack of family in a part of the country where family ties mattered greatly. It held me back from making close friends.

Even my name, Lacey, had set its mark on me. It seemed old-fashioned and different—as *I* was forced to be different.

I knew only that I was named after a grandmother whom my mother had loved. So this, at least, was a slim tie with the past.

My mother believed, however mistakenly, that she was protecting me. But from what? Her refusal to tell me anything had set me apart. My few "romances" had never worked out. Men didn't like that sort of mystery in the women they dated. It hinted of some scandal that had to be concealed. I was always on guard, holding back my inner feelings, lest I be hurt. So of course I was hurt all the more, and had learned that it was safer to give myself to my work.

My mother had always encouraged me to develop my own talents, and I had created a one-woman business that partly supported us. My mother received a check once a year in a Christmas letter—though she banked it herself, and I had no idea who signed it, or what the amount might be. When we needed cash to buy a car, or some other expensive item, the money would be there. Otherwise, we lived comfortably on my earnings from the brochures I designed and illustrated for various merchants around the city. I no longer had to look for work. My reputation was such that clients came to me. My main interest at the moment, however, lay in a special sort of book I'd created for children.

"Place books" I called them, and so far two had been published and were well received. My editor liked my presentation of some special setting with drawings, photographs, and a text that touched on the area's local history. For these books I developed imaginative, illustrated maps that took young readers on a journey through each place I wrote about. This side of my life was very satisfying, but I always knew that it wasn't enough. Now perhaps this out-of-order letter could open some door, offer some knowledge of my mother and myself that I needed.

Each year when the Christmas letter came, Mother would take it to her bedroom and close the door. Some time later, when she came out, I would catch the odor of burnt paper and know that the letter had been destroyed immediately. I would see that she'd been crying and that her mouth was set in a straight line that warned me not to ask questions. I had no idea whether she ever answered the writer. Her pain was so great, so obvious, that I could not bring myself to question her.

Since my mother used the name Amelia Elliot, and refused
to talk about my father, I might never have known his first
name if these annual envelopes had not been addressed to
"Mrs. Bradley Elliot." But that was the extent of my information. Sometimes I'd wondered if my father had committed
some crime so terrible that my mother had taken me and run
away, perhaps fearing for her life. But *someone* knew where we
were—the writer of the letters.

The fact that I was in my early thirties and regarded myself
as sensibly mature meant nothing to my mother, who still
thought of me as her young daughter. The bond between us
was strong, but it was completely limiting for me. Whatever
this letter contained, I must use it to gain my own freedom.
The freedom to know who I was.

I went upstairs to her room and stood in the doorway. She
sat listlessly in a wheelchair she didn't really need. Her heart
and interest were not in getting well. Perhaps she'd invited her
own illness. When I was small I'd counted on her quiet inner
strength. Now I was the stronger one, and she could not take
this letter and run away with it.

I watched her for a moment before she saw me. Even with
her present pallor, she was still a beautiful woman. I'd often
wished I looked more like her. My hair was a dark chestnut—
not brown, not quite red—while hers was a lovely light brown
that was just beginning to gray. Once I'd asked if my father's
hair had been red, but the question had so upset her that it had
caused her to drop a steaming mug of tea and I'd never asked
again.

I would often stare in the mirror, desperate for clues as I was
growing up. I didn't like my own features. They added up to
what an artist acquaintance had damned with the word "interesting." I was larger of bone than my mother, and taller. Now
her look of fragility made me dread what I must do. I hid the
envelope behind my back as I bent to kiss her cheek, my
feeling of love for her so strong that it choked me. She was all
I had. There had always been only the two of us.

She read my hesitation quickly. "What is it, Lacey? What's happened?"

I glanced at Mrs. Brewster, her nurse. She understood and put aside her book. "Call me when you want me," she said, and gave me a slight frown of warning as she went out the door. It was a look that indicated that this had been a bad day, and I felt all the more anxious about what I must do.

I drew a chair close to my mother's and plunged in. "A letter came for you this morning."

She looked at the familiar blue envelope I held out, and seemed to shrivel. "Take it away! I'm not up to whatever she wants." A grayish look tinged her pallor and her hand trembled as she waved the letter aside.

I tried to will some of my own strength into her. "Do you want me to open it?"

I could see the conflict of emotions in her face. The old habit of secrecy was so long ingrained that it was hard for her to let it go.

"Let me help you," I said. "This time there's a different postmark—Harpers Ferry. The pattern of writing at Christmastime has never been broken before, so something must have happened. Let me help you deal with this. Whatever it means, I should know about it."

I suppose that a time comes in every mother-daughter relationship when the old pattern of child leaning on parent is reversed. Perhaps there was even a touch of relief as she laid her hands limply in her lap in a gesture of surrender.

"Open it, Lacey. Read it to me."

I slit the flap with my forefinger and drew out the handwritten sheets. For an instant I wondered if I should read the letter first and perhaps edit. But there was no time, and I read the words aloud steadily, even though they sent a twinge of alarm through me. At least I had a relative—a woman who signed herself "Aunt Vinnie." Her plea was for my mother to come "home" to Harpers Ferry, and she was someone who had loved me when I was little.

My mother covered her face with her hands as I began to read, and I heard her wail of distress.

"I can't go! I'm too sick. Vinnie doesn't know what she's asking. After what happened I never want to go back there."

"Of course she doesn't understand," I said. "She has no idea of what you've just been through. If she's your aunt, where does she fit into the family tree? Who is Vinnie?"

Her answer was so faint that I could hardly hear her. "Lavinia Griffin is my aunt and your great-aunt. She is your grandfather's sister."

"Is the man she mentions having seen my father?"

Her eyes widened as though she couldn't believe I'd asked this. "No, of course not! Your father is dead."

"You've never told me that," I reminded her, my voice filled with old resentment. We stared at each other for a long moment. "How did he die?"

Something in her seemed to steady for the moment, as though the letter had broken through her barrier of defense, reaching into some inner reserve that had once made her strong.

"He was murdered," she told me. "Though no one was ever punished and his murderer was never caught."

Her words stunned me and I could say nothing at all. As I was growing up, I'd often created fantasies about my father—about meeting him and filling in all those empty spaces in my life with the love and friendship that would grow between us. Then the past would no longer matter. My mother's words had wiped away these imaginings, and substituted two terrible words: "murder" and "murderer." Robbed of this dream, I felt unreasonably angry.

"How could you? How could you let me believe he was alive all these years?"

Her face seemed to crumple; it was as though she grew older as I watched. "I'm so sorry, Lacey. In the beginning I only wanted to protect you. I wanted to hold all the terrible things that had happened away, so they wouldn't scar your life. He wasn't a good man, your father." I could hear the love for me in her voice, but now I could think only of myself.

"Not knowing has scarred me in ways that you aren't even aware of. The letter says that my grandmother died tragically. I don't know about her death, either. It's time to fill me in on my family history."

Strength drained away, leaving her weak and sick and hopeless. At once I blamed myself. She must have suffered a great deal. She needn't have suffered in silence, but I couldn't blame her for that now. She had done what seemed wise at the time.

I put my arm around her painfully thin shoulders. "Never mind. I'm sorry. We can talk another time when you're feeling stronger. Shall I write and tell this woman how ill you've been, and that there's no way you can help her?"

She closed her eyes, her hands lying uselessly in her lap. Then she seemed to pull herself together and I recognized the dawning of new resolution.

"As I said, her name is Lavinia Griffin. If you really want to learn about the family I've kept from you, don't answer her letter, just go there yourself. She can fill in all the gaps I've left empty. I owe you that, but I can't manage it now myself. Help her if you can. But be careful. Harpers Ferry is bloody ground for our family—not just because of its history. If old ghosts are walking, I don't want you hurt. That's why I've kept you apart from all of that."

Her words alarmed me, yet at the same time I felt a stirring of excitement. My need to know was stronger than any vague threat. All my life I'd felt alone. Now it seemed that relatives existed, not so far away. A great-aunt who had cared about me and wrote wistfully of her affection.

"I'd like to go," I told my mother. "I *need* to go. But shouldn't you tell me what Aunt Vinnie is afraid of?"

She showed signs of weakness again. "I'm not sure. I can't explain."

"Is it the man she mentions in her letter?"

"Why would he ever return to Harpers Ferry? How can he dare to come back?"

Her sudden fierceness startled me. Although I didn't know what she was talking about, I felt uncomfortable asking her to explain. I told her again not to worry and summoned Mrs. Brewster. Then I went downstairs.

The old houses in our town had often been built with "second parlors"—perhaps the equivalent of today's family room. I'd turned the one in our house into a workroom for me. Because of my interest in maps, I kept shelves of them from all around the country. I had several maps, both old and new, of Harpers Ferry because of its connection with John Brown and its importance in the history of the South.

The location and configuration of the town were unusual, and these had obviously limited its growth. In the northeast corner of West Virginia, where that state met Maryland and Virginia, a wedge of land, wide where it began, but narrowing to a low point, separated two rivers—the Potomac and the Shenandoah. Harpers Ferry (the apostrophe had been dropped sometime in the 1940s) occupied the sharp triangle where the rivers met and flowed together through a gap in the Blue Ridge to become the Potomac. The text told me that this place had first been called The Hole, and it was here that Mr. Harper had provided his ferry.

The town itself appeared to be tiny, the lower section now designated as a National Historic Park. Residents lived outside this area on higher ground, away from flooding. That was probably where I would find Lavinia Griffin.

I might as well leave immediately, I decided. No brochures were pending that couldn't be postponed, so only my concern for my mother held me back. She was clearly torn between wanting me to go, and being mysteriously fearful of my safety.

When I went to tell her my plans, she was full of suggestions, prompted by her concern. "Perhaps it's best if you don't let Vinnie know right away that you've come. If you stay in some tourist place and say you're there to do another of your children's books, you can ask all the questions you like."

"Why shouldn't I let her know at once who I am?"

"Harpers Ferry is a small town and there's always gossip. Ask around and listen. There'll be talk about this stranger in town. Don't use your real name in the beginning. It's too well known. See what you can learn. Then, if there's anything at all that makes you uneasy, just come home."

I had no intention of coming home until I knew as much about the past that concerned me as I could possibly learn. But I didn't tell my mother this. Perhaps, when I knew enough, I could come home and allay her fears.

So it was settled, and the next morning I drove north through the Shenandoah Valley. After I'd crossed the high Blue Ridge and gone over Afton Mountain, the course of the highway lay well to the west of the river, so its broad, muddy expanse didn't come into view until I had reached my destination.

During the drive I felt increasingly elated because I was finally taking some action about my life. I wouldn't allow my mother's nebulous anxieties to become contagious. Promise was in the air, along with spring, and a feeling of anticipation, of adventure, filled me. I'd never before experienced such a sense of giddy delight in throwing off the bonds that had held me, and letting myself go.

In my optimism I hadn't the least suspicion of the events that awaited me in Harpers Ferry.

But even if I'd known, I would have gone anyway.

TWO

ALTHOUGH the drive took only two and a half hours—my mother hadn't run too far from home—it might as well have been a thousand miles, a lifetime away, and into unknown territory.

When I reached Harpers Ferry, the route I followed led me onto Washington Street along the higher road of the peninsula. As it descended into what was called, oddly enough, High Street, I began to catch the historic flavor of the town. The streets were narrow and crowded with gabled houses from the last century built wall against wall. Some were of the original brick or stone, while others had been restored. Most fronted on the sidewalk without porches. Decorous signs indicated an assortment of shops. Nothing had been allowed to clash with the old and the authentic, so that I had a sense of stepping back into history.

Last night I'd again studied old and new maps of the area, so I knew where I wanted to go first—just to gain some perspective about this unique place. When I'd found a spot where I could park, I descended on foot to Shenandoah Street, which curved around the foot of the wedge. I walked past Arsenal Square, from which the historic United States Arsenal, the object of John Brown's raid, was long gone. A bright green expanse of park occupied what had been a busy, built-up section in the last century.

A railroad trestle followed the water and I noticed that the trees along the way wore the tender greens of early spring. I'd already passed a redbud tree alive with purple-red blossoms. The season was less advanced than in Charlottesville farther south, so it was like enjoying spring twice. I walked out to what was called the Point and stood with my hands on the protective iron rail. The two wide rivers flowed on either side, the one on my left smoothly, the river on the right more turbulent, tumbling over rapids. As they flowed together and moved toward the Gap, sunlight caught the sparkle of seemingly calm water, and I breathed deeply, feeling refreshed. It was hard to believe that this peaceful place had once been "bloody ground," or that these quiet rivers could rampage over the land, destroying everything man had built—as I'd read that they'd done several times in the past.

Last night I'd managed to do a little cramming about Harpers Ferry, so I knew some of its geography and history. On my left a footbridge ran beside railroad tracks, before crossing to the Maryland side. Steep, rocky cliffs rose to the heights above—Maryland Heights. One colorful account had told me that the Confederates had once held that high ground, overlooking a Federal garrison at Harpers Ferry far below. Surrounded on all sides and occupying an exposed space, the garrison had surrendered and Stonewall Jackson had made the largest single capture of Union troops of the entire war.

Across the water on my right rose the somewhat less precipitous Loudoun Heights in Virginia. Where I stood was, of course, West Virginia.

A voice spoke, startling me. "I like the way Thomas Jefferson phrased it," the man said, coming to stand near me at the rail. " 'On the right comes up the Shenandoah . . .' "

And indeed it did, pouring like shining white lace over rocks that broke the surface.

He was looking at me in a friendly way and, as I never minded talking to strangers, I smiled. A little taller than I, he seemed rather thin, with short brown hair that curled tightly and showed a glint of gold in sunlight. His eyes reminded me of the rivers—a lively blue-gray, with a spark in their depths. His manner was easy and matter-of-fact, so I answered him readily. "I've always liked the name Shenandoah best. There's a rolling sound to the syllables. So why is it that when the rivers merge they both become the Potomac?"

He looked ahead of us, toward the Gap, where a bridge now crossed from shore to shore. "The story goes that the Potomac was a mighty warrior and the Shenandoah a feisty maiden who could be dangerously tempestuous at times. There was a union when the two met, and she took her husband's name when they became one—as the custom had always been."

I liked his easy manner, and I welcomed a chance to talk to someone who knew Harpers Ferry. "Do you know what 'Shenandoah' means?"

"There are various claims about where the name comes from, but I like the legend best—that it's an Indian word which translates as Daughter of the Stars."

"Daughter of the Stars." I repeated the words aloud, savoring their sound. "That's beautiful. Are you a historian?"

"In a way. I'm Ryan Pearce and I teach history at Shepherd College. I'm on sabbatical now, doing a book about Jefferson County—this county. A pretty rich historical brew from the beginning, I can tell you."

"Including John Brown, I suppose?"

"He's certainly an important part of it. Harpers Ferry is famous because of him. The torch old John Brown lighted probably helped to spark the Civil War two years before Fort Sumter." He held out his hand. "Tell me your name."

I hesitated, because I knew that once I'd told him my real name, my identity would be known and I could not do as my mother had advised.

"I'm Lacey Dennis," I said, using a surname I'd picked out of the phone book before I left Charlottesville. "I'm here to collect material for a children's book."

His handclasp was strong, but brief, presuming nothing.

"Lacey is an uncommon name these days. Do you know that there's a distinguished lady in this town who has the same first name—Lacey Enright?"

I looked down at the waters mingling beyond the place where I stood and my fingers tightened on cold iron. Lacey Enright must be the great-grandmother for whom I was named. It was exciting to know that she was still alive. I wondered if my mother was aware of this. I'd been starved for relatives all my life, so knowing my great-grandmother existed—lived in this town—stirred something in me that I'd never felt before.

I let his words pass as though they meant nothing to me. "Perhaps you can tell me where I might stay for a few days while I'm in town. I'm looking for something small and simple."

He considered for a moment. "Well, there are several bed-and-breakfast choices in this area. In fact, I'm staying at a very good place right here in Harpers Ferry. If you like, I can show you where it is and introduce you to the woman who owns it. But first, I was about to go up to the Anvil for lunch. If you'd care to join me, we can go by Miss Lavinia Griffin's place after lunch and you can see if she has a room for you."

Too many emotions must have crossed my face at the mention of Lavinia's name, for he looked startled. "I'm sorry—I know we've only been acquainted a short time, but I thought you might be hungry and I'm sure I can simplify your problem of where to stay."

I didn't want him to apologize. "It isn't that. I'd like to join you for lunch. I don't know anyone in town, and I'm grateful for your kindness."

He looked mildly pleased. "Fine. Shall we go in my car, and then I'll bring you back to wherever you've left yours."

"Fine," I said and smiled, although I still felt a bit shaken. This man not only knew of my great-grandmother, but he was staying with my mother's aunt Vinnie. I couldn't let this easy opportunity to meet my great-aunt slip away. I made myself relax as we walked toward High Street. I meant to enjoy lunch and find out all I could about Harpers Ferry.

For a little we seemed to have nothing to say. When we came to a small red brick building, Ryan Pearce stopped.

"Here's a bit of Harpers Ferry history," he said. "They call this place John Brown's Fort, because it's the building in which he and his raiders made their last stand."

The old fire engine house looked peaceful enough on this sunny day. It was topped by an empty white bell tower, and three arched doorways opened into the one-room interior.

"Once there was a bell in that tower, but now it tops an engine house in Marlboro, Massachusetts. The building itself has been moved a few times—even out to Chicago for the World's Fair. It was finally brought back here, close to the spot where it originally stood. An interesting historical fact: The United States officer who effected John Brown's capture was none other than Colonel Robert E. Lee. Two years later his uniform would be gray instead of blue."

The historian had taken over in the man beside me. "Tell me more," I said, delighted to be with someone who had a real feeling for what had happened here.

"Close your eyes. Imagine that it's night. There has already been bloodshed, and Brown has taken hostages he's holding inside. The town is angry, up in arms. There are torches burning and the sound of gunfire everywhere. All night long it goes on, until the marines arrive and the capture is made."

I'd closed my eyes and the sound of his voice as he told me the story sent a shiver down my spine. Somehow he aroused unexpected emotions in me—a sense of something long past that had left its mark on Harpers Ferry.

When I looked at him, I saw the dreamy, faraway expression on his face—as though he had forgotten the present in his re-creation of the past. He sensed my attention and smiled.

"I get carried away," he said. "Sometimes I think what happened a hundred years ago is more important to me than what's happening now."

I asked a prosaic question as we walked on. "Is there a good bookstore in town? I need to know a great deal about Harpers Ferry for my own book."

He pointed. "There's a very good shop right over there on Shenandoah Street. It's run by the Historical Society, and you'll find one of the best Civil War collections in the country on its shelves."

I noted the shop's location so I could find it later, and we walked on in silence. Now I found myself suddenly focusing on what to do about Lavinia Griffin. My mother's warning to find out a few things before I approached her was still in my mind, but I was still undecided.

We climbed High Street to where Ryan Pearce's modest blue Chevy was parked, and then drove up Washington Street to the restaurant.

The Anvil, he told me, was also the name of a play about John Brown. While the building dated back only to 1985, the attractive interior was more typical of a nineteenth-century pub.

We walked into a front room with a low ceiling and a good deal of dark wood, and were seated in a high-backed booth. At night a larger room would be opened for dinner, Ryan told me, but at noon the fare was simple. We both ordered salads and homemade tomato-vegetable soup.

"Tell me about your writing for children," Ryan Pearce said when the waitress had gone.

I explained that I chose small places that interested me and wrote short histories of them. The maps I drew illustrated certain key locations, and I would add little houses and buildings that would seem to stand up from the page in three dimensions, as the viewer looked down on them.

"Of course I take a lot of pictures that I can use as a memory grid when I'm working at my desk at home."

"Where is home?"

I told him Charlottesville and he said he knew the city well and found it attractive. Again I was drawn to his friendliness and felt a genuine interest in him. If it hadn't been for the question of Lavinia Griffin and how I was to act when I met her, I could have simply enjoyed his company and forgotten everything else.

"When you go to the bookstore," he went on, "look for a volume of legends about Harpers Ferry. You'll find stories that may be useful and interesting. Of course there are lots of ghost stories too. A local woman has collected a good many and even conducts lively tours for those interested in haunted places."

"That sounds pretty exciting. Have you ever gone?"

"No, but I've been meaning to. Perhaps we could arrange to do the tour together."

"I'd like that," I said, briefly averting my gaze.

Our food arrived and as I began to eat, I found myself thinking again of my problem with the bed-and-breakfast. It was going to simplify my real mission if I just went with Ryan Pearce to my great-aunt's house and took a room there. In that case, however, concealment wouldn't be possible. The moment I was asked to show my driver's license, she would know. But did that matter as much as my mother had seemed to think? I was no longer sure that a masquerade was necessary.

"Speaking of ghosts . . ." Ryan said, breaking in on my thoughts. "I think one just walked in. There's been talk around town—half-joking, of course—that John Brown has returned. Or at least someone who resembles him."

Startled, I glanced toward the corner table where a tall, wiry old man was being seated. His thick salt-and-pepper hair framed a bony forehead, while a mustache concealed his mouth, and a flowing, spade-shaped gray beard completed the effect. Indeed, he did look vaguely like pictures I'd seen of John Brown. I was disconcerted when his eyes met mine in a look that was chillingly direct. I felt as though his cold gray eyes were saying, "Don't mess with me or you'll be sorry," and I turned away quickly.

"Who is he?" I asked Ryan Pearce.

"No one knows. He appears and disappears very effectively. He seems to talk only when he has to and nobody seems to know where he stays."

I wondered if this could be the man Vinnie had referred to in her letter. My mother had seemed alarmed by her reference to him, which only increased my interest, though I took care not to look toward the corner table again.

When we'd finished our light meal, Ryan Pearce asked a question that made me realize he'd known I was rethinking his offer. "Have you made up your mind, Lacey?" He used my name easily, and I liked that.

"Yes. I'd like to stay at the place you mentioned if there's room for me."

He looked pleased. "Then let me take you back to your car, and you can follow me up the hill."

There was no time to explain the complicated matter of who I was and why I was here. All I could do was play this by ear and see what happened.

Once in my car, I trailed Ryan up High Street. He took a zigzag turn that led to a parallel street above and parked near a square-faced brick house from the last century. When I pulled into the space next to him and got out of my car, I began to feel increasingly uncomfortable. Lavinia Griffin hadn't asked for *me* in her letter, and I knew my mother would say that I was doing this all wrong.

The two-story house was set on a grassy bank above the street, so we climbed two sets of brick steps to reach the small, columned portico. This higher section of town seemed quiet and residential, with none of the pedestrian bustle I'd witnessed in the Park area below. Near the house another redbud tree bloomed in glorious blossom.

Ryan opened the unlocked front door and gestured me into a narrow hall that seemed to run the length of the house from front to back. I stepped in hesitantly, still uncertain of what I would say or do. This wasn't like me. I usually made up my mind quickly and flew into action. Now I felt like a child, with all of a child's uncertainties. Perhaps I'd been in this house when I was small. Perhaps my mother had once lived here. Something strange was happening to me.

A faint scent lingered in the air—both sweet and spicy and wonderfully familiar. Something in me remembered, even though I had no conscious recognition of anything I saw. It was as though in some long-ago time that fragrance had signified a state of safety and happiness.

A half circle of desk had been tucked under slanting stairs that ran steeply to the floor above. Since no one had appeared, Ryan rang a small brass bell and a tinkling sounded clearly in the orderly silence.

A woman appeared from an inner room and I experienced a sense of immediate recognition. Though she was nearly thirty years older than when my mother had taken me away, and well into her sixties, I knew I'd loved her when I was small. For just a moment I had a foolish urge to run into her embrace, but instead I merely stood and looked at her.

Lavinia Griffin's hair, from which pins were slipping, was gray and thick, dipping over her forehead in a sort of pompadour. Her skin seemed remarkably free of wrinkles, giving her a youthful look. She would never have been beautiful, as my mother was, but she had aged well.

She greeted Ryan with a warm smile, and the long-forgotten child in me wanted that look of affection to be turned on me. I gave myself a sensible inner shake.

"Vinnie," Ryan said, "I've brought you a guest. This is Miss Dennis. She's going to do a book for children about Harpers Ferry. I hope you have a room for her."

Without hesitation, her friendliness turned on me. "Of course. The room in the garden corner is free and we can put you there, Miss Dennis. That is, if you like it."

The moment of truth had come as she opened the register and handed me a pen. I spoke quickly, not looking at Ryan. "Dennis isn't my real name. I hope you'll forgive the deceit, but I didn't want to tell anyone my last name until I'd been here for a little while."

I wrote *Lacey Elliot* and my Charlottesville address firmly along the line her finger indicated, and then waited to see how it would be received.

My great-aunt put on her glasses and turned the book around. As she read what I had written, a flush of excitement rose in her cheeks.

"No—you can't be! I asked Amelia to come. I never dreamed . . ."

"I'm sorry," I said. "My mother has been very ill, so I've come in her stead." I threw an apologetic look at Ryan, but he was staring at the register, his face telling me nothing.

Vinnie stood looking at me, her hands resting palms down on the sheet I had just signed. Then she held them out to me and tears came into her eyes.

"Little Lacey! I've thought of you so often."

"I'm not very little now," I said awkwardly. "I didn't know anything about you until your letter came yesterday and I read it to my mother."

She walked from behind the desk, dabbing at her eyes with a handkerchief. I wanted to put my arms around her, but that wasn't an easy gesture for me to make. Mother was seldom demonstrative, but Vinnie had no such reservations and she wrapped me in her warm embrace.

Ryan broke in, his tone guarded. "What is all this about? Will someone clue me in?"

Vinnie smiled at him through tears. "The last time I saw Lacey she was four years old. So I'm a bit overcome."

"I'm sorry," I told Ryan. "I know I've handled this very badly. I didn't mean—"

"Oh, I don't know," he spoke dryly. "You seem to have handled everything perfectly. You came here to find Vinnie Griffin, and you've managed to move right into her house within hours of your arrival. I simply don't understand why I had to be misled."

I stared at him, unable to explain the complicated details of my mother's warnings or the rigors of a childhood and adolescence spent wondering if everyone's life was marred by secrets. Vinnie shook her head at him. "Don't be grouchy, Ryan. She was right to be cautious. My letter must have upset her mother. I'm grateful to you for bringing her here."

His look remained remote, focusing somewhere beyond me. "So our Miss Lacey is your great-grandmother?"

I tried feebly to explain. "I'd never known about my great-grandmother, even though I'd been named for her. I didn't even know of Aunt Vinnie's existence until her letter came."

Vinnie kept an arm around me. "Well, I'm glad you're here and glad that you'll be in my garden room. I'll take you there in a moment, but first I want to speak to Ryan."

"And I'd like to phone my mother," I told her.

While I dialed the phone on the desk, Vinnie and Ryan walked to the front door together. I hadn't thanked Ryan, but I hoped I'd have a chance to later.

Mrs. Brewster answered and put Mother on the line at once. She was feeling stronger, though anxious, and wanted to know all about what I was doing. I quickly explained where I would be staying and promised to keep in touch with her daily. I couldn't deal with questions right now—too much was up in the air—so I said I'd call soon and tell her all my news.

Ryan was nowhere in sight as Vinnie returned to take a key from a hook behind the desk. She walked ahead of me, leading the way, as I tried to find some memory of this house that I must have known well as a young child.

THREE

AS I FOLLOWED Vinnie, I found that while the house must
have been built foursquare originally, a more recent addition
dropped down a few steps to a long hall at the rear. Its carpet
was a cheerful turkey red and led past windows on one side,
and closed doors of guest rooms on the other. There were only
four rooms, so the number of guests would be limited.

When we reached the far end, she inserted a key that opened
a door into a sunny room with windows that looked out upon
a garden. I was delighted to see that an inside door at the far
end of my room gave me access to the garden.

The moment I stepped into the room a familiar scent enveloped me and I breathed deeply.

"I remember!" I cried in delight. "Rose petals!"

She gestured toward a crystal bowl set on a drop-leaf table.
Colorful, aromatic particles filled it nearly to the brim, and
when she stirred the contents with a finger, the aroma of the
potpourri wafted pungently on the light breeze from an open
window.

I closed my eyes, trying to recapture something that just
managed to elude me. I wanted so much to remember.

"You were so little," Vinnie said softly. "You loved that old
rose bush out there in the corner of my herb garden. I was
lucky to have antique roses on my property. That bush must
date back a hundred years and more. Only antique roses have

that special scent. I dry the petals and add a few more herbs
to spice the sweetness."

I sniffed again, almost recovering some distant happiness.
"There's sassafras in there too, isn't there? I wouldn't have
thought I'd recognize the smell, but my nose remembers."

She laughed—a sound that ran lightly up the scale. I had
loved to hear her laugh—I knew that.

"What a lively, into-everything child you were! 'Sassafras'
was one of your favorite words—though you said the smell
made your nose tickle. You'd crush a leaf in your little fingers
and sniff to your heart's delight—even when it made you
sneeze."

We were both silent for a moment. Without any doubt, I
knew that I had loved Vinnie Griffin dearly. There was so
much she could tell me—and not all of it would be sad.

She drew me farther into the room, and now she sounded
brisk and matter-of-fact, perhaps to hide her own emotion.

"How do you like the room?" she asked.

"I love it!" I looked around at the four-poster bed with its
patchwork quilt, the kneehole desk, a tall polished bureau
with brass pulls on the drawers, and a comfortable-looking,
chintz-covered armchair. A rug in the center of the floor was
a large oval in shape, and undoubtedly handbraided in its
multi-colors. The frames of the two windows on the long side
of the room had been painted white, their small panes offering
ledges for rows of colored stones.

Through the screened door in the far corner sunny air
poured in and I could hear the birds in the garden beyond. An
herb garden with lumaria brightly pink against a white picket
fence caught my eye. Much as I wanted to simply enjoy what
was being offered to me, I couldn't relax. Not yet. There were
too many unanswered questions—some that Vinnie might not
want to discuss, but I had to begin somewhere.

"Please tell me why you wrote to my mother—why you
wanted her to come here now."

"I shouldn't have written. That letter was sent out of my

own weakness. Though I can't be sorry since it brought you here."

"What can I do to help?"

"There's nothing anyone can do, really. I can only wait to see what *he* intends."

She looked so vulnerable, so open to being wounded, that this time I did what I hadn't quite dared to do before. I put my arms around her and held her tightly. She smelled fragrantly of some herbal mixture and again I felt the tug of something almost remembered.

"I'll wait until you're ready to tell me, Aunt Vinnie. It's just that I know so little. I don't know why my mother ran away, or what happened to my father."

She held me away from her and looked into my face. "But that's terrible! You should know, although it's a hard story to tell because of the complicated emotions involved. I don't know where to begin."

"Just begin anywhere, if you feel up to it now."

"Let's go outside," she said. "There's a bench in the garden, and perhaps I can relax a little and talk better there."

She opened the screen door, but before we could descend the two brick steps to the ground, we saw a small boy looking up at us gravely. He was about the age I was when I left Harpers Ferry, maybe a year or so older. His hair, the color of ripe corn, was cut in bangs across his forehead. Blue eyes, fringed by long lashes only a little darker, looked up at us. On one shoulder rested a calico kitten—black and brown and white—its nose nestled sleepily in the boy's neck.

"This is Egan," Vinnie told me, and left the introduction at that.

Egan dealt with first things first. "Her name is Shenandoah," he told me, and the kitten opened her blue eyes to examine me with interest. "You have to be careful because she bites at fingers. It's only playing, so don't scold her."

"I wouldn't scold her for anything," I promised. "That's a very big name for such a small kitten. Did you name her?"

"She told me her name," he informed me solemnly.

Of course! Kitten and boy were young enough to understand each other perfectly.

Vinnie was looking anxious, and as she spoke to the boy, she watched me. "Egan, this is Lacey Elliot. Lacey, Egan is your half sister Caryl's son."

I had asked for information but this news had come so suddenly that I reacted with shock. Vinnie put her hand on my arm gently.

"Are you all right, Lacey dear?"

I wasn't all right. How could I have a sister I knew *nothing* about? Somehow I managed to take the small hand Egan held out to me. He let me squeeze his fingers, and that instant of contact sparked a communication we both understood. Strange that reassurance could come from so small a person, but it had and I managed a response.

"I'm happy to know that we're related, Egan."

He accepted this as though it were his due. "Egan means 'Little Fire' in Gaelic. My daddy was Irish. He died when I was little, but he still looks after me. Now Grandma Ardra has gone away, and Jasmine says she's never coming back."

Was Ardra my mother's sister? I had no idea where she fit into the family tree. Mother had never mentioned a sister.

"Jasmine talks too much," Vinnie told the little boy. "And she doesn't know everything."

Egan paid no attention, still intent on informing me. "My mommy's gone to get Grandma Ardra, and I know *she'll* come back. She promised me." Then he changed the subject. "Would you like to hold Shenandoah?"

"I'd like that very much," I said.

He pried the kitten's claws from his T-shirt and held the silky little creature up to me, whispering as he did so. "She's a friend, Shenna. You'll be all right."

The kitten was too young for doubts. She cocked her head to one side, the better to examine me as I held her. A diamond-shaped black patch covered one side of her nose, with a matching dab of black on the white fur under her chin. I set her against my shoulder and stroked her gently so that a deep, rolling purr resulted. A very large purr for something so small. "She likes you," Egan approved. "But she won't stay still long."

Trying to think of nothing but the scrap of warm life under my chin, I walked away from Vinnie and the boy, following a brick path.

"The bench is over there, Lacey," Vinnie said, coming after me. "Let's sit down."

I was happy to feel the cool support of marble under me. I hadn't expected that the first revelations would jolt me like this and I was feeling impatient with my own reactions. From having no one but my mother, I had been thrust into possession of a great-aunt, a great-grandmother, a nephew—and a sister!

The kitten began to squirm and I gave her back to Egan, who set her on the ground where she began to chase her own multicolored tail enthusiastically.

Vinnie smiled at her performance. "Egan, will you please tell Jasmine there will be one more person for supper tonight?" And then she added to me, "I don't serve meals to guests, except for breakfast, but you're family and Ryan is a permanent resident right now, so he joins us at night."

The boy gave her an enchanting smile that showed a deep dimple in one cheek. The sight made me touch my own cheek, where I'd always regretted just such an indentation.

Egan ran off and Vinnie watched him go.

"Tell me about my half sister," I said. "Did my father have an earlier marriage?"

"I only wish!" Vinnie took a deep breath and plunged into her story. "Brad was married only once—to your mother. He had an affair with her younger sister, Ardra, while he was still living with you and your mother. Caryl is four years younger than you and was born before your mother left Harpers Ferry."

I was beginning to see what my mother had endured. "No wonder she left!"

"She didn't leave because of that. She left after Brad was possibly murdered and—"

"Possibly? Don't you know for sure?"

"There were suspicions, but no one really knows what happened. You see, dear, your father's body was never found. A jacket with a single bullet hole was found on some rocks downriver, but without a body nothing could ever be proved."

Somehow this conversation didn't seem real. This couldn't be my father Vinnie was talking about. "My mother believes he was murdered."

"She is not alone. There was some circumstantial evidence that seemed to point to my brother, Daniel Griffin, who is your mother's father—your grandfather. Suspicion increased when he too disappeared. People said he ran away to save his own neck."

She seemed to speak almost by rote and I knew she was holding her feelings starkly under control.

"There's more, isn't there?" I asked.

She nodded stiffly. "Daniel has returned, and I'm afraid, though he hasn't been near me. Not yet. He is older than I am and we were never close, but I remember what he was like—a violent man when he was young. I can't imagine why he has come here now, unless it's for revenge."

"So many years later?"

"That's what makes it strange and all the more frightening. For some reason I feel as though he's been brooding for all these years, and now means to take some sort of action. He was only wanted for questioning, so there's no charge hanging over him. Your mother was the only person who ever stood up to him and got away with it. She was his favorite daughter. He always frightened Ardra—and me. Perhaps if Amelia were here—oh, I know I shouldn't have asked her to come. There's probably nothing anyone can do."

"I don't think you should keep saying that. Since I'm here,

perhaps I should try to meet him. I believe I saw him today when I had lunch at the Anvil with Ryan Pearce." When I thought of the chilling look he had given me, I wasn't sure I really wanted to meet him, but if it would help Vinnie, I'd try.

My great-aunt was already shaking her head, but we heard someone coming through the garden from the front of the house, so she said nothing more. Ryan walked toward us between beds of thyme and sweet marjoram and Vinnie straightened on the bench beside me.

"I sent Ryan on an errand and we must hear how it turned out."

He stepped over a patch of borage to reach us, looking both amused and annoyed.

"Did you see her, Ryan? What did she say?"

"You might guess," he said. "I've been given my orders. Lacey, your great-grandmother wants to meet you. I'm to bring you to her house immediately."

Vinnie's distress was clear. "Oh, no! Lacey isn't ready for this yet—there's been too much for her to deal with in so short a period of time."

"You sent me to see Mrs. Enright," Ryan said. "What else could you expect?"

"I didn't dare not let Miss Lacey know that her great-granddaughter was in town. I expect it will be all right. She was fond of Amelia." Vinnie looked at me. "After all, you're her namesake, and she can't blame you for going away with your mother when you were so little. You'd better go see her and get it over with. Ryan will go with you, won't you, Ryan?"

I didn't care for this autocratic summons. Vinnie was right, I had been through a lot. "Must I?"

Ryan's expression gave me no choice. "I expect you'll do all right facing the dragon in her castle."

Vinnie snorted impatiently. "Stop it, Ryan! Miss Lacey's not a dragon, and while her house may be impressive, it's hardly a castle. Just watch your step, dear, and don't let yourself trust her too easily. Don't let her blow you down! Unfortunately, she has me under her thumb, but that needn't happen to you."

"I'll bet *this* Lacey can hold her own," Ryan said.

Clearly he hadn't forgiven me, and I prickled at his words. Vinnie saw my face and broke in. "Take it a step at a time. Ryan, I expect Lacey's feeling a bit overwhelmed right now. She's only just learned that she has a half sister she never knew existed. And there's a great deal about her father that she's only beginning to understand."

Ryan considered this and when he spoke the faint needling was gone from his words. "Maybe we'll just let Miss Lacey wait a little while and take our time about getting to her house." He pointed off beyond a clump of nearby trees. "Do you see the church steeple sticking up through the trees over there, Lacey? There's a parking space near the church where we can leave my car. Then, if you're willing, we'll take the long way up the hill. It's a climb, but maybe the exercise will give you a chance to put things into perspective."

"A very good idea!" Vinnie said. She gave me a quick hug of reassurance, and I followed Ryan out to his car.

When I was in the seat beside him, he spoke reassuringly. "Don't worry. She's an elderly lady who's used to having her way. I don't mind—I just tease her and she seems to take it. Anyway, we can't have you in a state of nerves when you're presented to her. I promise you'll feel better soon."

I already felt better, now that Ryan was friendly again. With him there to back me up, perhaps the meeting with my great-grandmother, "the dragon," wouldn't be so bad after all.

As Ryan turned the car from the curb and started down the street, I tried not to remember that my mother had never been in touch with Miss Lacey, and that what letters had come from home had never been from my mother's grandmother.

★ ★
FOUR
★ ★

RYAN PARKED his car in the small area that overlooked St. Peter's Roman Catholic Church, and I got out to look around. The present handsome building, with its steeple and peaked roofs, had been built just before the turn of the century to replace a small earlier structure, Ryan told me. The tall white spire could be seen from almost anywhere in Harpers Ferry—a landmark that I'd already noted.

We climbed wide steps to follow a stone walk that slanted uphill between groves of trees. Steep cliffs dropped off on our left, with the Shenandoah far below. On our right were the picturesque ruins of what Ryan said had once been an Episcopal church. I'd always been drawn to old ruins, so I would probably come back here to explore with my camera. These old stones might become part of the book I would be writing.

Soon the path changed to dirt, moving uphill in easy rises. As we climbed I became aware that Ryan was watching me covertly every now and then. Such observation made me uncomfortable. His impression of me certainly hadn't been favorable since he'd learned of my earlier deception, but I thought he'd forgiven me.

When we'd climbed partway up, we stopped to look down on the wonderful view of the Shenandoah, where white water broke over the rocks of the rapids.

"There's an even better view farther up," Ryan said, and we

went on along the upward curving hillside until a great slab of
rock came into sight ahead.

"That's called Jefferson's Rock," Ryan told me. "It's where
he is supposed to have sat looking across the river toward
Maryland Heights. He set it all down in a published book—
Notes on the State of Virginia. He wrote about the two great
rivers coming up on each side of Harpers Ferry, seeking a way
through the mountains. I remember Jefferson's words. He said
that at the moment of their junction they 'rush together
against the mountain, rend it asunder and pass off to the sea.'
So we have the Gap out there, where the rivers broke through
in prehistoric times."

He savored the words as he spoke them, and again I was
drawn to the way he could be excited about history.

When we came opposite the rock, he held out his hand. "We
can climb out there, if you like. Take hold—it's rough going."

The gesture of steadying me was casual enough, yet I was
suddenly conscious of his hand, warm about my own and
somehow comforting. I let go of him too quickly, and barely
managed not to stumble.

He smiled slightly and didn't try to help me again, which
made me feel a little foolish and impatient with myself.

We crossed an uneven rocky space to stand on a great
boulder that was propped on four short legs, supporting a
slab of gray shale. Ryan explained that these legs had been
added in the last century, when the natural supports of the
rock were worn away by storms, changing seasons, and
climbing visitors. Now the rock rested securely on red sandstone supports.

I sat down on the gray slab and tried to let all tension flow
out of me, so that I was aware only of the beauty around me.
I began to feel strangely contented, and more at ease, even
accepting of the presence of this stranger beside me. He
seemed relaxed, and a little dreamy. As though his own
thoughts and feelings took him far away from the present and
into the past that he found so exciting and interesting. I won-

dered about his life—did he have a wife and family?—but I hadn't a clue beyond the little he had told me.

"When Jefferson first saw this view, he wrote that it was something worth crossing the Atlantic to see."

This I could believe.

Far below the Shenandoah flowed with her own excitement, forever anticipating her meeting with the Potomac.

"That's Virginius Island down there," Ryan said, pointing toward a narrow, wooded island stretching along the near side of the river with a strip of canal between island and shore. "It's a historic place in itself. When the water power of the rivers was harnessed, grain and pulp mills and an iron foundry were built down there. And there were houses too, for those who worked there. Some two hundred people lived on the island at one time. The canal was dug to enable boats to bypass the rapids. It isn't used anymore, but the Park has cleaned up the canal and the island as an attraction for visitors."

"What happened to all the buildings and people on the island?"

"The river won out. Floods washed everything away, and took the lives of those who didn't escape across bridges to high ground in time. There are nothing but ruins down there now. Your great-grandmother can probably tell you stories about the island that have been handed down by her family. *Your* family, Lacey."

I didn't want to ask my great-grandmother about the distant past. My interest had to do with events much closer to the present. If I found the courage, perhaps I would ask the alarming Miss Lacey a few pointed questions. Right now it seemed safer to talk about geography and history.

"Why is there a West Virginia? Why not one state?"

"When the war broke out, part of Virginia sided with the South and seceded. But some of the state remained loyal to the North and refused to separate. During the fighting Harpers Ferry was taken over by one side and then the other—several times. A good many people who lived here left and never came back. In 1867 the part of the state that had sided with the North voted to become West Virginia, an independent state."

Undoubtedly men in my family had fought in that war—though I didn't know on which side. I didn't know anything. "If you lived then, which state would you have belonged to?"

He smiled at me. "My wife asked me that once, but I could never give her a certain answer. My sympathies—and my grief—are still for both sides. *She* was always very certain about everything. I suppose that's one reason why we divorced."

I shouldn't have felt so relieved, but somehow I did.

He stood up and held out his hand. "We'd better go on now. Miss Lacey doesn't like to be kept waiting, and we're already late. When she's not pleased, sparks can fly."

"I don't think I'll like her," I said as he helped me up. "I wish I didn't have to meet her at all."

"Being her great-granddaughter, you can't stay in Harpers Ferry for a week and not hear about her, so you might as well form your own opinions. Besides, how many people get to meet a great-grandmother? She's very old and she's special. You may even find you like her when you get used to her ways. So let's get started. We still have a climb ahead."

I went with him up past the enclosure of an old cemetery. At another time I might have stopped to look at the gravestones, but Ryan was walking faster now, making up for lost time.

The path we followed wound above shale cliffs that dropped straight down to a road that edged the river. Most roads up here were farther inland, and we turned away from the cliffs as we rounded a turn. Suddenly Ryan stopped me.

"There it is—Miss Lacey's house. It survived the war and, of course, way up here it was safe from floods, so there's a lot of history inside those walls. Miss Lacey has lived in that house all her life—Lacey Fenwick Enright. Now there's a name to roll on your tongue!"

This was the first time I'd heard her full name, and somehow it had a foreboding ring. It was a name that stood for position, perhaps wealth, and clearly power. At least Ryan seemed to admire her, and I put a little hope in that.

Now that our destination was in sight, I took a moment to examine the house. Whether I liked it or not, this place was sure to mean something in my life, both because of its history and because of the woman who lived there.

It stood alone, without neighbors, plain and sturdy—an independent structure that knew its own worth. A house like this had no need to be beautiful in order to possess its own distinctive character.

Narrow gray clapboards rose two stories above a high brick foundation, its width only three green-shuttered windows across. The rest stretched into a long space at the back. Across the front at the first-floor level a railed gallery offered a spacious place to sit outside.

Four slender white pillars supported the gallery roof—not at all like the great Greek Revival columns of the storybook South. Beyond the gallery and off to one side stood a tall closed front door. I was sure that the house observed us suspiciously from behind curtained windows as we approached. Perhaps, already, we didn't like each other.

I told myself this was whimsical nonsense and went with Ryan up steps that rose steeply from the ground at one side. A curtain moved slightly at one window, and I knew that someone had seen us approach. Before Ryan could ring, a woman opened the door and stood looking at us, her expression anything but welcoming. She wore a shapeless black dress that enveloped her bony frame.

"Hello, Anne-Marie," Ryan said and bent to kiss a cheek that wasn't offered. She pushed him away crossly and he laughed. "I know we're later than Miss Lacey expected. We walked up from the church, so *this* Lacey could see Jefferson's Rock and the view."

"You took your time," the woman told him. "Miss Lacey isn't pleased."

Ryan made a mock-despairing face. "I'll take the blame. Lacey, this is Anne-Marie St. Pol and she is very much in charge around here, so be respectful. Anne-Marie, this is Miss Lacey Elliot."

His teasing approach to this guardian suggested that she wasn't as fierce as she looked, and I gave her my hand.

Though her clasp was firm, it was brief and I had the feeling that she already disapproved of me.

I watched as she turned again to Ryan. She was probably in her late fifties—close to my mother's age—quite tall and thin, with carefully tinted brown hair.

"Come on in," she said curtly. "I'll tell Miss Lacey you're here."

As she held the door open, I walked into a narrow hall, with a steep staircase running up along the wall on my right. Anne-Marie gestured us into a room on the left, opposite the stairs— an old-fashioned parlor that might have come out of a book of Victoriana.

At any other time I would have delighted in this lovely room, but now my focus was on the coming meeting with the family matriarch. I registered only that a soft rosy aura, laced with bits of ferny green, gave the room a dreamy ambience that was not intimidating.

A black sofa with a scalloped walnut frame made the one discordant note in the room's soft colors, but its very distinction drew me and I sat down, once more bracing myself. There was nothing soft about the upholstery that cushioned me, and I wondered if this piece of furniture was still stuffed with the original horsehair.

Ryan's eyes were watchful and I had the uncomfortable feeling that he might be looking forward to the coming encounter. I must remember that he was first of all a historian and an observer.

Anne-Marie had disappeared and, as we waited, my body seemed to take on the stiffness of the upholstery under me.

Ryan had chosen a more comfortable-looking chair, and he

still seemed entirely relaxed. "You'll be fine," he assured me. "She likes to keep people waiting so she can make an entrance."

I reminded myself that I owed this woman nothing. Whatever problems had broken up the family had nothing to do with me.

I was still revving myself up when she suddenly appeared, entering from the hallway. Whatever I had expected, whatever the word "formidable" had conjured up in my mind, it was not this woman who stood framed in the double doorway.

From her slightly yellowed white hair to the tips of satin slippers that showed beneath the hem of her long gown, she was a small figure that might have been carved in ivory. Large silvery blue eyes seemed incongruous in so small a face, and a wide, soft, rose-tinted mouth broke the one-tone color scheme.

Ryan stood at once, and I found myself following his example, feeling like a schoolgirl waiting to be inspected. As she took a few steps into the room, she propped herself on a cane that was topped with the fanciful carving of a gryphon's head. Her short hair had been combed back from a remarkably unwrinkled forehead. Her face formed a small triangle, with a chin that might once have been pointed, but now blended into the folds of the neck below. Her gown, cut from a length of Chinese brocade in a chrysanthemum design, was the same ivory color as the rest of her. The standard Chinese collar partially concealed her neck, as was undoubtedly intended. She was neither fat nor thin, and the otherwise concealing gown revealed that her back was straight, making no concession to old age.

As she came a few steps into the room, her eyes never left my face. Then, startling me, she slipped her hand down along the cane, grasping it in the middle and raising the gryphon's head at me. As I would learn, this was a characteristic gesture of command. Gryphons, however legendary, had been fierce creatures, and I wondered if whoever had made the cane for

Miss Lacey had seen something of that same fierce spirit in her.

"Come here," she ordered.

In spite of Vinnie's warning that I must not let her "blow me down," I could never have found the courage to disobey this summons. She wore no glasses, and probably saw more clearly close up. She waited while I crossed the room to stand before her. Under her probing look, I felt clumsy and oversized, and suspected that she enjoyed making people feel uncomfortable.

"Why do you suppose they named you after me?" she asked, cocking one eyebrow.

Her manner, her tone of voice, challenged me, and I recovered a bit of my own spirit. "I have no idea. I didn't choose the name."

"Let me see your hand," she said. "Your right hand."

Mystified, I held it out, palm down. She took it into her own small fingers and turned it over so she could study the palm.

"Humph!" she snorted. "I might have expected as much."

I hadn't come for a palm reading, and I took my hand back quickly. "What did you expect?"

"I never cared for your father—and his presence is there in your hand."

I had no idea what she was talking about and perhaps I didn't want to know. I'd experienced no feeling of kinship with this woman, and I was sure she'd felt none toward me.

She'd paid no attention to Ryan since she'd entered the room, but now he came to stand beside her, almost protectively.

"I don't think introductions are necessary, are they? So I'll leave you two to get acquainted."

"Yes. Go talk to Anne-Marie," Miss Lacey said and flicked a dismissive hand at him.

He glanced at me with a look that seemed to convey some message I couldn't read, and went out the door. I suspected that he'd been happy to retreat and leave me to face my great-grandmother on my own.

★ ★ ★
F I V E
★ ★

WHEN HE'D gone, Miss Lacey walked regally to the armchair Ryan had occupied, the one that looked more comfortable than the unwelcoming sofa, and seated herself.

"Sit down, Lacey," she ordered. "Tell me why you're here
after all these years." Her voice was strong, with none of the
cracking that sometimes came with age.

I sat again on the stiff sofa, feeling that I didn't want to let
down my guard for an instant with this woman. Vinnie had
seemed in awe of her, perhaps even a little afraid, but I meant
to pay attention to her warning to stand up to this great-
grandmother.

"My mother is recovering from a cancer operation," I said.
"Lavinia Griffin wrote asking her to come here. There was an
urgency in her letter, and my mother sent me instead."

"Amelia was the best of my grandchildren, yet she could
behave foolishly. You are *her* child, but you're also Bradley
Elliot's daughter. So who do you take after?"

I don't know what prompted me to say what I did, but the
words came out filled with challenge, like a glove thrown
down. "Perhaps I take after you." She was silent for a moment
as her scrutiny grew intense, then she smiled slightly as though
I'd pleased her. "That remains to be seen. Why did Vinnie
write to your mother?"

"I'm not sure, exactly. I think she's afraid of her brother,
Daniel Griffin; she thinks he's back in town."

The ivory hair over Miss Lacey's forehead trembled as she nodded. "Vinnie's a nincompoop. She scares too easily."

"I like Aunt Vinnie very much," I said in quick defense. "She doesn't strike me as a foolish woman. Perhaps she's too gentle and that makes her vulnerable."

"You haven't known her as long as I have. Go on with your story."

"There isn't any more. It was important to me to come to Harpers Ferry and find out who my family was. I've known of no one I was related to but my mother until that letter arrived."

"How much do you know about what happened in the past?"

"Almost nothing. My mother must have wanted to make a clean break. I didn't even know Harpers Ferry was where I was from. I'd never heard of *you* before today."

That seemed to shock her, suggesting, I supposed, an affront to her own sense of importance.

"Do you know how your father died?"

I answered her quietly. "My mother told me yesterday that he was murdered. I don't know anything else."

Miss Lacey rose and walked down the room toward a small grand piano at the far end. I had a feeling that her cane was more like a useful prop than anything she really needed.

"Come here," she said over her shoulder.

I went to stand beside her and saw that the top of the piano was crowded with small framed photographs. She picked up one and set it before me.

"That is my daughter, Ida, when she was young. She was your grandmother. The man is Ida's husband, Daniel Griffin. Vinnie's brother, of course. They are your mother's parents."

I picked up the photograph and looked at two young faces—the girl's happy and hopeful, while her husband's was more serious, suggesting that he had been grim even in his youth. His was a strong, rugged face with dark eyes that seemed to have had a chilling quality to them even as a young

man. I was more sure than ever that I had seen Daniel Griffin
at the Anvil.

"This man is here in Harpers Ferry now, isn't he?" I asked.
"Vinnie seems afraid of him. Why? What really happened all
those years ago? What is all this about? Or don't you know?"

"Oh, I know." She spoke with a snap in the words, as
though I'd challenged her again.

"Then tell me, please." I wanted to hear her version, so that
I could compare it with what Vinnie had told me.

She hesitated briefly, and then seemed to make up her mind.
"My husband and I had only one child—Ida. She was born in
this house. And she didn't take after either of us—she was a
timid little thing. She grew up to marry *him.*" Her forefinger
touched the face of the man in the picture. "He and his sister
Vinnie came here when they were children and their parents
moved to Harpers Ferry. Vinnie became closer to our family
than he ever did. My husband and I never liked him or trusted
him. But Ida was besotted."

She reached out abruptly to take the picture from me and
laid it facedown on the piano.

Besotted, I thought. An old-fashioned word that said a great
deal. I had never known what it was like to be besotted and I
hoped I would never find out.

"Do you play the piano?" she asked abruptly.

"I'm afraid not."

"Of course you wouldn't. In my day, young ladies were
taught a few graceful talents."

"I can play the guitar," I offered, smiling.

Her expression told me what she thought of guitars, but this
bit of chatter was taking us down a side road that didn't
interest me.

"I would still like to know what happened. 'Murder' is a
frightening word."

"We don't even know if it really applies. But I'll tell you
what little I do know." She straightened her shoulders beneath
the ivory brocade, as though facing once again what had to be

faced. "Ida and Daniel had two daughters. The older is Amelia, your mother. Ardra is a year younger. Amelia married Bradley Elliot. He was a local boy, but he was never much good for anything except attracting silly young women."

I heard the bite in her words, and knew that a lifetime of anger had built up in this woman.

"We didn't want Amelia to marry him, but she was stubborn like Ida, and in love with someone she should never have looked at twice. Amelia had good sense in every other way. Ardra, on the other hand, had no sense at all, but, physically, she was very attractive—and spoiled. She'd always had just about anything she wanted, except her sister's husband. And of course she got him in the end."

Miss Lacey broke off and moved away from the piano, as though to be free of any support. When she continued she didn't look at me. "When your father seduced your mother's sister and got her pregnant, Daniel went crazy. He threatened Brad."

"Vinnie told me that his jacket was found on a rock downriver with a bullet hole in it."

Miss Lacey answered carefully. "I suppose his body could have been carried all the way to the sea by the strong river current. Once out in the ocean, it would never have been found. When Daniel saw circumstantial evidence closing in on him, he disappeared too, no doubt to save himself from arrest and a possible trial."

"Poor Ida," I said.

"Oh phoo, she didn't have the gumption of a canary." Scorn for her daughter cut through Miss Lacey's words. "The rest of us had to take what happened and live with it, but she chose the easy way out. She threw herself off the Point in Harpers Ferry. Your mother couldn't accept what had happened either. After Ida's suicide, her choice was to run away and take you with her. So, in a sense, you disappeared, too."

By this time I couldn't blame anyone for anything. This was a dreadful story—much worse than I could have imagined—

and both Ida and my mother deserved everyone's sympathy.

Miss Lacey put both hands on the gryphon's head and leaned heavily on her cane for the first time. "Vinnie took Ardra and her baby girl into her home and cared for them. I give her credit for that."

"Why didn't *you* take in your granddaughter and her baby?" I asked. "You have this big house with plenty of room. It would have been easier for you to do."

She stared at me. "My husband was ill. All these terrible events had made him worse. I couldn't bring Ardra—the cause of all that tragedy—into my house."

All the while, as she poured out words of explanation, her eyes had avoided mine, and I wondered if all she told me was true.

Instead of confronting her, I asked about my grandfather. "Why would Daniel Griffin come back here now?"

"Perhaps for revenge? That would be in character."

"Revenge on whom? And why after all these years?"

Her face took on a wry look and a smile twisted her mouth. "Why don't you ask him?"

When I stared at her in surprise, she walked to the hall door and motioned me through. Neither Anne-Marie nor Ryan was in sight as I followed her down the hall to the rear of the house. There a door opened to an expanse of yard set above a thick grove of oak trees that ran down to where the cliffs began.

Miss Lacey pointed toward a small cottage that stood at one end of the yard. "That used to be a cookhouse out there. Mostly it's used for storage these days, although it does have a phone. I told him he could stay there if he cleaned it out."

I looked toward the small building, but there was no one in sight. "You mean you actually allow that man to stay here?"

"He had no place else to go," she said, as though that explained everything. "Daniel's an angry man and I thought he might be more likely to stay out of trouble down there, where we could watch him. Go talk to him, if you like. Ask *him* your questions. If you have that much nerve."

"Who is he angry with?" I asked.

"A better question might be, who isn't he angry with? I was just testing you. I wouldn't have allowed you to go out there. I want you to stay away from your grandfather."

I didn't want to expose myself to anyone's anger, certainly not to a crazy man who may have killed my father. Once I could get away from this woman and her unsettling presence, I would go back to Vinnie's and find out what she really wanted from my mother. If there was anything I could do for her, I would do it gladly. Then I would go home to Charlottesville, where I belonged, and I suspected that I would be far more contented with my life there than I'd ever been before.

Miss Lacey gave me a sharp look and closed the back door, before leading the way along the narrow hallway. I spoke before she could suggest anything else she might want of me.

"If we could find Ryan, I'd like to leave now." I sounded stiff and unfriendly, and that was the way I wanted it.

But she wasn't through with me. "Wouldn't you like to go upstairs and see the rest of the house?"

"Why should I?"

Her eyes flashed. "Because you belong to this house as much as I do. Part of you is Fenwick, whether you like it or not. A Fenwick built this house, and Fenwicks have always lived here. Perhaps I'll leave it to you when I die."

The last thing I wanted was to own this white elephant or to have anything further to do with the woman who lived here. I wasn't surprised that my mother had never talked about her.

She stopped to face me in the dim hallway, and I was aware of a portrait on the wall above her head, lost in murky light. It seemed to be an oil painting of a man.

My arrested attention caught hers, and she flicked on the hall lights. "That is Jud Fenwick, an ancestor who is part of your remarkable heritage. There is so much I have to tell you, show you."

The intense gaze of the portrait seemed to challenge me, but I rejected him, as I wanted to reject everything else in this house.

"I don't belong here, Miss Lacey. My mother was right to leave what happened here behind and escape."

She tilted her strong chin a fraction higher. "You can never leave behind what is in your blood. Certainly not before you know enough to make a choice."

I'd already made my choice and I tried a last effort to get away. "Perhaps I can visit you again before I leave Harpers Ferry. Vinnie is expecting us for supper, and I'd like to rest a little first. . . ."

She dismissed this excuse impatiently. *"First* I want you to go upstairs. Just go up and see what's there. It won't take long. You'll know if anything speaks to you. Young Egan can sense what's there and perhaps you will too."

I didn't like the sound of this. "Sense what?"

"History. I've never let Ryan go up there, though he's wanted to because of the book he's writing. But *you* are a Fenwick. The house recognizes that and you are free to move about it at will."

I wondered about her sanity. Perhaps it would be easier to do as she wished, and then get away. "All right. Is there anything special I should look for up there?"

"You'll know if you find it. History leaves a mark. Go up quickly while there's still light outside. You'll find candles, if you need them. Don't touch an electric switch. That would be an intrusion and foreign to the climate up there."

I refused to be spooked and I started up the steep flight with my hand firmly on the rail. I turned and asked one more question before I reached the top.

"What does Anne-Marie think of your letting Daniel Griffin stay out there in your cottage?"

Her smile was almost roguish. "She'd like to feed him ground glass, but of course she does what I tell her to."

As she expected everyone else to do, as well! I stepped quickly into the dim hallway above. The draperies were drawn, so I could see that candles would be needed despite the sunshine outside. A small table near the head of the stairs held

several candlesticks, and there were matchbooks, as well. I
chose an old-fashioned tin candle holder, with a looped handle
at the rim, and struck a match. The flame burned high and
unwavering in the still air. I picked up the holder with its fat
candle and held it over my head. Moving shadows leaped up
the walls with a life of their own. Since I belonged to the age
of steady electricity, these wavering shapes made me uneasy.

I walked first toward the front of the house. The hall and
stairs ran along the outer wall, with a large room across the
front. The door stood open and I stepped into a room with a
wide four-poster bed and furnishings that belonged to the
past. A commode held a china washbasin and water pitcher
with a flowered design. A rack along one side held fresh tow-
els, as though awaiting a guest. A bar of lavender soap rested
in a dish, and scented the air when I raised it to my nose.

Against one wall stood an old-fashioned wardrobe with an
oval mirror set into a door on one side. A space between
heavily draped windows was occupied by a dressing table with
a flounced skirt. A bench drawn up to face the round mirror
offered a lady a place to sit while she combed her hair.

I moved about the room, trying to sense whatever it was
that Miss Lacey thought I should feel, but I received no message, no sense of the men and women who had dressed and
slept and lived a good part of their lives in this room. Clearly,
it was unoccupied now.

An adjoining door led into another large bedroom that
reached toward the back of the house. The furnishings were
similar, and only the wallpaper in the two rooms expressed a
difference in tastes. Faded yellow paper with a faint geometric
pattern must have made the front room seem bright and
sunny, while this second room had walls that were covered
with tiny blue violets tied together in bunches. These too were
faded and somehow melancholy. But in neither room did I
sense anything that Miss Lacey might have meant when she
referred to history leaving its mark.

I wandered back to the hall and discovered that a third

room remained to be explored—a rear room set into a back corner beyond the top of the stairs. The door was closed. I put my hand on the china knob, but though it turned, the door didn't open. I wondered why this one room was locked. There seemed no point in continuing this futile exploration. A woman as old as Miss Lacey must be allowed her fantasies. I could go downstairs now, having done as she wished.

"The door isn't locked." A voice spoke behind me.

Startled, I nearly dropped the candle. I swung around to find Anne-Marie St. Pol watching me from the top of the stairs. She must have come up with a deliberately quiet step in order to take me by surprise. In this light her black clothing seemed to fade into the gloom.

"Miss Lacey thought you might need help," she said matter-of-factly. "Here—let me." She put her own hand on the knob and her shoulder against the dark wood panel.

The door opened with an unnerving shriek and stale, dusty air made me cough. The woman touched a switch at the side of the door and a light fixture that hung from the ceiling sprang to life with a yellow glow. Apparently Anne-Marie didn't bother to heed the edict about candles.

"This is where it happened," she said. "Miss Lacey prefers us to stay out of this room. It has been left as it was and never refurbished, even to the old wallpaper. Perhaps keeping it closed up shuts away any echo of the screams that must have sounded in this room."

Her hand on my shoulder gave me a slight thrust forward, and I stepped reluctantly into the room. Here the wallpaper was stained and torn in patches, so that strips hung down, leaving the wall bare. What was left on the walls showed strands of green ivy that seemed to creep along the paper.

Anne-Marie went to one of two high, rear windows and flung the tattered draperies aside, so that choking dust flew out from their folds. The woman fanned it away from her face in annoyance, and I suspected that she would have preferred to do a little housecleaning here. She raised a window and fresh air blew into the room. She didn't move from the window, but remained there, staring down into the backyard.

As I went to stand beside her and breathe fresh air, I saw what held her attention. Daniel Griffin lounged outside the door of the cottage, staring off through the trees. He held a ceramic mug in one hand and now and then drank from it. Perhaps he felt our eyes upon him, for he turned suddenly and looked up at the window where we stood. Instinctively, I stepped back out of sight, but Anne-Marie stood her ground. He saw her at the window and raised the mug in mocking salute.

She slammed down the window and drew the draperies, so that dust flew again and I sneezed.

When she moved toward the door I spoke to her. "If that man down there murdered my father, why does Miss Lacey let him stay here?"

She regarded me with impatient scorn. "You'd better ask her. We might all be finished off in our beds anytime, if you ask me."

"What do you know about him?" I ventured.

"I know that *you* should never have come here. You could be the spark that blows everything to smithereens."

I tried another question. "What happened in this room? Is this where history is supposed to have left its mark, as Miss Lacey suggests?"

She nodded solemnly. "If you are very still and listen with all your being, perhaps you'll hear her crying. *I* heard her once." She shivered in an exaggerated fashion.

"I'm afraid I don't believe in ghosts."

"Then you're a fool. How could Harpers Ferry not be awash in ghosts, considering its history?"

"Tell me what happened in this room."

She seemed to consider my question seriously, weighing the words before coming to a decision. "It's no secret—what was done in this room more than a hundred years ago. There were often renegades from both North and South roaming about during the war, victimizing old people and women who had no one left to defend them. Most of the men in that war came from towns and country farms—they weren't trained soldiers. Some of the deserters were rough men, stealing and murdering. Three men who had deserted from Union forces broke into this house. Ellen Fenwick was sleeping in that very bed. They raped her—the three of them! Jud Fenwick, Ellen's father, was away fighting, and her mother had died just a month before. Only the servants were here—freedmen, not slaves—but the deserters had guns and there was nobody who could stand against them. Poor little Ellen."

I looked at the bed, and a feeling of pain and despair filled me. When I closed my eyes to shut out the sight of the bed, I could almost hear her cries and pleading. Green vines growing lushly across the remnants of wallpaper gave me a sick feeling of vertigo when I opened my eyes.

Anne-Marie went on in a whisper. "Nine months later Ellen Fenwick died in childbirth in that very bed where she was violated."

"What happened to the baby?" I asked.

"That poor little bastard baby with a father she never knew? She was cared for by the servants until the men came home from fighting, and then she was disposed of."

I heard the words in horror. "You mean . . ."

She shook her head. "Not that way. It's thought that she was given to a couple who had lost their own child. The family never saw the baby again."

"How terrible! You'd think Ellen's father would have wanted something left of *her.*"

"Not Jud Fenwick. He must have been a hard man. There're plenty of stories about him. You can ask Miss Lacey all about it, if you want."

I didn't want to ask Miss Lacey anything. I'd had enough of tragedy, both ancient and recent. I left Anne-Marie to close up, and hurried downstairs to look for Ryan. All I wanted was to get away from the ominous climate of this house and back to Vinnie's.

SIX

MISS LACEY sat outside on the front gallery with Ryan, who was toeing himself back and forth in a swing. I stood for a moment in the doorway watching before they saw me. I was glad to see Ryan—happy to see him—as he represented sanity and the appreciation of small, safe things. He had given me the breathing space of the climb to Jefferson's Rock because he'd understood the ordeal I was about to face better than I had. I realized now that I'd not been properly grateful. I spoke to Miss Lacey briefly, without mentioning what Anne-Marie had told me. Then I turned to Ryan.

I wanted to see him alone and tell him of my experience in Miss Lacey's house, and when I smiled at him brightly, he looked a little surprised.

"I'd like to go back to Vinnie's now," I told him.

He stood up at once. "Of course. We should start back, it's getting late."

But Miss Lacey wasn't quite through with me. "Well?" she challenged. "Did you get a sense of what is up there?"

"Anne-Marie told me what happened in that room, so of course I was horrified. That poor young girl!"

"There's more than emotion in that room," she told me sharply. "That's why I keep it closed. Whatever is in there must stay shut in. I wanted you to feel it because you are a Fenwick."

"That was all a long time ago." I paused and then went on recklessly, because my feelings about the room were so strong. "It should be aired out and the tattered furnishings and wallpaper should be removed."

She stared at me in astonishment, and Ryan raised his eyebrows slightly, so I realized how out of order I was. But when she spoke it was as though she hadn't heard what I said.

"It's a particular disgrace that those miscreants were *Union* renegades. Now, at least, you know a little of the history of your family. But not all of it, by any means."

I'd learned enough in one day to last me for a long while. I hadn't begun to digest even a fraction of this experience.

"Please, may we go?" I said to Ryan.

He bent to kiss Miss Lacey's papery white cheek and there was affection in the gesture.

"I'll want to see *her* again," she told him, as though I were a child.

"Of course," he said calmly, putting a hand on my arm. "I'll bring her up in a day or two. Perhaps Lacey needs to settle in a bit first."

That wasn't going to happen, but I took the hand she held out to me, and felt a cool brittleness in her fingers. There was nothing left to say but good-bye, and I started across the gallery to the side steps. I was still badly shaken, and I didn't watch where I was stepping, until something tripped my toe and I stumbled. Ryan was quick to catch me by the arm and prevent a fall. I looked down to see that a large trap door had been set into the gallery floor. What had tripped me was a circular iron ring that protruded slightly. A handle to the door, undoubtedly.

"The root cellar is down there," Ryan said. "With refrigeration it's not in use anymore."

I nodded absently and held on to the rail as I went down the steps, uninterested in root cellars. The entire visit with Miss Lacey and her household had disturbed me more than I'd expected.

As we started back along the cliffs above the river, I tried to tell Ryan what I'd felt in that upstairs room. Even though he'd never been in the room, he knew its history and he listened quietly to my outburst.

"It's terrible that she keeps that room as a sort of shrine! I didn't like her. I hate being related to all that horror. Besides, in recent times, she must have treated my grandmother Ida dreadfully. I don't want to see her again."

He spoke to me in the same calm, reasonable manner he had used with Miss Lacey. "When you get to know her, you may feel better about the relationship. I suspect that she's lonely living in that old house with only Anne-Marie as a companion. She probably thinks about the past too much."

"I can understand why people leave her alone. Who would want to spend time with her?" I changed the subject. "Tell me about Anne-Marie."

"There isn't that much to tell. She came to town from Winnepeg, Canada, when she was about eighteen. Her mother had died a few months before and her father was long gone, so she had no family. Somehow she and Miss Lacey found each other and she started working for your great-grandmother as a maid. Eventually, she graduated to housekeeper, the position she still holds."

"Hasn't Anne-Marie tried to do anything else with her life?"

"Miss Lacey sent her to a vocational school, but she never seemed to fit in anywhere. She has that sort of personality. Working for Miss Lacey seems to be what she likes best. If there's any affection in her, she keeps it for the woman who took her in when she needed a job and a place to stay. I try to tease her and treat her in a friendly way, and she tolerates me most of the time."

"Miss Lacey actually spoke of leaving that house to me in her will. She doesn't even know me! She's seen me once. Besides, I don't want it, to begin with."

"For Miss Lacey, once may be enough. You're her great-granddaughter, after all. Perhaps she hasn't anyone else."

"What about Caryl?"

"Unfortunately, Caryl is Ardra's daughter, and Miss Lacey has never forgiven Ardra for sleeping with your father. She still blames her for all the unhappy things that happened because of their affair."

This made me all the more impatient with my great-grandmother and I lost myself in gloomy thoughts as we walked on. I found that I was placing blame too—against my mother whose long silence had resulted in nothing but confusion for me and an onslaught of information that was all coming at once.

Perhaps Ryan sensed what I was feeling. "Give it time," he said. "You'll feel better tomorrow."

We'd reached the steps that led down to the church grounds, where he'd left his car. I found his assurance about tomorrow meaningless and didn't answer. When we were in the car, he went on talking quietly.

"You're upset right now and what you'd probably like is somebody with whom you can get really angry. I'm afraid I can't serve that purpose, but the best cure for me when I feel upset is to find something so interesting to do that it uses up the excess anger that's turning me inside out. If you still want to do your book about Harpers Ferry, why not go out tomorrow and explore the Lower Town? There's plenty to see and the best way to see it is on foot. You could distract yourself for a while, and give everything time to fall into perspective. You do have roots in this place and that could make the exploration even more exciting."

"Thank you, but I've had enough excitement connected with my roots to last for a while." I didn't want to sound irritable, so I asked a question. "Did Miss Lacey tell you that Daniel Griffin is staying in the cottage behind her house? He's the man we saw at the Anvil. The one you've been noticing around town."

That surprised him. "She never said a word."

"He's my grandfather. I seem to have more unwelcome

relatives than I can count. I know you must have heard all about Daniel Griffin from my family. Why is Vinnie afraid of him?"

He studied me for a moment, still not starting the car. When he began to talk, he stared away from me through the windshield as he turned the key in the ignition.

"I'll tell you what little I know. Vinnie and Daniel were never close as brother and sister. He's quite a bit older than Vinnie. After Brad died—this is hearsay, you know, since I was pretty young when all this was happening—Vinnie suspected her brother of killing him. Apparently Daniel and Brad had a fierce quarrel—Vinnie has told me that her brother had a terrible temper. She was ready to testify against Daniel. I've seen the old newspaper accounts of what happened. Brad disappeared and only his jacket was found later. It had a bullet hole in it. Daniel disappeared at the same time. So what could anyone think? Vinnie believes that he has come back for revenge, and she's afraid."

"Why now?" I asked as he drove slowly back to Vinnie's through the quiet streets. "He must have made a life for himself somewhere else. Brad's gone—so who is there for him to feel angry with? Surely not his sister."

"I can't even guess at the answers, but it might be interesting if you could talk with your grandfather."

We'd reached the house, and he pulled up before the brick steps. When we'd climbed to the front door, Vinnie met us, her eyes sparkling with excitement.

"Caryl's home, Lacey! Your sister's very excited about meeting you. And perhaps a little scared. So be gentle with her."

I needed somebody to be gentle with me. I wasn't in the least ready to meet a sister I hadn't known existed until today. I hadn't had time to wonder about the outcome of Ardra's pregnancy with my father's child, and I couldn't deal with any more family just now. I felt tired to my fingertips, and when I closed my eyes green vines seemed to shimmer beneath my lids.

"Please, Vinnie," I said. "I'd like to rest for a little while. Tomorrow I'm going back to Charlottesville."

She seemed to understand. "It was as bad as that? I'm sorry, but you mustn't think of leaving now. We need you here." She turned to Ryan. "Can't you talk to her?"

His smile was sympathetic. "Take it easy, Vinnie. Lacey really has had a hard day. Give her a little time to collect herself. I don't think she's ready to meet Caryl right this minute."

Vinnie looked down the hall nervously, as Ryan held out a hand to me.

"When things get to be too much, just think yourself back to Jefferson's Rock. That's one of the most peaceful and beautiful spots I know. Sometimes I find it helps if I go there in my mind when the going gets rough. I'll see you later, Lacey."

He told Vinnie he had some work to do and went upstairs to his own apartment.

Vinnie put an arm around me. "Ryan's right. I can see that Miss Lacey has upset you. She has a talent for that. I don't think she realizes the effect she has on people."

"I think she does," I said, and hurried away toward my room.

Once inside, with the door safely closed behind me, I kicked off my shoes and lay down on the bed. But when I closed my eyes green ivy was there again, and I tried to think of Jefferson's Rock. That brought Ryan sharply to mind, and I remembered the small kindnesses he'd shown me, and the patience.

As I lay there trying to relax, a faint, plaintive mew sounded nearby. I rolled over and propped myself on one elbow to consider the source. Shenandoah sat on her small haunches a few feet from the bed, her head cocked to one side as she regarded me hopefully.

"Hello, Shenna," I said.

Clearly she took this as an invitation and flew over to the bed, where she paused to consider the height of the necessary leap. She gathered herself and sprang into the air, landing inches from my face. A kitten was exactly what I needed. I reached out

two fingers and she sniffed at them, examining each one carefully. Then she licked my forefinger with a raspy tongue and
curled herself into a ball of bright calico within the curve of my
arm. I wondered if Egan had put her in my room to welcome me
back. I stroked her soft fur, feeling comforted, and fell asleep.

The tap on my door could have been part of a dream and
I lay still to hear if it would come again. When it was repeated,
I called to whomever it was to come in.

A young woman walked into the room looking both uncertain and expectant. I knew who she must be and I sat up on
the side of the bed. Shenna uncurled herself and watched with
lively interest.

"You're Caryl?" I said.

"And you're my sister, Lacey. I hope you don't mind. I
couldn't wait to meet you."

Half sister, I thought. She wasn't my mother's child, though
strangely she resembled my mother more than I did. All those
mixed-up genes! Caryl was a slighter, more fragile version of
Amelia. Her fair hair, cut just above her ears, fluffed naturally
about her face and her blue eyes regarded me with open curiosity. I found myself at a complete loss. I hoped she would be
the one to bridge the silence in which we regarded each other
and she didn't disappoint me.

"Aunt Vinnie says you went to visit Miss Lacey. Did she
scare you, the way she does me?"

Though there were only four years between us, Caryl
seemed much younger than I was.

"I suppose I was in awe of her at first," I said. "She's pretty
imposing. But I didn't like her. And I hated her spooky old
house."

Caryl went to the crystal bowl of potpourri and lifted a few
dried rose petals to sniff. A delaying action, I suspected.

"I know what you mean about that house," she said over
her shoulder. "I only go there because Egan loves it and Miss
Lacey dotes on him."

Of course. Caryl was Egan's mother. In the confusion I

hadn't quite put it all together. At least all my relatives weren't unpleasant.

"Miss Lacey doesn't think much of me," she went on, "even though all that bad history that produced me isn't my fault. She can't seem to forgive me for being alive, but you're her namesake—that gives you an in."

She turned to look at me speculatively, and I suspected that Miss Lacey had hurt her deeply in the past.

"You know so much more than I've ever been told about the family history," I said. "This is all new to me."

"I met Ryan on the stairs a little while ago and he told me you had seen *him.*"

"Him?"

"Our grandfather. The scary one. The one who's supposed to have . . ." Again she broke off. "Maybe I've pushed all that painful stuff away because I don't want to think about it. I don't know all of the story, either. Nobody wants to answer questions, but I've put bits and pieces together."

"I never even knew Aunt Vinnie existed until a letter came yesterday for my mother."

She was still focused in one direction and didn't seem to hear me. "Tell me about our grandfather." She sat down at the dressing table and her reflection looked back at me in the mirror. Shenna leaped onto her knees, to be absently stroked.

"Miss Lacey is allowing him to use a cottage behind her house. I don't know why he's returned, but he makes me very uncomfortable."

"I wish I could meet him," Caryl said.

I felt sad watching her. We might have grown up as close sisters if things had been different. "I don't want to stay here, Caryl, but I wonder if you would come visit me in Charlottesville?"

She brightened at once. "I'd love to visit you, if I can bring Egan with me."

"Oh, I'd like that very much." I wasn't sure how my mother would feel, but I would manage somehow.

"Perhaps I can go back with you when you leave," Caryl suggested. "Though I can't leave for at least a few days. I have to meet him first."

That startled me. "Our grandfather? Why do you want to do that?"

"He's the only one who can tell me what really happened. I want to ask him face-to-face how my—our—father died."

"But why would he tell you?"

Her eyes shone as she stared at me in the mirror. "No one really knows who killed Bradley Elliot. Everyone was supposed to believe that Daniel Griffin was guilty and that's why he ran away. I've been picking up hints all my life, but I'm not sure which ones are true. There were so many contradictions."

"From Miss Lacey?"

She turned around to look directly at me. "I told you she doesn't like me. She sees me because of Egan. But otherwise she wants nothing to do with me."

"But you weren't responsible for what happened."

"Try telling her that. She's been really rotten to my mother and, because of that, I've stood up to her now and then."

"Where *is* your mother?"

"She's gone to visit friends over in Maryland, because she's terribly afraid of her father, which, naturally, makes me want to see him all the more."

"Perhaps we could see him together."

When she smiled, she was very pretty. "Do you think that's possible?"

"We'll find a way. In fact, we could go out to the cottage to see him without telling Miss Lacey first."

Her laughter was like Vinnie's, running up the scale. When she came to give me a quick hug, I knew I would enjoy having her as a coconspirator.

Daniel Griffin, watch out! I said to myself. Suddenly, I felt more lighthearted than I had since coming to Harpers Ferry. Foolishly lighthearted.

S E V E N

CARYL WAITED for me while I got ready for supper. As I washed my face and combed my hair, tentative plans began to form in my mind. It might not be easy to bypass Miss Lacey and Anne-Marie in an effort to see Daniel Griffin, but together we could act boldly. Miss Lacey's displeasure didn't really matter to me. We'd deal with that when the time came.

I rejoined Caryl and we went together to the long dining room opposite the two parlors. The others were already at the table and Vinnie looked mildly impatient.

"Do hurry and join us," she said and motioned toward our places at the table. There were five of us—Vinnie, Ryan, Egan, Caryl, and I. As we sat down, Egan was busy asking Ryan questions about John Brown, but when he saw me he broke off and looked at me with eyes that were as beautiful as his mother's.

"Hey, did you get to see Miss Lacey's house?" he asked. "Did you go upstairs?"

I said I had and we compared notes on the creepy wallpaper. He was too young to know what had happened in that room, but he clearly knew that it was something bad.

Vinnie drew the talk back to the safer subject of John Brown. "How is your book coming along, Ryan?"

He shook his head. "It's not always easy. Right now I'm trying to find out more about what Brown was really like as a man. There's plenty of material about what he did and its consequences, but I'd like to dig a little deeper. I'm trying to follow up on what happened to his raiders and find descendants who might be willing to share their family records with me. That's more difficult than you might think, because they came from all over—Kansas, Iowa, Connecticut, and other states. His home was in upstate New York."

I watched him as he talked and I liked what I saw. Ryan's eyes had a dreamy, faraway look, even as his voice quickened with an inner enthusiasm. He cared about what he did, and the past was as real to him as the present.

"Aren't there descendants of the men and women who were here at that time still living in Harpers Ferry?" I asked.

"War and floods drove a good many families away, and most of them never returned. I showed you Virginius Island today. Once it was crowded, thriving. Now there's nothing there but old stones."

"Miss Lacey's family never moved away," Vinnie said.

"I know, and I've talked to her a bit. But up where she lives the John Brown episode seemed a long way off. She doesn't even like to talk about him because she feels he opened up the path to war."

I glanced at Caryl and was startled. She was watching Ryan with her heart in her eyes, and I realized that my new sister was in love with Ryan Pearce. I found this somehow disturbing, but I didn't want to examine my own reactions.

"Was John Brown really a madman?" I asked to distract myself.

Ryan smiled. "That depends on whether your sympathies lie with the North or the South. There was insanity in his family—he admitted to that himself. In fact, one of his lawyers brought it up at the trial, hoping to get him off on a plea of insanity. But Brown wouldn't allow that. In fact, he read a clearly written statement in court attesting to his own sanity."

As Ryan talked, I looked out a nearby window toward the streets below, where once a terrible night had been filled with shots and the flames of torches in the darkness. This morning Ryan had showed me the old firehouse where many of Brown's men had died.

"He took hostages, didn't he?" I asked.

"Yes, and fortunately none of them was hurt. If Brown hadn't been hanged, what he tried to do might have been only a footnote in history. But he was a fierce abolitionist and when he died, the North turned him into a martyr and the war drums began to beat."

"Tell about bloody Kansas," Egan said eagerly, as he grabbed a piece of cornbread from a basket being passed around the table.

"Brown was mixed up in another fracas in Kansas," Ryan began, "and when he came here he brought fourteen whites and five Negroes with him. Nobody used the term 'black' in those days. He picked Harpers Ferry because the United States arsenal was here, with nearly a hundred thousand weapons available."

"There's a farm near here where he stayed," Vinnie said. "It's a tourist attraction now—and very popular."

Ryan went on. "That's where he made his plans. He meant to take over the arsenal and provide weapons for his antislavery army. He thought the slaves would leave their plantations and come with him. The mountains around Harpers Ferry would give them good hiding places. Then strikes could be made against slave owners to free more slaves. Without slaves, he was convinced that the economy of the South would collapse. That way war could be averted. His plans were visionary and in their own way idealistic."

"But there was a war," Egan said.

"There certainly was, and Brown made a few mistakes. The most important was that he kept his plans so secret—due to security fears—that none of the slaves knew about what he intended until everything burst into the open. They didn't expect him, knew nothing about him, and were afraid to follow his lead. The second mistake was a strange one. The raid had succeeded to the extent that Brown was in charge of the arsenal, but he allowed a B & O train to go through to Baltimore and that spread news of the raid. Word was sent to Washington that Harpers Ferry needed help. One man had already been killed—Heyward Shepherd—a railroad employee who walked innocently out on the tracks to find out what was happening. When he was told to halt, he started to run and drew first blood. Ironically, he was a black man and already free."

Vinnie had been caught up in the story. "I've heard that the townspeople were so angry they poured out into the streets, and then the local militia moved in to attack the firehouse where Brown had taken refuge with his men and the hostages. It must have been a frightening, crazy night."

"It was. Men were wounded in the fighting, but it was a standoff between Brown and the locals until ninety U.S. marines arrived under the command of Colonel Robert E. Lee and charged the firehouse. Some of the raiders died. A few escaped. Five were captured, including the wounded Brown. His own sons were involved and died in the attack. The hostages were rescued and it was all over very quickly, except for the trial and the hangings in Charles Town, a few miles away.

"When John Brown died on the scaffold, church bells rang in New England. He was called St. John the Just, while of course Southern newspapers denounced him as the devil himself. Before he died, Brown prophesied that slavery would cause a great civil war and that Harpers Ferry would be destroyed. He was right on both counts. I want to learn more about what went into making him the fanatic that he became."

"So now you know a bit of history, Lacey," Vinnie said. "But Harpers Ferry survived through war and floods and economic disasters. Now it's thriving. Both because of what the Park has done to attract tourists, and because it's become a bedroom community for Washington. With the railroad station here, it's less than a two-hour commute. This has all been good for the town, but I still liked the quiet times better."

As we talked, we had been enjoying Jasmine's tender chicken and dumplings, with a mixed green salad and hot cornbread. Now she cleared away the dishes and brought servings of strawberry shortcake made with luscious early strawberries.

The doorbell rang while we were lingering over dessert and Jasmine went to answer it. She returned quickly, looking upset.

"Miss Vinnie, there's a man asking to see you. He wouldn't give his name. He's got a long beard, and he's—I don't know—sort of old-looking."

Ryan saw Vinnie's quick alarm and set down his napkin. "I'll talk to him, if you like, Vinnie."

"Please." Vinnie choked over the word. "I know who it is, and I don't want to see him."

"I'll get rid of him," Ryan promised and went out to the front door.

Caryl and I looked at each other, but we both knew this wasn't the time or place to meet Daniel Griffin. Only Egan continued to eat his shortcake, unconcerned. The rest of us waited uneasily for Ryan's return. Vinnie looked shaken, and I knew I was seeing the same frightened woman who had written to my mother.

Ryan returned quickly and went over to reassure Vinnie. "He's gone. He left this envelope for you. He didn't seem to care about seeing you, he just wanted to deliver this. When I offered to give it to you, he went away peacefully enough."

Vinnie took the white envelope as though she hated to touch it, and set it beside her plate. Caryl leaned toward her.

"I should have gone to the door for you. I *want* to meet my grandfather."

"No!" Vinnie cried. "He's only here to cause trouble. I never thought I'd see him again. I thought he'd be dead by now."

"I should think any trouble he might cause would be for himself," Ryan said. "If there's a murder charge, it would still be on the books."

Vinnie shook her head. "There was never enough proof about what happened, the police said. Not even a body. I would have testified about the quarrel he had with Brad Elliot, but I didn't know anything else. Threats were made, that's all I knew. But if he was innocent he should have stayed to see it through. When he ran away we all thought he was guilty. There've been thirty years of silence, so why come back now?" Her hand shook as she lifted her coffee cup.

"Why don't you open the envelope?" Ryan asked.

She shook her head, regarding it with repugnance. "I'll open it later."

"Would you really have testified against your own brother?" Caryl asked.

Vinnie's voice sharpened as she answered. "He was always violent. I was afraid of him when I was little. I could believe easily enough that he'd murdered Brad. He was so angry about what had been done to your mother, Caryl."

Caryl made a face. "He can't blame me for that. And he is my grandfather."

"Amelia always stood up to him." Vinnie looked at me. "She tried to warn Ardra about Brad, but in those days, Caryl, your mother was pretty flighty, and she was crazy about that man."

"Even though he was married to her sister?" I said, incredulously.

"Neither Ardra nor Brad was thinking clearly, I'm sorry to say."

That seemed an understatement! I felt a little sick, hearing all this, and I looked at Egan. He was listening, but how much could a child his age understand?

Ryan spoke to the little boy. "How about going out in the garden with me for a while—before it gets too dark?"

Egan agreed happily, and Caryl watched them go. "Isn't Ryan wonderful?" she said to nobody in particular. "I think I'll go and join them."

When she'd gone, Vinnie rose, picking up the envelope from beside her plate. When she left the room, I followed her.

"Could I talk with you, please, Vinnie?" I asked.

Already on her way to the stairs, she looked over her shoulder wearily. "I'm very tired, Lacey."

"I'm sorry," I said, "but there's been no opportunity to see you alone. Caryl is determined to meet our grandfather, so I'd like to tell you what we're planning."

That got her attention and she gestured me to follow her up the stairs.

Her room was over the front part of the house, and looked out toward the street below. She held the door open for me and when I stepped in I saw that she'd made this a quiet place for resting and reading—for privacy. A tea table was drawn before the open fireplace, and beside it an armchair wore a slipcover of chintz in a tiny green design, perhaps of some herb that grew in her garden. The wallpaper was a calm mossy green—with no design.

Set apart from this sitting room area stood a single bed, covered by a handsome quilt done in patches of warm reds and earth colors.

Vinnie stretched out in a chaise longue, kicking off her shoes, and waved me into the armchair opposite her. When I sat down, she picked up an ivory paper knife and slit open the envelope Griffin had left. When she took out the single folded sheet of paper and looked at it, she cried out in alarm and let the paper flutter from her fingers. Then she lay back against the cushions and closed her eyes as though she felt faint.

"Are you all right, Aunt Vinnie—can I get you some water?"

Again she waved her hand at me, and I picked up the sheet from the floor. There were no words, but only a rough sketch. Daniel Griffin had drawn a knife form on the paper—perhaps a dagger. The cross handle was clearly ready for the grip of a hand.

Vinnie opened her eyes, and looked at me indignantly. "A dagger! For stabbing in the back, I suppose. He was always good at playing tricks like this. I mustn't let him frighten me, must I? What can he do?"

"Perhaps it *will* help if Caryl and I go up to Miss Lacey's to talk with him."

"I told you I don't want you to get involved with him. And as for Miss Lacey, I don't trust her, either. Why has she taken him in as she has?"

She was becoming upset again, and I went to kneel beside her chair and took her hand in mine. The veins resembled map lines on the thin skin, and her fingers felt fragile in mine. I smoothed the back of her hand gently. I'd often done this with my mother when she was keyed up, and it had a quieting effect now on Vinnie. Her tension seemed to lessen, and she smiled at me tremulously.

"I'm glad you've come, Lacey, but the thought of your confronting Daniel alarms me."

"You mustn't be alarmed, Aunt Vinnie. I'm a big girl and so is Caryl. We need to speak to our grandfather. Please understand."

"When will you go?"

"Tomorrow, if that suits Caryl. We'll probably bypass Miss Lacey and just go around to the back of the house. Daniel Griffin is an old man now—he seems much older than you do—and I don't think he is going to hurt anyone. I'd like to take this dagger sketch with me and see what he has to say about it. Do you mind?"

"No, take it, if you like. But don't be too sure that he can't hurt you. He has subtle ways, and if he chooses, I think he can do some damage we'll all regret."

She was quieter now, but as I rose to go, she had a question for me.

"Did you stand up to Miss Lacey as I asked you to?"

"In a way, though if there was a contest of wills, I think she won. I didn't like her very much."

"I hope you'll keep it that way—not liking her. It's safer than falling under her spell—the way I did a long time ago.

And don't let Caryl do anything foolish. In fact, it might even
be better if you went alone."

"I suppose you know that Caryl is in love with Ryan
Pearce?"

"I guess it's pretty obvious," she answered, pulling a shawl
about her shoulders.

"How does he feel about this?"

"I don't think he's accepted yet how much he cares about
her. It would be a good match—they need each other. Caryl's
been alone since her husband died, and Ryan is recovering
from an unpleasant divorce."

"What was his wife like?"

"Pretty as anything, but they couldn't talk to each other.
She wasn't interested in what he does, and mostly she just
wanted to be flattered and admired. I think he got pretty tired
of that. But he's devoted to Egan, and Caryl is a dear person.
I hope you'll get along well as sisters."

I hoped we would too, but a curious splitting seemed to be
taking place inside me. I'd only just met Ryan, but I knew he
was someone I would like to have as a friend. That was all. Yet
some stranger I didn't know seemed to be whispering inside
me that if Ryan was in love with Caryl I wouldn't be able to
bear it.

"Caryl's younger than you are, Lacey, and I don't mean just
in years. She has a bit of her mother in her—the way Ardra
used to be. Ardra loved to stir things up. But she's different
now. All those things that happened changed her, I think."

"Does Caryl hold what her mother did against her?"

"Not at all. She loves Ardra devotedly, and she's very good
to her. Ardra is the one who needed me most, and I've loved
her like a daughter."

"Perhaps it's time for things to be stirred up again—just to
clear the air."

"And you could do that so easily," Vinnie said, and shivered. "Everything would have been fine if my brother had just
stayed away. Now I don't know what will happen. Although,

I must say that getting you back has made some of this bearable, but, please, please be careful."

"What can he do to me?"

"I don't know. But there's plenty he can do to those he feels revengeful toward."

I said nothing more, but I think she sensed my determination and strength. I kissed her cheek lightly, but she lay with her eyes closed, not responding, and I went quietly away.

When I reached my room, the door I had closed stood open and Shenandoah lay asleep on my bed. Caryl sat waiting for me in the rocking chair, and I knew by her expression that she needed to tell me whatever was troubling her.

EIGHT

I WASN'T in the mood for a visit with my sister just then, but I managed a smile that she happily returned.

"I won't be able to sleep tonight until I know our plans," she said. "How do we go about meeting our grandfather?"

She was leaving the decisions up to me, and perhaps that was what I wanted. "I've had a change of heart," I told her. "I think we should talk to Miss Lacey first. Perhaps I should do this alone."

"That would be fine. But if she says we can't see him?"

"Then we'll just bypass her. He leaves her property at will; it shouldn't be hard, but I'd prefer to have her blessing."

"Ryan knows her pretty well, so he might talk to her if we ask him."

"Just be a little patient. I'll see her tomorrow. How does your mother get along with her?"

"Mostly Miss Lacey pretends that she doesn't exist. But I hear she loved your mother."

I had no idea whether or not this was true. "Where did you say your mother is now?"

"She's gone to Hagerstown, Maryland, to stay with friends. But I suppose she can come home now. I don't think he'll bother her."

In my mind's eye I saw the dagger sketch Griffin had sent Vinnie, and I wondered who he was threatening.

"Tell me about you, Caryl. I know so little. Was your marriage happy?"

She thought about that. "I miss him, but it wasn't working out very well. At least he gave me Egan, and Egan has some of his father's Irish magic in him—the best part. Sometimes Egan can even remember bits about where he came from."

I could almost believe that. The little boy had an air at times of belonging to another world.

"Never mind about me," Caryl said. "Do you work, Lacey? What do you do? Is there a man in your life?"

I answered the last question first. "There's no one at present." I opened my briefcase and showed her my published books. She was interested and full of praise, so that we were able to avoid dangerous topics for the time being.

When Caryl left she picked up the sleepy kitten and carried it off on her shoulder. I sat down in the rocking chair feeling suddenly exhausted—both physically and emotionally. Too much had happened in this crowded day—too much that was confusing and unsettling.

Not least on my problem list was the question of how I felt about Ryan Pearce. He was not a complication I'd expected, or wanted. But when I thought about him I knew he wasn't someone I could easily dismiss. When I saw him I felt a faint beat of excitement that I didn't want. Especially not in the face of the way Caryl felt about him.

After a half hour of futile arguments with myself, I gave up and went to bed. Whenever I dozed off some new face from my day would intrude and wake me up. Toward morning I fell asleep for two or three hours, and then rose early, eager to be out and about. I didn't want to call on my great-grandmother at this early hour, but I could explore the Lower Town, as Ryan had suggested, and perhaps take some pictures to help with my book.

None of Vinnie's guests was stirring and I saw nothing of my great-aunt, so I ate a light breakfast that Jasmine fixed for me, and then asked her to let Vinnie know that I intended to walk down and visit some of the shops in the Lower Town. When I'd packed my camera and a sketchbook into my shoulder bag, I was off.

The air outside was fresh and cool, with a breeze that carried the scent of spring flowers. A white dogwood coming into bloom lifted my spirits.

None of the shops was open yet, and I had the town mostly to myself. Below Shenandoah Street, and beyond the high trestle of the railroad tracks, stretched an expanse of grass and trees, ending at a sandy bank that sloped down to the water. Sycamores and poplars grew along the bank, and some of the trees were knee-deep in water. Through the crosspieces of the trestle I could glimpse the river where it rushed into rapids. Across the Potomac, on the other side of the Point was Maryland Heights, while Loudoun Heights in Virginia rose across the Shenandoah. Both had been occupied by troops during the war.

An old building at the end of the grassy park sported a marker that had been placed there to show the height of various floods. I could see that the water had risen the highest in 1936. When I'd taken several snapshots, I found a bench where I could sit while I waited for the shops to open.

About half an hour later, a busload of children arrived with their teachers. Bright sweaters made patches of red and green and yellow and young voices filled the air. I watched the children race about before being pulled into a scraggly line by their teachers.

My map had told me that this area was part of Arsenal Square, named for the arsenal that had been seized by John Brown and his raiders, only to be burned to the ground a few years later when Federal troops retreated. Now only traces of stone ruins remained.

Across Shenandoah Street buildings of red brick and white stone edged the sidewalk—some old, some restored. Most were three stories high, with gables set into the roofs. On the hill directly above, the white steeple of St. Peter's pointed into a great blue space of sky. Between the buildings that almost touched rose high, steep steps cutting upward to the church. I snapped more pictures and drew a few rough sketches. Though I liked to have maps in my books, I was not a mapmaker. I adapted existing maps for my own use and put in my little three-dimensional buildings to lend interest and character. That meant that I must sketch each real house so that I could present it accurately.

John Brown's Fort was close by, its three arched doorways standing open. I walked over to it and went inside. Brick walls made the interior cool and quiet, and the sound of children's voices faded away. When I stood still, listening, I could sense the heavy presence of history here. I could imagine the darkness, stabbed with slashes of light from guns. There would have been moans from the wounded, and a terrible clamor outside the walls of the small engine house. Ryan's account had made the story seem very real and I was relieved to step back outside.

The bookstore Ryan had pointed out to me was at the end of a walk built above the street. I climbed a few steps to follow the walk to the door and found that it was open. The shop was small, but good use had been made of its space. A remarkable collection of Civil War books filled the shelves, and more were displayed on tables. While exploring, I found a section devoted to Harpers Ferry and selected several handbooks with maps and illustrations that I thought would be useful to me.

The collection of Harpers Ferry legends that Ryan had mentioned was among the books on another shelf and I began to page through it. As I did, a name caught my eye—Fenwick. The Fenwicks had built the house in which Miss Lacey lived and where Ellen Fenwick had lived her short life and died.

A particularly engrossing story had to do with the vengeance Jud Fenwick and his son had visited upon three renegades they had tracked to Bolivar Heights in a near-dawn hour. While they thought they had killed all three, one of the men, though near death, had survived. Since I had stood so recently in Ellen's room, this was eerie stuff to read.

I wondered again about the baby girl Ellen had borne and what had happened to her. I must ask Miss Lacey if she knew more than Anne-Marie had told me.

When I'd paid for my books, I walked up High Street until I came to a shop that sold an assortment of herbs. I went in and looked around the enticing crowded interior. The scented air smelled heavenly, and I saw interesting and sometimes exotic objects on shelves all around me.

A collection of dragons fascinated me. One was made cleverly of rope; several were ceramic. The largest and fiercest had been carved from the branch of a tree, and it regarded me with a smile full of sharp teeth. I had the feeling that it might snap at me if I went too close.

"Hello, Lacey," a pleasant voice said from the back of the shop. I looked around to see Caryl smiling at me as she secured a hook in the low, wood-beamed ceiling.

She was hanging up a set of melodious wind chimes and I walked back through the shop in surprise. "Do you work here, Caryl?"

"Mother and I own the shop. This is what we do, Lacey. Mother travels all around to find unique treasures, and sometimes we get customers from a long way off who hear about us because we specialize in the unusual. We're proud of what we've collected here."

On a nearby counter were boxes of Georgia O'Keeffe notepaper with one of her black iris paintings on the lid. Vivid watercolors of Harpers Ferry hung on the walls, along with quilts and beautiful tapestries.

"That carved dragon is from Indonesia," Caryl told me. "As is that new display of silks behind him."

I wandered around for a few moments in delight. In a glass case I found a collection of handmade jewelry, and in one crowded corner several small cats carved from wood. There was one that resembled Shenandoah.

Today Caryl wore a pale green smock with a spray of white dogwood embroidered over one shoulder. She looked happy and a little excited, and I wondered if anything had happened since the last time I'd seen her.

The chimes she was hanging had a lovely sound. She reached up and touched the black clapper, so that it swung, releasing its music. I turned back, caught by the unusual tones. Long black metal tubes hung on nylon cords were suspended from a round cap at the top. The long tongue, a smoky charcoal black, moved gently at Caryl's touch.

"These are from Sweden—they've just come in," Caryl said, setting off the music again.

The chimes gave me an idea. "I want to find a gift for Aunt Vinnie, and I wonder if she'd like these."

"That's a wonderful idea. Let's find out." She unhooked the chimes and held them up for me to take. "Bring them over here and we'll let her hear the sound."

I smiled as I waited for Caryl to get Vinnie on the phone. Not all of Egan's imaginative notions came from his father.

When Vinnie answered, Caryl said, "We want you to listen to something. Lacey has picked out a gift for you, but we want to make sure you'll like it."

I held the tubes high, so the swinging clapper would send musical sounds into the telephone's ear. After a moment, Caryl held out the phone.

"What do you think?" I asked Vinnie.

"What a beautiful sound," she said, clearly delighted. "And I know just the place we can hang them—out in my herb garden. Thank you, Lacey. I accept!"

When she hung up, Caryl wrapped the chimes in a long box. As she worked with tissue and ribbon, she told me what had lifted her spirits.

"Mother is coming home. I talked to her early this morning and told her that Daniel Griffin is staying up at Miss Lacey's, so she needn't see him. And that *you* are here. I think that troubles her a little, since you're Amelia's daughter and she hasn't been in touch with her sister in all these years. Oh, I do hope you'll like her, Lacey. She's a gentle woman and she hasn't had a happy life."

I thought of what Ardra had done to my mother, and couldn't feel much sympathy for her. I said nothing, and Caryl looked at me sadly, seeming to understand.

"If you like, you can leave your package here until after you've made your trip up to see Miss Lacey," she offered, as I paid her for my purchase.

"Thank you," I said, realizing there could be no more postponing of what I had to do. Caryl came to the door with me. "You'll be fine, Lacey. You can talk to her, where I can't. It will work out better if we involve her in our decision to see our grandfather."

"Don't count on anything," I warned.

She came with me to the door and gave me a little push. "You can use the shortcut—those steps over there—if you don't mind the climb."

I walked down High Street to Shenandoah and found the narrow, very steep steps leading to the church. I started up quickly, but slowed down a bit as I passed the halfway point. The steps matched the steep pitch of the hill, and I came out at the top near the church. There was still a long walk ahead of me, but now I looked forward to retracing the climb I'd made yesterday with Ryan.

As I followed the walk along the cliffs, I noticed again the ruins of what had been the Episcopal church. Now I could take time to explore. Crumbling walls, with no roof overhead, were constructed entirely of shale slabs that I supposed had come from this area. An opening in one wall had been a door, and a protecting beam still stretched overhead.

I crossed intervening patches of grass and walked through the empty space of the door to stand in what had once been the interior of the church. There must have been rows of benches and pews to hold the congregation, but all the woodwork was long gone. The floor was only stone-strewn grass, with a wild bush springing up here and there, and a multitude of weeds. For me, the spell of past events would always haunt old ruins and I stood very still within these broken walls, with the vault of high blue sky overhead. There was little wind today and the clouds seemed hardly to move.

My eyes were drawn to what had once been an altar. Beyond a keystone arch an empty window stood against the sky, its space once filled, I imagined, by stained glass. Thick stone walls rose all around me, and for a few moments I was filled with a sense of complete isolation from the rest of the world.

When a rabbit scuttled out from some hidden burrow, I turned around to discover that I was not alone.

DOWN THE length of one side wall a man sat on a pile of rocks watching me. His eyes gleamed with amusement as he saw my startled response.

I tilted my chin defensively and stared back. Apparently I was to meet Daniel Griffin a lot sooner than I'd expected.

"Good morning," I said, disliking the way nervousness made my voice reach a higher level than I intended.

He looked as much like Moses as he did John Brown, and he seemed to be studying me judgmentally. He didn't answer my greeting, but continued to examine me as though I were something to dissect.

I tried again. "I'm Lacey Elliot and you're my grandfather, Daniel Griffin, aren't you?"

Thin lips, almost hidden by beard and mustache, seemed to move faintly—whether in a smile or merely in dismissal, I couldn't be sure. When he finally spoke, his voice startled me, seeming to rouse echoes with its deep resonance.

"I never could figure out why Amelia named you Lacey. Do you know?"

"I haven't a clue. *I* didn't choose my name. Did Miss Lacey tell you I'd come to Harpers Ferry?"

Before he could answer, a small figure emerged from behind scraggly bushes, and Egan ran toward me happily.

"Hi, Lacey. This is my great-grandpa Daniel. He's taking

me to see Grandma Lacey. She says I don't have to call her great-great-grandma because there are too many 'greats' already. He lives up there with her now, you know."

I didn't trust Daniel Griffin and I wondered if either Vinnie or Caryl knew that Egan was with him.

Egan seemed to read my mind. "It's all right. Shenna will tell Aunt Vinnie where I am," he said airily.

"When we get to Miss Lacey's, I'll phone Aunt Vinnie and your mother, just in case Shenna forgets to tell them."

Daniel Griffin stood up and stretched long arms above his head. For the first time I realized how tall he was. Beneath a green plaid shirt his shoulders stretched broad and powerful.

Meeting him like this, under such strange circumstances, was beginning to give me courage, and I risked a direct question.

"Why have you come back to Harpers Ferry?"

His lips moved more in a grimace than a smile. "Maybe I've come for my pound of flesh."

I didn't hold back my resentment. "After all these years— with a suspicion of murder hanging over your head?"

"It's best not to chatter, girl, when you have nothing to say."

I turned toward the opening in the wall and spoke over my shoulder. "I'm going up to see Miss Lacey, Egan. Let's go together?"

But Egan wasn't ready to leave. He spread his arms suddenly and went dancing across the rough grass. "I like this place, don't you?" he asked as he stopped whirling and looked at me.

"I've always liked old ruins," I said.

He nodded his approval. "Do you know where all the wood went that used to be inside this church? Great-grandpa Daniel told me that during the war soldiers came in here for shelter. They burned up all the wood inside to keep warm! The floors and walls and pews and everything was torn out and burned— even the altar!"

Within these walls everything was quiet, but when I closed my eyes, shadows from the past seemed to swirl around me, as they did so often in Harpers Ferry. Soldiers had huddled in this empty space, trying to keep warm with piles of burning wood that sent flames flaring upward in the darkness. There would have been the sounds of men laughing, shouting, moaning in pain.

My grandfather's voice brought me back to the world. "What does it say to you—this place?"

Again I closed my eyes. "I feel a—a sort of pulsing in the air, as though events from the past are still happening here. It sounds silly, but I feel as though this ground can never forget."

He was silent, and when I opened my eyes to a sunny morning, crumbling walls and the blue sky overhead, I found him watching me, his strange steely eyes intent, but no longer angry.

"Yes, it's like that, when we take the time to stop and feel what's here. Have you been on Virginius Island, girl? There's your place for shadow spirits."

"I've seen the island from the cliffs, but I haven't been there yet."

Suddenly he turned to Egan. "Come along now. We're going up to Miss Lacey's."

The little boy went with him happily, and I followed them away from the ruined church and up the path I'd climbed yesterday with Ryan.

Halfway to the top, Daniel turned to look back at me. "What about your mother, girl? Is she coming home to Harpers Ferry?"

"My mother is recovering from a cancer operation," I told him. "She sent me in her stead."

He heard this without visible reaction. My feelings toward him were mixed. He could easily alarm me, but I was beginning to sense that much more lay behind his grim manner than I could have guessed. At least we could settle one thing between us, since his habit of calling me "girl" had begun to rankle.

"I do have a name," I said.

"It's not a name I care for. There are too many Laceys."

"One of them appears to be helping you," I said pointedly, knowing that I was pushing. Daniel Griffin could be a source of information for me, if ever he were willing to talk.

He gave me a dismissive look and continued on up the hill.

The three of us had covered ground a good deal faster than Ryan and I had done yesterday, and when we'd cut up past the cemetery, Miss Lacey's house came into view.

I looked across the gravel road that ran past it, and saw again that narrow, forbidding front, and the gallery with its four thin white pillars. I hadn't liked the house when I'd first seen it, and I still didn't.

Daniel stopped ahead of us, and he too was staring at the house. When he spoke, it was to Egan. "I'm going around back. Come visit me when she gets through with you." Clearly I wasn't included in the invitation, and he didn't look at me again as his long legs carried him around the side of the house.

Egan looked after him, bright-eyed. "I like Grandpa Daniel. I like him lots."

"Why do you like him?" I asked as we started toward the side steps that led up to the gallery.

He considered my question gravely. "Aunt Vinnie says he did bad things and hurt people. But maybe she doesn't know what he's like inside. I do bad things sometimes, but I'm not a bad boy—am I?"

I gave him a quick hug as we climbed the steps. "No— you're certainly not." But I couldn't be that trusting about Daniel Griffin. Some purpose drove him—perhaps an angry purpose that might result in damage to people I was coming to like.

Again Anne-Marie met us at the door, no more friendly than she'd been yesterday. "Is *she* expecting you?"

I understood her disapproval a little better than I had yesterday. Her devoted task was to protect Miss Lacey from anyone who might upset her.

"Who is it?" The challenge came from a room behind the long drawing room where Miss Lacey had received me yesterday.

Egan ran past Anne-Marie, crying out, "I've brought another Lacey to see you, Grandma."

She came into the hall a few steps, the carved head of the gryphon hidden by her hand, as she spoke to Anne-Marie. "I'll take care of them."

Before the housekeeper could leave, I asked her to phone Vinnie and tell her Egan was here. I'd explain about Daniel Griffin's high-handedness later. Anne-Marie went off, clearly disapproving of unexpected visitors. Miss Lacey walked to the far door, and I knew we were expected to follow.

Egan ran ahead, and I went after him into a small, comfortably furnished back parlor. The boy went at once to a big drum that was sitting on the floor in a corner, and Miss Lacey watched his eagerness fondly. This morning she had dressed less formally in a flowing summery gown that draped her small body in a field of cornflowers. I couldn't imagine her in jeans or even a knee-length skirt.

"Come and see!" Egan called to me, patting the rug beside him.

Miss Lacey smiled. Yesterday she had never smiled. The difference in her puzzled me and gave me an uneasy feeling.

I knelt beside Egan, waiting to be instructed.

"This drum is from the war," he told me. "It's got a special secret."

There was, of course, only one war that deserved the emphasis of being referred to as *the* war. The drum was tall, and looked as though it might have been heavy for a young drummer boy to carry. Its sides were covered with faded paintings—of pistols and cannons and flags. Cross cords bound the drum all the way around, a bit frayed here and there, but still holding.

Egan turned the drum and pointed to an almost invisible peephole. "Look in there, Lacey."

I put my eye to the tiny opening and saw that whoever had made this drum had set a name in clear letters on the interior wall opposite the peephole. The name was *Royal Fenwick.* I looked up at Miss Lacey and she nodded proudly.

"Royal Fenwick is a distinguished name on our family tree—even if he did fight for the South. He was Jud Fenwick's older brother, and our line is descended from him."

I was relieved to know that I wasn't directly descended from Jud, whose fierce vengeance I had just read about. But there was a question I hadn't asked Miss Lacey.

"What became of Ellen's baby?"

"There's no record. We only know that Jud gave her away for adoption. By the time Royal came home, all that was over.

Royal Fenwick caught my imagination and I wondered if *he* would have kept the baby in the family, no matter who her father was. I told Miss Lacey about the book I had found in the store on Shenandoah Street.

"It gave an account of what Jud and his son did to avenge poor Ellen. The book said that one of the three men Jud and his son attacked actually lived. So weren't they accused of murder?"

Miss Lacey looked affronted. "Certainly not. The man who lived—Orin Lang—kept his mouth shut until many years later. For a long time the story of what happened was told only by the little boy who witnessed it."

"What became of Jud Fenwick?"

"It's not a pretty story. When Royal came home he was once again the head of the family and this house belonged to him. The brothers quarreled and Jud moved to Charles Town. In his later years he became deranged and thought the men he'd killed on Bolivar Heights had come back to hunt him down. When he became violent he was placed in an asylum, where he eventually died. The asylums of that day were dreadful places."

"What became of Jud's son?"

"He died in one of the last battles of the war. I'm thankful that our line of descent is from Royal, who was a good man and a master drum maker. After the war he made drums for musicians. This is one of his few war drums that has survived and it's one of my treasures. When I'm gone it will be given to a museum. But first I'm going to send it to the Preservation Department of the National Park Service to be restored. They do wonderful work on pieces sent to them from all around the country."

"Do you have to give it away, Grandma?" Egan asked.

Miss Lacey's look was affectionate. "Perhaps I will lend you the drum, Egan. And then *you* can give it to a museum."

Egan got up from the floor to face her eagerly. "I'd like that! When can I take it home, Grandma?"

She hadn't expected him to assume such quick ownership, but she gave in promptly. "Soon, if you like. Just for a short time until it goes to Charles Town for repairs. I know you'll take very good care of it."

When he'd promised that he would, she turned her attention to me. "I'm sure you came to see me this morning for a reason, Lacey. So tell me what it is."

I stayed where I was, kneeling beside Royal Fenwick's drum, as I answered her. "I've just met a sister I didn't know I had—Egan's mother, Caryl—and I like her. I think we'll become friends. Now we both want to meet our grandfather. Since he's staying in your cottage, we'd like your permission . . ."

She stopped me sharply. "No! Stay away from that man—he'll do you no good."

Her vehemence surprised me. "Why do you feel that way?"

"This is not something I care to discuss."

I pushed myself up so that I would be standing and therefore better braced as I faced her again. "You can't keep us from talking to him, but we'd rather have your permission."

Her look of outrage seemed to give her more stature and she appeared to grow taller in her chair. I felt certain she wasn't used to being confronted, and the look she gave me made me quake inwardly.

"You will not see him! He is a dangerous man. There may even be blood on his hands."

"Why do you allow him to stay here if you believe that?"

"I told you, I want him where I can watch him. I want to know his real purpose in coming here. Believe me, he isn't to be trusted."

"Did he kill my father?" I asked.

Egan, for all his interest in the drum, was listening intently, and he gave Miss Lacey an angelic smile. "Grandpa Daniel brought me up here today. He said I could come see him anytime I liked, so maybe I'll take Lacey with me."

Miss Lacey threw her hands up despairingly. She might tell me off in a rage, but a softness toward Egan held her silent for the moment. I never got an answer to my question because at that moment a commotion sounded from the direction of the front door.

Anne-Marie's voice rose in shrill protest as a man's rough tones overrode her words. "Get out of my way!"

The intruder must have pushed past her, for she cried out in pain, and I heard a thud as though she had fallen. It all happened so suddenly that neither Miss Lacey nor I had time to move before a man came stomping down the hall, looking into one room after another, until he found us in the rear parlor.

When he saw us, he held on to the doorjamb to steady himself, clearly drunk. Beneath thinning, rusty hair, his face looked red and bloated. Though a big man, he had none of Daniel Griffin's lean strength. He was middle-aged and time had larded his body with fat that overflowed his belted pants.

As I stared, he raised one hand and I saw that he held a gun. Miss Lacey stood up, facing him with no outward sign of fear, while I pushed Egan behind me protectively.

"What do you want, Henry?"

He rocked on his heels, glaring at us both. Whoever he was, he obviously meant trouble.

TEN

THE MAN Miss Lacey had called Henry made an effort to focus his wild-eyed look on her. "I know who's hiding here! I've heard the talk clear to Charles Town. Where is he? I want to see him!" The gun waved so unsteadily that I expected to hear the crash of a shot at any moment.

"Put that thing down," Miss Lacey told him quietly. "You're likely to shoot yourself, Henry."

She looked tiny facing him, but her courage and her words seemed to reach him. He regarded the unsteady weapon as if in surprise and lowered his arm to his side. "Just tell me where he is!"

"I don't know what you're talking about." In spite of her reasonable tone, Miss Lacey had tightened her grip on her cane. When the intruder came a few more steps into the room, she raised the cane by its middle and waved the gryphon's head at him. "Don't come any closer, Henry. You're very drunk. Liquor is the only thing that ever gave you courage. What help were you when your brother died? You didn't even like him."

"I want to see Dan Griffin! I know he's here. I owe him—because of Brad."

I listened in dismay. No one had told me that my father had a brother, and I didn't relish the fact that this wild-eyed man was my uncle.

Anne-Marie, recovered from her encounter with Henry, came running into the room. "Shall I call the police, Miss Lacey?"

"No, of course not. I've seen Henry like this before, and he's going to leave quietly. Daniel Griffin isn't in this house, Henry, and I wouldn't turn him over to you if he were. You know he'd make mincemeat out of you. Even if you were sober you wouldn't stand a chance. It's been thirty years since Brad was lost to the river. You didn't do anything then, so why should you be concerned now?"

He raked his hand through his hair, looking almost helpless. "How could I do anything when Dan ran away? Maybe you've cooled off—but not me. Brad wasn't all that good a brother, but he never deserved to die. Dan Griffin killed my brother."

"What do you know about what happened?" Miss Lacey asked, still outwardly calm.

"I know plenty."

Miss Lacey tried to distract him. "Perhaps you'd like to meet your niece, Henry. This is Lacey Elliot. Lacey, Henry Elliot is your father's brother."

For the first time he seemed to notice me. "Amelia's kid? You know *she* was really the one to blame for this whole mess. If Amelia had been a better wife to Brad, he'd never have looked at Ardra."

Egan slipped from behind me and surprised Henry by coming to stand in front of him.

"Can I see your gun, please?"

Henry made an effort to pull Egan into focus. He held the gun out of Egan's reach, shaking his head unsteadily.

"You don't want anything to do with guns, boy." Perhaps he was sobering up a little. "I only brought this so Daniel wouldn't try to hurt me. I need to show him something."

The sound of a car stopping before the house reached us through the open windows. Henry looked even more alarmed as he listened.

When Anne-Marie started toward the hall door, Miss Lacey stopped her. "Wait. I'm not expecting anyone. Are you?"

Anne-Marie shook her head. A car door slammed loudly in the late-morning quiet. A moment later the front door opened and closed without any knocking and Vinnie came running down the hall and into the room. After a glance at us, all of her attention was on Egan.

"What made you go off without telling me? You always let me know when you go away. We were worried."

Egan returned her look calmly. "I'm sorry, Aunt Vinnie. Grandpa Daniel said it would be all right. And I told Shenna to tell you where I was."

"I don't speak kitten-talk," Vinnie said, her manner softening as she looked at the little boy.

"I'm going out back to see Grandpa Daniel now," Egan told her. "He said I could visit him."

"Out back!" Henry echoed. "So that's where he is." For a moment he looked as though he would rush out of the house to find Daniel, but some glimmer of reason seemed to stop him. He addressed Miss Lacey with a last show of bluster.

"You tell him I'll be back, whether he likes it or not. I have to see him."

He pushed past Vinnie, who suddenly noticed the gun and looked alarmed, as he ran out the door.

"Why did *he* come here, Miss Lacey? What did he want?"

Miss Lacey lowered herself into a chair, moving slowly, regally, both hands clasping her cane. "Maybe he came gunning for Daniel—and then changed his mind. He's drunk, of course."

Vinnie held out a hand to Egan. "Come along, dear. We'll go home now."

I looked at Egan, who was smiling cheerfully, even as he shook his head.

"I have to see Grandpa Daniel first," he told her, and then looked at me. "Will you come with me, Lacey?"

Vinnie tried to object, but Miss Lacey tapped her cane

decisively on the floor. "Let him go, Vinnie." With a concealing dignity that hinted at how badly Henry had shaken her,
Miss Lacey rose and moved toward the door. "If you'll excuse
me, it's time for me to rest." She nodded at Anne-Marie and
then turned to me before leaving. "Thank you for coming to
see me, Lacey. Next time we'll have a real visit. I hope you'll
come again soon."

Egan ran after her as she moved toward the door. "Can I
take the drum home today, Grandma Lacey?" he asked.

She paused to reconsider her earlier decision. "I think I
should keep it for you right now. But you can come up anytime you like to play with it."

Egan agreed cheerfully enough, though I could tell by Vinnie's face that she wasn't happy about the bait of the drum
that would bring Egan here more often.

The energetic little boy didn't wait for any further interfer-
ence with his plans. He ran past us before anyone could stop
him and we heard the back door slam. Miss Lacey shrugged
and started down the hall, with Anne-Marie following her.

"Oh dear!" Vinnie wailed. "I don't want Egan to spend time
with Daniel. Will you come with me, Lacey, so we can get him
and take him home."

I agreed and we headed toward the back door. Miss Lacey
and Anne-Marie had disappeared behind Miss Lacey's bedroom door.

In the backyard everything seemed peaceful, the scene
empty of movement. Egan had apparently disappeared into
the cottage and the door was closed. Beyond the grove of
trees, I caught a shining glimpse of the river far below. From
here the Shenandoah's voice was only a whisper down by the
rapids, but, of course, today the lady was in a sunny mood.

Vinnie hesitated a moment, gathering up her courage, and
then went to the cottage door and rapped smartly. It opened at
once, as though Daniel Griffin had been expecting us.

"Come in, ladies." He spoke sardonically. "What's this
Egan tells me about Henry Elliot turning up with a gun?"

"Seems to me he was gunning for you," Vinnie said. "I guess he changed his mind. Of course he'd never come near you if he was sober. Why have you come back, Daniel?"

I remembered that these two hadn't met face-to-face in thirty years, yet this was no warm reunion between brother and sister. Griffin moved out of the doorway to allow us to step into the main room of the little house. It was stocked with pieces that were probably castoffs from the big house. A large faded couch, two shabby chairs, and a desk with a lamp made up the furnishings.

"I've come to take Egan home," Vinnie said, remaining in the doorway. "You should never have taken him away from my house without asking." She reminded me of a fly who was desperately afraid of the spider, but was nevertheless facing the web with her own quiet courage.

His smile was as grim as ever. "I didn't think you'd give your permission if we asked, my dear sister. After all, the boy is my great-grandson, and it's time we got to know each other." He turned to Egan, who was watching us intently. "Do you like cornbread?" he asked the boy. "I stirred up a batch this morning before I went to fetch you. Go out in the kitchen and help yourself. Maybe you can bring some in for our guests."

Egan dashed off happily through a door that stood ajar, and Daniel gestured toward the two worn armchairs. I walked in and sat down, but Vinnie stubbornly remained where she was.

Two wooden boxes had been turned over to form a crude table, with several yellowing newspapers spread open upon them.

"Take a look, if you like," he invited me. "These papers may interest you too, Vinnie, since you're concerned. And it's time for Egan to be told a few things that nobody seems to have revealed about what happened thirty years ago."

"Egan is a small boy," Vinnie reminded him sharply. "He's too young to understand what is so long past."

"He's smart beyond his years, and he's been soaking up a

lot from what's been said around him. I suspect he's collecting some wrong ideas."

"Why have you come back?" Vinnie repeated. It was the old question, and once more he didn't answer.

"You are in those papers," Daniel told her. "Or have you forgotten? You might take a look and refresh your memory. You told the police assorted stories—all a little different. I suspect that you got mixed up when you lied and forgot what you'd said before."

Vinnie ignored him and repeated her question for the third time. "Why have you returned to Harpers Ferry?"

He went to a tall chest of drawers and took out a framed photograph. For a moment he stood looking at it. Then he handed it to me. "This is my wife when she was young. My second wife—my *real* marriage. Before we married twenty-five years ago, I told her the whole story of what happened here— as far as I knew it—before I 'escaped' from Harpers Ferry. That's the word they use in those accounts. 'Escaped.'"

"I don't know anything about that time," I said. "My mother would never talk about where we were from or who we were before we moved."

He seemed to approve. "Then you can learn without prejudice. Over the years my wife kept urging me to return and clear everything up, but I knew I couldn't do that—not at the time. I was caught in a trap. I felt my life had been taken away from me as surely as Brad's was."

I examined the calm, beautiful face in the photograph. An inner goodness shone in her wide eyes.

"What is her name?" I asked.

"Virginia, after the state where she was born. Her maiden name was Driscoll. I would never have come here if she hadn't died. We had one child—a son. He's grown up and lives out West. There was no one left, so I decided to do as Virginia wanted and come back. Though not for her reasons." His voice hardened. "I came to persuade a few people to tell the truth."

"At the possible risk of your own neck?" Vinnie asked. She had finally taken a few steps into the room, but did not sit down.

"I believe the phrase is 'worthless neck,' isn't it?" The dark look he turned on her disturbed me. There was so much suppressed anger in this man and I could tell Vinnie recognized it too, for she shrank away from him.

When she spoke, her voice sounded shrill. "I can't see why Miss Lacey would allow you to stay here!"

Daniel's heavy eyebrows drew down in a fierce scowl. "Miss Lacey feels safer if she believes that she's keeping an eye on me. It's pretty funny that Henry Elliot has turned up—looking for *me!* Maybe we'll have the whole cast on stage for the last act. Except for those who have gone on to their final reward, of course."

Vinnie made an effort to steady herself. "Your real wife was Ida, as far as I'm concerned, and she threw herself into the river because her younger daughter had betrayed her, and because she thought her husband was a murderer."

Daniel dismissed that scornfully. "Ida died because she couldn't take what living meant. She died because of her own weakness. She never had Amelia's courage. Maybe Amelia's handed this trait on to her own daughter. Anyway, Amelia did the right thing in taking her child and getting away to make a new life for herself. Just the way I did."

There was a subject I knew Vinnie wouldn't bring up, and I took the sketch he'd left at the house from my purse. "Why did you send Aunt Vinnie this sketch of a dagger?"

"I think she knows why." He threw a mocking look at his sister.

Vinnie had turned so pale that I went to put an arm around her so that we faced Daniel Griffin together. "We don't need to stay any longer, Vinnie. We can take Egan and leave now."

But Vinnie had to try once more. "Please go away, Daniel. Stay forgotten." She lifted her chin so she could look into his eyes. "If you stay, I might have to let the police know that you're here."

"You won't do that, Lavinia. And neither will Miss Lacey. Because you can't be sure what I may have up my sleeve. You'll wait for whatever move I may make, and in the meantime you'll start to be afraid of shadows. As for me, I'll watch my back every minute."

Vinnie called out to Egan. "We're going home now, dear. Come along right away."

The little boy came at once, but he had clearly been busy in the kitchen. He emerged carrying a large plate on which he'd placed ragged chunks of cornbread that he must have cut from the pan.

"It's real good," he told Vinnie. "Have a piece." He'd found paper plates, as well, and there was no immediate way to do as she wished and leave.

When Vinnie sat down, supplied with plate and cornbread, and I had been served, Egan carried the plate to Daniel, who helped himself, smiling slightly. We must have made a curious Alice-in-Wonderland tea party. The warm morsels were dry in my mouth and hard to swallow, but somehow Vinnie ate every crumb and then spoke to the boy.

"We'll leave as soon as you're finished, Egan." Then she rose and faced her brother. "I think you're making a mistake to stay where you aren't wanted. The past was sleeping quietly, but if you wake it up, goodness knows what may happen."

"*Is* Brad dead? Do you *know* that?" he asked her.

She turned so white that she frightened me. Her hands rose in a despairing gesture, and dropped to her sides. "I'll just ask one thing of you, Daniel. Don't hurt Miss Lacey. She's had enough to bear in her life."

His look mocked her. "That lady can take care of herself."

Vinnie went out the door and for some reason I found myself feeling apologetic. But when I tried to say something, no words came, and I went outside to wait with Vinnie until Egan joined us.

She had walked across scraggly grass to where an iron fence offered protection from the straight plunge of the cliff, and I joined her there. She looked so badly shaken that I made an effort to distract her.

"That's Virginius Island down there, isn't it? Ryan told me about the mills and foundries and homes that once covered the island until floods swept everything away."

Vinnie held on to the fence as though she needed support. "So many died when the waters rose. You can see how easily water would cover the island. Why would they ever build there? But they did. Once it must have been a busy, happy place. Perhaps it's even more beautiful with wildflowers growing among the ruins. But it's a haunted place too. I used to go there when I was young and I'd try to listen. Sometimes I felt they could talk to me, those who had gone before."

"What did they say?" I asked softly.

My question seemed to call her back from some distant place. "I don't remember. I never go there anymore. Probably if I went to the island now they'd just tell me to go home and mind my own business. There's nothing I have to give them." She turned her back on island and river and faced me earnestly. "I'm glad you've come. You were my darling little girl when you were small. We had lovely times together. But now that you've seen how things are, you must go back to Charlottesville and get away from the unhappiness here."

"What is here that could threaten me? Where is it supposed to come from? I don't think your brother is dangerous. Perhaps he just wants to know the truth, so he can be free of old suspicions against him."

Vinnie put an arm around me. "Whatever he intends, I hope he won't hurt you, but there are others he can injure. None of us is safe from him. Only Egan. He's taken a liking to the boy, and I hate to see Egan turning to him as though he were some kind of hero."

"What if he is? What if he was made a scapegoat?"

She looked off across the river, but had nothing to say.

"What has Henry Elliot to do with any of this?" I asked. "Why is he so angry with Daniel Griffin?"

Vinnie sighed. "There was so much treachery in the old days; Brad and Henry were both in love with Amelia—and neither one worth a hill of beans!"

"Yet it was Brad my mother chose."

"Brad always knew how to charm a woman. Ardra wasn't entirely to blame. She could never have resisted him when he went after her. I'm sorry to tell you these things about your father, Lacey, but you wanted to know."

"It doesn't matter," I said. I had no attachment to this man who seemed to have injured both my mother and Ardra, to say nothing of Ida. All I wanted was to see the mystery of my background cleared up.

Egan came to the door of the cottage, licking crumbs of cornbread from his fingers and looking thoroughly happy. Daniel stood behind him.

"I'm ready to go now," he called to Vinnie. "Grandpa Daniel says I can come see him anytime I like." He looked up at the tall, old man and I saw a gentling in that grim face.

Egan's words caused Vinnie distress, but she merely held out a hand to him and we started toward the house.

Daniel called after him. "Next time bring your mother with you, boy. I've never met my other granddaughter."

So the matter of Caryl's visit was settled as easily as that.

Vinnie led us quickly toward the house where she told us we could cut through the hall to the front door. The house was quiet as we entered, but when we reached the foot of the stairs, she stopped with a hand on the banister and looked upward, listening. Then she shook her head and went out to the car with Egan and me following.

I had listened too as we stood at the bottom of the stairs, and I had heard a faint murmur of voices in the direction of Ellen's room. I couldn't make out the words, but for some reason the sound made me shiver.

ELEVEN

WHEN WE WERE in the car I asked about the voices we had heard upstairs. Vinnie didn't answer until we were back on the road. Then she seemed hesitant, and perhaps a little too casual.

"It's just a ritual Miss Lacey and Anne-Marie have concocted. Don't pay any attention."

"I think it bothers you and I'd like to know why. Don't you see, Aunt Vinnie—there's so much I don't know. Everything counts."

She decided to tell me. "They do this once a year—on the anniversary."

"What anniversary?"

"The day and hour of Ellen Fenwick's death. I don't know what they do up there, but I suspect Miss Lacey believes she has some sort of pact with the past."

"After more than a hundred years? That's dreadful!"

"I know. But old people can get curious notions. Let's not talk about it. I'm not in her confidence and I shouldn't even be speculating."

I had to respect her feelings about this, and I let the matter go for now. Remembering that I had wanted to pick up my gift of chimes for Aunt Vinnie, I asked her to let me out near the top of the steps that ran down to Shenandoah Street and she obliged.

I told her I would see her in a little while and went down the steps a lot faster than I'd come up and then hurried along High Street to Caryl's shop. She seemed glad to see me when I went in, and I knew she was excited about something.

She placed the handsome blue and silver package containing the chimes on the counter, then she glanced toward the back of the room, her eyes alight with anticipation.

"Mother's here. So you'll get to meet her right away. Try not to say anything about where you've been, unless she asks you directly. It'll only upset her."

If it had been possible, I'd have taken my package and left the shop at once. Though I knew our eventual meeting couldn't be avoided, I wasn't ready yet to face my mother's sister. Her role in what had happened had resulted in too many ruined lives for me to feel comfortable with her. However, it was already too late to get away.

A woman had emerged from a rear room of the store, and I had only a few moments of grace before we met there in the aisle. In those few moments I was able to see her clearly before she knew who I was.

Ardra Griffin didn't look at all as I'd pictured her. Her fragility surprised me. I'd expected someone more forceful, considering her tempestuous past. This woman looked rather timid, and she was no longer as pretty as she must have been in the days when she'd caught my father's eye.

As she came toward me down the crowded aisle, Caryl introduced us. "Mother, this is Lacey Elliot." Then, as the bell over the shop door sounded, she excused herself to take care of a customer, leaving Ardra and me to confront each other.

For just an instant, Ardra looked uncomfortable. Then she seemed to pull herself together, and I could see traces of the Southern belle she had once been. Her blouse was the color of heliotrope and her fawn-colored trousers were too well cut to have been purchased in a country store. She placed a small hand on the nearest counter, perhaps to steady herself, and the smile she managed lighted her face.

I went to her holding out my hand. "Hello, Aunt Ardra."

She took my hand graciously enough, but then let it go quickly. Her touch suggested that she was wary of me and that she was on guard against any criticism I might level at her.

I tried to help us both feel more relaxed. "I didn't even know I had a sister until yesterday. Now I'm very glad I've found her."

Ardra moistened her lips with the tip of her tongue. "How is your mother?"

"She's convalescing from an operation, but every day sees her stronger and more herself. I think the worst is behind her."

"Caryl tells me that she never told you anything about me?"

"She's never spoken of Harpers Ferry, or anyone here," I said gently. "I'm not sure that was right, though I can understand how she must have felt about the past."

Her pointed little tongue touched her lips again. "Have you seen him since you came?" she asked quietly.

She meant her father, of course, and I nodded. Caryl's customer had gone, so she joined us again.

"I've seen him a few times," I told Ardra. "But today was the first time that I've talked with him."

Ardra lapsed into silence, though I could sense there were questions she wanted to ask. I began to relax a little. Whatever I'd expected from Caryl's mother, Ardra was far from alarming. I went on to tell them both about coming upon Daniel Griffin and Egan in the ruins of the old church, and of going up to Miss Lacey's with them. I left it there, not wanting to talk about what had happened at Miss Lacey's and later, out in the cottage. At least, I could reassure Caryl.

"Your grandfather is very fond of Egan and I don't think he meant any harm in taking him for a walk to Miss Lacey's. *And* he's asked to meet you. I thought we might go see him tomorrow, if you'd like."

Ardra made a little protesting sound in the back of her throat and Caryl patted her arm and told her not to worry. "It'll be all right, Momma. I want to meet him."

I told them about Egan's excitement at being at Miss Lacey's and that I thought she might be using the drum as bait to win Egan over.

Caryl and Ardra looked at each other, and Caryl nodded. "I know she'd like to take him away from me. She doesn't think I'm raising him properly. If Egan began to respond to her and wanted to live up there with her, she might have a strong weapon to use. But I won't let that happen."

When I thought of Miss Lacey's autocratic ways, I could only hope that Caryl would have the strength to stand against her. I didn't think that either Ardra or Vinnie would be able to oppose her effectively in such a struggle.

It was nearly twelve o'clock as Caryl went about closing up early for the day, so that she could go home with her mother. She told me that she often walked down to the shop, so she didn't have her car with her today. When we were ready, the three of us went out to where Ardra's car was parked.

Tension was visible in the way Ardra drove and I was glad the distance was short. When we reached the street on the higher level, she touched the horn and called out the window to a man who was walking along the sidewalk ahead of us.

"Ryan! Do you want a lift?"

He came over to the car at once and smiled at Ardra. "Welcome home. And thanks." His smile included Caryl and turned on me in the back seat. I moved over to give him room, feeling a familiar rush of pleasure at seeing him. I felt as though I'd known him for a great deal longer than I had, even though this was a man I'd met for the first time yesterday.

Caryl was openly glad to see him, bouncing a little in the front seat beside Ardra. Her mother gave her an observant sidelong glance, and I thought that she missed nothing of her daughter's reaction to Ryan.

When he'd settled next to me in the back seat, he began to talk eagerly. "I'm about to be handed a gold mine of old papers and letters that go way back to Civil War times and before. Would any of you care to come with me when I pick them up?"

"Thank you, dear," Ardra said, "but I'd like to spend the rest of the afternoon with my daughter and my grandson, that is, of course, unless Caryl would like to go."

"Any other time I'd love to, but, Mom's right; the three of us do need a little time together. Egan's never with us enough." She looked disappointed but sure of her duty.

"Well, Lacey," Ryan said, turning to me, "how about you?"

"Of course," I said quickly. "I'd be delighted." Ryan was the one I wanted most to talk to about everything I'd learned. Perhaps he could make some sense out of the strange morning I'd spent at Miss Lacey's.

When we reached the house Ryan brought in Ardra's suitcase and Caryl and Ardra went off together. Ryan went upstairs to his room and I carried my package out to the herb garden, where Egan was talking to Vinnie a mile a minute. Shenandoah was all over the place, leaping onto Vinnie's knees, and immediately off again. My package instantly drew the kitten's attention and she seemed poised to attack the wrappings, so I handed it to Vinnie.

She still looked strained after her meeting with her brother, but she smiled at me as she opened the paper with a careful thrust of her forefinger so the wrappings wouldn't be torn. My mother had always opened packages in just that way, so that paper and ribbon could be used another time.

When the box was open, she lifted out the smooth black tubes suspended from a disk shape at the top. She held them up and a breeze from the river played over the chimes, making a lovely sound.

"Thank you, dear," she said, kissing my cheek as she dangled the chimes at Egan. "Where do you think we should hang them?"

He considered this, closing his eyes, perhaps to visualize where they might hang. In a moment he opened them. "I know! Over there on the end of the wisteria trellis."

I looked toward the white framework and saw that a metal arm for holding hanging plants extended at one end.

"That's just the place I thought of, Egan!" she told him and sent him off to fetch her small ladder.

Shenandoah was having a marvelous time making a nest out of the wrappings, and Vinnie shooed her away and began to fold them neatly.

"After all that time we spent with him, we still don't know what Daniel means to do," she said.

"Why are you afraid of him?"

She went on smoothing blue paper, musing aloud. "We always had different interests. He was never like a big brother to me, though I wanted him to be. I never understood how he could marry Ida Enright when she was so very different from him. We all expected him to marry—" She broke off for a moment and then went on. "Oh, never mind. That's all ancient history. It's *now* that matters. He seems changed after all these years, but I'm not sure what that means. Perhaps he's just become a harder man and far more sure of himself than I remember him being. At least, he seems to have had a happy second marriage."

"You said that both Brad and Henry were in love with my mother. Did this upset my grandfather?"

She shook her head and smiled, remembering. "Your mother had so much appeal. She was so lively and funny. All the boys were crazy about her. But Daniel didn't pay much mind. He just wanted his daughter to be pretty and good. Beyond that, his attention was somewhere else."

I couldn't remember my mother being all that lively, and certainly not lighthearted enough to be funny. The events that had driven her from Harpers Ferry must have subdued and changed her. I wished that I could have known her the way she used to be.

"Were you able to discern anything really different about your brother when you saw him today?" I asked Vinnie.

"He's a stranger. I don't think I'd really be able to judge. Can you understand that?"

I nodded. "He doesn't seem afraid of arrest."

"He knows there was never enough proof."

"Then why did he go away in the first place?"

She lifted the chimes and played them with her fingers. "There was circumstantial evidence, and perhaps he knew that if he stayed, more would be found. His word wouldn't have been good for much, under the circumstances, and maybe he was smart when he decided not to risk it." She shook her head as though in confusion. *"I* helped with what evidence there was. I felt I had no other choice at the time. He had a reputation for being rough and violent and I'd seen the fight he had with Brad. I'd heard the threats he made—" Her voice broke and she stopped.

"But you don't think he was guilty of whatever happened to Brad?"

She set the chimes down on her knees with a clatter. "Let it go, Lacey. I only hope that *he* will give up and not try to get even with anyone."

"Getting even might include you?"

She looked so miserable that I was instantly sorry I had asked the question. To give her time to recover, I fished Shenna out of some shredded tissue paper and held her on my shoulder. She tucked her small head under my chin and started a great rolling purr that made her seem much larger than she was.

Egan came running back with a wooden kitchen stool that was almost as big as he was. "I couldn't find the ladder, Aunt Vinnie, but maybe this will work."

I handed the kitten to Vinnie and held the stool while Egan scrambled up and managed the simple task of hanging the chimes. The sleek black tubes looked beautiful against the green backdrop and a gentle wind obliged to set them ringing.

Just then Jasmine came out to tell us that lunch was ready. A table had been set up in another part of the garden and at this hour, with the sun warmly overhead, it was pleasant to eat outdoors. The others came out to join us and Vinnie and Egan had a chance to hug and kiss Ardra and welcome her home.

Ardra seemed every bit as happy to see them as they were to
see her, although I detected something amiss once we sat down
to lunch. Jasmine served a simple meal of homemade chicken
salad, tender spring lettuce, and hot biscuits. The fragrant iced
green tea was Vinnie's idea, and pungent lemon slices en-
hanced the flavor.

Caryl was the talkative one, with an amusing story about
one of the customers in her shop that morning. Ardra seemed
too quiet, and ate without much appetite, hardly looking at
her plate. In the midday light she looked older and even more
fragile than she'd appeared in the shop. When she spoke it was
directly to me.

"When you saw my father this morning, Lacey, did he tell
you why he's come back?"

"I don't think he's explained that to anyone," I said.

She mused aloud, as though talking to herself. "When I was
young I thought he was wonderful. I really loved him, but he
never forgave me for what happened. Finally he turned
against all of us. He was terribly angry—he frightened me. I'll
never be able to forget what he was like then. When he went
off, he didn't tell any of us good-bye. I don't think you should
be friendly with him, Lacey."

"What happened was a long time ago," Ryan said. "Ardra,
perhaps you could be the one to convince your father that
everyone concerned has been punished enough."

Ardra looked horrified. "I could never talk to him—even if
he would listen."

"You don't need to," Caryl reassured her, reaching out to
touch her mother's arm comfortingly.

I liked Caryl more all the time, but I couldn't warm to her
mother.

When we finished our meal, Ryan told Vinnie that I was
going with him to see Laura Kelly and she looked surprised.
"I haven't seen Laura in a couple of years, though she used to
be active in village affairs. I was always very fond of her."

"Just who is she?" I asked.

"I'll tell you when we're on our way," Ryan said. "I've made an appointment for two o'clock, and it's almost that now. So we'd better get started."

We weren't going far, he assured me as we drove up High Street in his car. Just to a remarkable house on Bolivar Heights.

"Laura Kelly has lived in Harpers Ferry all her life and she's something of a historian. She's been helping me with my book. Only recently, someone in Charles Town who knew Laura from a long time ago died and left her his collection of letters and papers. She said I could help sort and tabulate them, in case there's anything there I can use. Of course I jumped at the chance. She tells me she's found something she thinks will especially interest me."

He went on to tell me a little about the house we were to visit. "It was designed by Stanford White early in the century. Those were his great days before he was shot by Harry K. Thaw in a notorious love triangle."

We were following a high ridge of road that he told me would lead past Laura's house. However, before the house came into view, Ryan parked at the side of the road and sat for a few moments looking down over a hillside that sloped gradually to the Potomac unlike the cliffs on the Shenandoah side.

"Before you meet her, I'd like to tell you a little about Laura. When she was quite young she expected to marry Daniel Griffin. The story goes that he jilted her for Ida. How Laura feels about Griffin now, I don't know, or even whether she knows he's returned. I've never talked to her about any of these matters, and I don't know how she'll feel about meeting Griffin's granddaughter, though I suspect she doesn't indulge in old resentments."

"Did she marry anyone else?"

"Yes. Albert Kelly died some time ago. Over the years, Laura has been a lot more active in Harpers Ferry affairs than Miss Lacey ever has. Miss Lacey sits on her hilltop and reigns,

but Laura digs in and plays a real role. Or at least she used to.
She's been on the library board and active in civic matters.
She's even been a consultant to the Park Service in their resto-
ration projects. But she's never chosen to make too many
friends, so few people have been invited to her home. I'm one
of the lucky ones, probably because of the book I'm writing.
I called her before we left Vinnie's and told her I was bringing
a writer friend with me."

"Have you told her who I am?"

"It didn't seem necessary on the phone."

"Won't she recognize my name?"

"Probably. We'll play it by ear and see what happens."

It was going to be interesting to meet a woman who had
once been engaged to my formidable grandfather.

TWELVE

AS WE DROVE on, the house came into view. It was big and white and built in a manner that resembled no architecture I'd ever seen. A large gable with a pointed roof and three windows rose above the arches, set well back on the roof. In one of the windows a figure stood watching us. It was not the woman who owned the house, but a man, and he drew out of sight as we came near, as though not wanting to be seen.

The road ran past the wide front of the house, and we parked near steps that rose to a terrace. We got out to cross an expanse of lawn and I saw that more white arches ran the full width of the house, with various gables and dormers set above in the high gray roof. Except for the roof, everything about the house was painted white. Old trees and evergreen shrubbery abounded, but the house itself stood free and impressive in its shining white dignity.

As we mounted the steps to the terrace, a woman came from inside and walked briskly toward us. Laura Kelly was thin and tall and her well-chiseled features were still strong, without the drooping of age to be seen in fleshier faces. She wore her gray hair drawn back from a center part, and folded into a thick braid that hung forward over one shoulder. The feathery ends of the braid were caught whimsically with a tiny red velvet bow. Her well-cut trousers were of mocha tweed, topped by a brown silk coat blouse with a rosy, knitted turtleneck showing at the V.

She came to greet us, her smile warm and beautiful as she held out a slim hand, first to Ryan, and then to me.

"Thanks for giving me this chance to see the papers, Laura," Ryan said. "This is my friend Lacey Elliot."

Her large brown eyes focused on me without surprise. "Ida's granddaughter." It was a statement, not a question. "Once, a long time ago, I was very fond of your mother. How is Amelia?"

"She's recovering from an illness right now, but she'll soon be fine," I said briefly.

She nodded pleasantly as she led us toward a long, tiled gallery that stretched behind the front arches. Laura Kelly crossed this to open a glass door and we walked into the house through a room with a massive stone fireplace covering the entire wall at one end. A curved wooden mantel extended from the stone, and a Civil War musket hung slanted above it. The room's furnishings were comfortable and informal, with a softly colored Aubusson rug covering a portion of the floor.

She led us into a hall where wide stairs ran up to a landing, and then rose along the wall to an upper floor. The woodwork had been left in its original dark varnish, surviving a later period when all woodwork in fashionable homes had been painted white. A dining room opened across the hall, its central feature the long, oval table that was now heaped with boxes and papers.

Mrs. Kelly waved a hand in the direction of the piles. "I've done a little sorting, Ryan, but you can decide how you want to handle this. I'm sure some of it will be useful, and you can spend as much time as you like on it." The timbre of her voice was attractive—deep and resonant.

I knew very little about Laura Kelly, but I liked what I saw.

"You mentioned a particular find that might interest me," Ryan reminded her.

"Yes, I did, and I'm sure it will. It's possible that Miss Elliot will find it interesting too. Do sit down. I've made some lemonade, so I'll bring a pitcher and this little book that I have to show you."

I sat down near the table and looked around the room. Oil paintings hung about the walls, all of men and women in various dress from the past. A portrait of a handsome soldier in gray occupied a prominent place.

Laura returned quickly, carrying a silver tray with a large glass pitcher and glasses. Ryan pushed aside papers on the table and she set down the tray. When she'd poured lemonade into the glasses, she took a small book from her pocket and handed it to Ryan.

I glimpsed faded violets and four-leaf clovers that someone had painted across the cover. The book had the look of an old-fashioned diary, and when Ryan opened it up at random, I saw cramped handwriting that slanted across yellowing pages.

Nothing seemed to catch his eye right away, and he set the book aside. "Thanks, Laura. I'm sure I'll find this interesting."

"Indeed you will," she said dryly, and her tone made me wonder what she had discovered in those pages.

Ryan picked up a sheaf of papers that had caught his attention, already absorbed and eager to explore this treasure from the past.

"Let's leave him to it for a while," Laura said. "Bring your glass and I'll show you my prize view."

Before we left the room I stopped before the portrait of the soldier in gray. "Do you know who he was?"

"Yes. That is Royal Fenwick. Perhaps you know about him? His younger brother Jud quarreled with him when Royal came back after the war because Jud considered him a traitor to the Union. Jud moved to Charles Town and Royal settled down here and continued making the drums for which he became famous."

I looked at the face of the young soldier—a contrast to the dark, unhappy countenance of his younger brother that I'd seen at Miss Lacey's house. The artist had managed to portray a handsome, open face that seemed filled with life. I liked Royal, while his brother gave me a chill.

"Miss Lacey has one of his drums," I said. "Caryl's son, Egan, showed it to me today. How do you happen to have his portrait?"

"His mother was a Kelly and an ancestor of my husband's. Those mixed Southern bloodlines again! There's a thread of relationship, so I inherited Royal's portrait. I suppose you and I are related in some way through all those tangled connections."

"I'd like that," I said.

Ryan had been looking through a box of papers, and before we left, he spoke again to Laura.

"Do you know that Daniel Griffin has come back to Harpers Ferry?"

She nodded gravely. "I know." When she left the room without further comment, I followed.

We walked through the house to an open porch that occupied a far corner. There we could look out across the narrowing wedge of land that ran gently downhill below us to eventually form the village of Harpers Ferry at water level. Scattered houses grew closer together as they formed the triangle that sloped to the Point. The Shenandoah was out of sight from where we stood, but on our left the Potomac swept toward its fated meeting with that turbulent body of water. The Gap where that meeting took place showed in the distance.

Laura pointed off to our right. "That large building over on the Shenandoah cliffs is on the grounds of what was once Storer College—it was the first college for blacks in this country. During the war thousands of freedmen gathered around Harpers Ferry for safety. After the fighting was over several of the old Armory buildings were used to start the school. Because John Brown's Fort was a symbol of freedom, it was moved up to the Storer College grounds for a time. That's

called Camp Hill over there—it's where Union soldiers biv-
ouacked."

All this was fascinating history, but there was a personal
question I wanted to ask and I decided not to wait any longer.
"Did you know my father?"

She pulled two deck chairs over to the railing, where we
could enjoy the view as we talked, and we sat down. I drank
lemonade as I waited for her answer. When she finally spoke
I sensed caution in her words.

"Brad belonged to a younger generation than mine, of
course, but I knew him socially."

"Please tell me about him. My mother has never been willing to tell me anything."

"I can understand why. He hurt her badly. He was a good-
looking man in his way, though he was rather slight and
unimpressive at first glance. What he had, more than looks or
a striking build, was charm. He knew how to win the friendship of women, and he took the trouble to understand them
better than most men ever do. Your mother caught his eye.
She had beauty and intelligence and spirit. They fell in love,
though Amelia's father didn't like or trust Brad. He opposed
the marriage and, of course, Ida always followed her husband's lead. The two young people had no other choice, so
they ran off to get married. When they returned they bought
a modest house on Bolivar Heights and settled down to married life. I suppose it could never have worked, given Brad's
nature. He wasn't the sort of man to stay committed to one
woman. It's unfortunate that the girl he chose to have a fling
with was your mother's sister. Brad foolishly thought he could
keep it a secret even after Ardra became pregnant."

"I met Ardra today," I said. "What was she like back
then?"

"She had a reckless quality about her that appealed to some
men. Brad was attracted to it and he never stopped when he
wanted something. He had little difficulty pulling Ardra into
what appears to have been a steamy love affair. When Ardra

became pregnant and Daniel found out, he couldn't endure what was happening. He could be a wild man when he got angry. Brad had betrayed one of his daughters and violated the other. He quarreled with Brad, threatened him, and put himself in a position where suspicion pointed in his direction when Brad disappeared and his jacket was found downriver with a bullet hole in it. It's all ancient history, Lacey. When Dan took to his heels and did his own disappearing act, it was just too much for Ida. She gave up and took her own way out. Amelia did the right thing to take you away and escape the whole miserable mess."

While some of the details were familiar by now, Laura had told me more than anyone else ever had. Her revelations, given reluctantly, pressed down on my spirit. For the first time I could fully understand the burden my mother must have carried for so long in silence.

"Thank you for telling me all this, Mrs. Kelly."

Her eyes were warm with sympathy. "Please call me Laura." She hesitated and then went on. "Now that Dan Griffin has come back, a lot of old stories may be dredged up. There was a time when I was ready to marry him, but sometimes he could frighten me and I backed away. He was angry with me for a while, and when he went right into his marriage to Ida, people said he'd jilted me." She smiled in wry amusement. "Dan was an exciting, fascinating man in those days. He knew he needed an anchor, and perhaps that's what he found in Ida. I was lucky to meet my husband—a man who could make me very happy—and I've never regretted the break with Daniel Griffin."

I asked the old question again, the one I couldn't get out of my mind. "Do you think he killed my father?"

She took a little time before answering. "Sometimes I've thought he must have. But I've never been sure and the evidence was all circumstantial. I'd rather give him the benefit of any doubt."

I told her what I had learned about Daniel's second wife,

and how her death seemed to have given him the impetus to come back to Harpers Ferry. "I don't know whether he wants to clear his name, or if he wants to even up the score with those who drove him into hiding."

My back was to the door that led into the house, so when I saw Laura stiffen, I looked over my shoulder. Henry Elliot stood there, watching us. He didn't seem as drunk as he'd been earlier, but he wasn't altogether steady on his feet. It must have been Henry who had watched our approach from the upstairs window. I couldn't imagine what he was doing here. Laura spoke to him. "Come and join us, Henry." And then to me, "Lacey, this is your father's brother, Henry Elliot."

"I know," I said. "We met earlier today up at Miss Lacey's."

Henry ignored the introduction. "Did you know that Dan Griffin is back and staying up at Miss Lacey's?" he asked Laura.

"I knew he had come to town," Laura said. "But I didn't know where he was staying. That's an interesting twist, since I didn't think she liked him."

"He has it in for me. That's why I went up to Miss Lacey's today with a gun—so I could protect myself. Everybody would be glad if I just finished him off."

"And you think that's a sensible solution?" Laura asked. "What happened?"

Henry began to sputter, and I answered for him. "Miss Lacey reasoned with him and Henry left."

He spat out more of his resentment. "Dan blames me for things I was never to blame for!"

Laura shook her head at him. "It was Brad who caused all the trouble—not you. I don't think he blames you for anything."

"Why is *she* here?" Henry turned a dark look on me. "She's trouble too. She's Amelia's kid. All that bad blood!"

"You're quite wrong, Henry. Neither Lacey nor her mother had anything to do with Brad's death. Lacey was only four when her mother took her away."

He gave me a last dismissive look and went back into the house. Laura spoke sadly. "I feel sorry for him, but if he gets out of hand, I can't let him stay here."

"Doesn't he have a home?"

"I believe he rents an apartment over in Charles Town. He has been working there as a custodian."

"You're right about my mother not having anything to do with my father's death. It's become clear to me that she was a victim of all that happened."

Laura shook her head. "Amelia was never a victim. She had too much spirit for that. Henry has always suffered from being the younger brother of a man who was everything he wasn't. Sometimes I take in strays and Henry is one of those."

"I hope my father wasn't anything like him."

"Strangely enough, when they were young, Henry was the big, handsome younger brother. But he never had Brad's charm or brains. He was devoted to Brad and jealous of him at the same time. Henry went a little crazy when Brad disappeared. It was Miss Lacey who took him in hand and talked some sense into him. He used to work for her sometimes when he was a boy and he was enough in awe of her then to pay attention."

"She told him today that he'd better stay away from Dan—who could make mincemeat out of him. It's strange to think of him as my uncle. I seem to be collecting a very strange batch of relatives."

Laura smiled. "Don't worry, Lacey. I can see Amelia in you at times. She had all the strength that Ardra lacked. And there's nothing wrong with Caryl, who is a dear. I love her wonderful little son too. *They* are also your relatives, you know."

A telephone rang inside, and she went to answer it. While I waited, I looked out toward the Gap and tried to let the view calm me. Henry's reappearance worried me. I suspected that he had a capacity for troublemaking.

When Laura returned, she looked bemused. "That was Dan

Griffin. He wants to see me and he asked if he could come up here now."

"Did he say what he wanted?"

"He didn't waste any time on chitchat, but he said it was important. I mentioned that you were here, and it didn't seem to change his mind."

I couldn't help wondering how she felt about seeing Daniel after all these years.

Laura played idly with the thick braid that hung over one shoulder, retying the little red bow. I could tell she wasn't completely calm about seeing Daniel Griffin again.

"I'll go and help Ryan when he comes," I offered.

"No! Stay with me, please. I don't wish to see him alone. Whatever he wants, I probably won't be able to do it. If he has come here to stir up old trouble, I don't want any part of that. It's finished—done—and nothing can be changed now."

I spoke quietly. "How can it ever be finished when no one knows what really happened to my father?"

"What if it's better not to know? Better for everyone?"

I pounced on her words. "What do *you* know?"

She dismissed my question at once. "I don't know anything. I was never involved. I'd parted company with Dan long before Brad was even born."

The door chimes sounded, and her apprehension seemed to increase. She held out her hand to me.

"Come with me, please." When I hesitated, she laughed. "If I'd married Dan, I might be your grandmother! So humor me."

"I wish you were," I said as I went with her, touched by her need of me, and feeling less like a stranger. When we reached the front hall and she opened the door, I stayed back so they could meet again without my presence.

Dan stood outside for a moment—a tall, strong figure. Only his beard made him look old. When Laura held out her hand in greeting, he didn't take it, but bent and kissed her on the cheek.

"Laura," he said. Just her name.

She turned away quickly and led him into the living room. Her look in my direction asked me to follow. Chairs were grouped near a decoratively carved coffee table, and she waved us toward them wordlessly. Then she took her place on the sofa, well away from Daniel. I sat down feeling that I didn't belong, though another look from Laura kept me there. Watching my grandfather, I had the feeling that he knew very well what Laura was experiencing and was grimly amused.

He seemed to notice me for the first time. "Hello, Lacey. This seems to be our day for running into each other."

I managed to give him a direct look. "Hello, Grandfather." This was the first time I'd called him that, but if he noticed, he gave no sign.

An uneasy silence settled on the room, as though each of us were busy with thoughts we couldn't express. Until Laura said, "Well, Daniel, why did you want to see me?"

Though nothing in his outward demeanor changed, I had the sense that he had not been altogether comfortable about meeting Laura again, but that he had now pulled himself together.

"I understand that Henry Elliot is staying here in your house, Laura. I'd like to talk to him."

He'd spoken her name again, but it wasn't the same. He sounded grim and distant now.

"I don't know if that's wise," Laura said. "He's been drinking; he's not in a reasonable state of mind. What can you hope to gain—?"

He broke in on her words. "Miss Lacey tells me that he came to her house with a gun, looking for me. I don't know what that's all about, but I've come back to Harpers Ferry for just one reason, and I want to ask him a question."

"We'd all like to know the reason behind your return," Laura said quietly.

He looked surprised, as though the answer should have been obvious. "I want to know who killed Brad Elliot."

"Why do you think Henry knows anything?"

"After I left this town I managed to get hold of Harpers Ferry papers for a while. I had one friend here who knew where I was and sent them to me, until I moved on and lost touch. I know from those news accounts that Henry was talking pretty wildly about his brother's murder. The police tried to pin him down, but he wriggled away, claiming that he'd been drunk and didn't know anything. I've always wondered about that. Perhaps now he'll talk."

Laura sat playing with her braid, and the red bow slipped off in her fingers. She tossed her hair over her shoulder and stood up. "I don't think this will do any good, Dan, but I'll see if he's upstairs. He's afraid of something and frightened men can be reckless, so go easy with him."

She rose gracefully from the sofa, her back straight, her head high. Only the gray braid, unraveling down her back, betrayed her uncertainty and admitted to something like anxiety. It was her nature, I was sure, to be neat and controlled about her person.

When she'd gone from the room, my grandfather spoke to me. "So you've decided to acknowledge our relationship, in spite of my being a murderer?"

"I don't think you're anything of the sort." I spoke with an impulsive conviction that surprised me and probably surprised him.

The smile he bestowed upon me didn't come easily—as though he hadn't used it for some time. He bowed slightly in my direction. "Thank you, Lacey. But I don't think you'll be popular if you spread that opinion around."

I heard a sound behind me and turned to find that Ryan had come across the hall. I introduced them. "Ryan, this is Daniel Griffin. Grandfather, Ryan Pearce."

Ryan crossed the room to shake hands with the older man, and Daniel repeated his name. "Ryan Pearce? I saw an article under that name recently—a piece about Virginius Island. I was interested in the digging that's been going on there."

That surprised me. "Digging?"

Ryan explained. "The island was populated once, Lacey, as I think I told you. Its history goes back more than a hundred years, so there's a lot to be learned about the people who once lived there. In a sense, it's become an archaeological treasure trove that's buried under silt from the floods."

Henry's voice reached us from the direction of the stairs, so we knew that he was coming down, though objecting all the way. When Laura had practically pushed him into the room, he stood looking about desperately—at anyone, anything, but Daniel Griffin.

"It's been a long time, Henry," Daniel said mildly.

"For heaven's sake, Henry," Laura said, giving him a slight shove that moved him in our direction. "Dan only wants to ask you a question."

Henry looked for the first time in Griffin's direction. "What question? I'm not good at answering questions."

"Maybe you can answer this one," Griffin said. "Who killed Brad Elliot?"

Henry's voice seemed to crack. "I don't know. I never did. Everybody says *you* killed him."

"But I think you know I didn't, and eventually you'll tell me what you do know. I suppose I can wait, but I'd rather have it come sooner than later."

"Oh, I have something to tell you," Henry said, "but now is not the time. I'll come see you when I'm ready. Until then, you will have to wait."

He turned abruptly and walked out of the room. We heard the front door slam moments later.

"I hope you're satisfied," she said to Daniel. "It doesn't seem worthwhile frightening a man like that."

"When he's scared enough, he'll talk," he said, tugging on his beard. "Thanks anyway for making him see me."

"It might help," Laura said, "if you'd talk to someone about what's driving *you.*"

"A confessional?" His scorn was biting. "And who's to play parish priest?"

Laura swung her braid forward and strands came loose in a thick mass. He'd made her angry and her cheeks were flushed. She looked beautiful and furious.

"I'm sorry," Daniel said stiffly. "There's no way anybody can help. Maybe I was a fool to come back and think I could find out what happened to Brad. I thought if people knew the truth, there wouldn't be sneaking suspicions about me. I don't know why I care."

I could sense pain in both Laura and Daniel and it made me want to do something. "When Ryan takes me back to Vinnie's, Grandfather, will you come with us? Caryl wants to meet you, and you said you'd like to meet her. Besides, Ardra's come home. Perhaps you could see your daughter—"

He stopped my words with a cutting slash of his hand. "My daughter and I have nothing to say to each other."

"Then you needn't see her. But I'll get Caryl out to the herb garden, and you can talk to her there."

"We'll leave now if you like," Ryan said, calmly.

Laura had recovered from her anger. "Go with them, Daniel. It will do you good."

"All right," Daniel said to Ryan. "I might as well come with you and Lacey."

We left quickly, before Daniel could change his mind. Laura came out on the porch with us and watched as we walked to Ryan's car. She stood framed by one of the white arches. Her braid had come entirely loose and soft gray hair blew about her shoulders. Daniel looked back. Whatever expression he might have worn was well hidden by his beard. Just then I had a sudden desire to see him clean shaven.

When he got into the back seat, he didn't look toward the house again, but as we drove away he spoke softly to himself.

"I didn't have much sense when I was young. But then— who has?"

I was the one who looked back one more time, but Laura had gone inside.

"Thank you for taking me there," I said to Ryan. "I feel as

though I've made a new friend. She knows all of my family, and she told me much more than my mother ever has."

"Amelia wouldn't tell you anything," Daniel said matter-of-factly and after that we were all silent on the way to Vinnie's house.

THIRTEEN

WHEN WE REACHED Vinnie's, Ryan offered to go inside to tell my great-aunt what was about to happen, so that I could take Daniel directly around to the garden.

It seemed as good a plan as any, though I knew Vinnie was not going to be pleased. The garden was empty when we reached it, and Daniel walked along a brick path, his shoulders hunched, lost in his own dark thoughts.

When I started to open the door of my room and leave him for a few minutes, he stopped me. "Don't go, Lacey. I may need you."

I stared in surprise that he would admit to needing anyone, and began to wonder about the man he had once been—the father of two daughters and Ida's husband. He had left his entire family, because he believed that if he stayed he would be charged with murder, perhaps convicted on trumped-up evidence. I shuddered at the thought of the pain and anger that must have filled him as he left Harpers Ferry so long ago.

I sat down on the bench and watched him pace. When he came near me, I asked a question. "Did you keep in touch with anyone after you left, besides the man who sent you papers?"

He looked down at me and I was aware again of his height and his powerful build. "There was no one in the family I could trust with my whereabouts."

"But you knew about Ida's death?"

"I knew. It was in the papers. I'd asked her to come with me and she refused. She believed I was guilty and she was afraid of me." He broke off, perhaps to hide what he might be feeling. When he went on, it was more quietly. "Aside from her illness, what is your mother like these days, Lacey?"

That was hard to answer. "I'm not sure I know anymore. I've only seen her as a woman with secrets she would never talk to me about. I know she wanted a better life for me than the one she'd had. But since I've come here I've heard stories about a very different woman from the one I thought I knew."

A door opened and Caryl came out, followed by Ardra. I suspected that Caryl had persuaded her mother to accompany her against Ardra's will. While Caryl stepped boldly into the sunlight and walked toward our grandfather, Ardra hung back in the shadow of the house. He stood looking at Caryl solemnly, making no move, saying nothing—simply waiting.

She threw me a nervous smile and stopped in front of him. "I've always wondered what you'd look like," she said. "I've heard so much about you, but I wanted to see for myself. I trust my own instincts."

He almost smiled. "So what do you think?"

"I don't believe all that I've heard. I don't think you killed my father."

"That's a foolish conclusion, isn't it? When most of Harpers Ferry thinks differently? Including your mother."

His dark look settled on Ardra, who was trying to be invisible. I was aware again of her faded prettiness, her air of fragility—as if she might break in two if anyone was rough with her.

"Well?" he said. "Are you coming to greet your long-lost father?"

She acted as though she hadn't heard him and walked hurriedly back into the house. He looked after her with distaste.

Caryl stood her ground. "You frighten her, but you don't frighten me. I don't know you, and I'm not sure I'll like you when I do get to know you. I just want to find out."

"How can you get to know me with everyone fighting to keep us from being together?"

"Lacey will help. You know, you've always seemed to me like the wild highwayman in a story I once read. But now you remind me of the pictures I've seen of John Brown. I guess he must have been about as wild as they come."

He laughed out loud, and it was as though some protective coating had begun to dissolve, leaving him more human and vulnerable. Nevertheless, I didn't trust him entirely. Something was still terribly wrong.

"So now I have two granddaughters who aren't afraid of me?"

I picked up the challenge of his words. "We are also Brad Elliot's daughters. Can you forgive us for that?"

"Thank God neither of you seems anything like Brad or his brother, Henry. Forgiving isn't the problem. You weren't to blame for what happened. But others are."

He looked past us and I turned to see Ryan coming out of the house with Vinnie and Ardra. Vinnie's arm was around Ardra, who looked as though she might run away at any moment. Ryan, at least, would lend a note of sanity to this strange meeting. Caryl moved toward her mother, but Vinnie shook her head. When she spoke it was directly to her brother.

"If you will promise to go away and leave us alone, I will tell you everything you want to know. Almost everything. I don't know it all."

Ardra cried out in shrill protest. "No! If you do that, he will kill again. That's why he's here."

"Bravo!" Daniel said derisively.

Vinnie gave her an odd look—a look that was almost distrustful. "Don't," she said to Ardra. "Don't go on like that. It isn't necessary."

Ardra grew very still. During this interchange, I was sharply aware of Ryan standing a little apart, the historian, watchful and aware. When I caught his eye, he gave me a faint nod of reassurance. It was as though he'd said, *Relax and let it hap-*

pen. But I was too much a part of all this, and I felt stiff with anxiety.

After her outburst, Daniel ignored Ardra completely. "I didn't kill him, but Brad got what was coming to him. It will all be out in the open soon, where it belongs. Is this to be a private session, Vinnie? Or do you want to invite a few more people? Miss Lacey, perhaps?"

Vinnie threw up her hands despairingly and came to sit beside me on the bench, leaving Ardra to her daughter.

"Go on, Vinnie," Daniel said. "I know there's plenty you can tell. And you won't sleep nights until you've spit it all out."

Vinnie looked so white that I thought she might faint, but Daniel pushed without mercy. "Do you want this to be an outdoor performance, Vinnie?"

This time she roused herself to answer. "Yes! If you want to call it a performance. All the actors are present. You, of course. And Brad's daughters. And me."

"So let's hear your story," Daniel said.

I noticed that the gray pallor was gone and her cheeks were pink again. When she began to speak her voice grew stronger. As she went on, a picture built in my mind of a dark evening long ago, with clouds blowing across the moon and a storm rising to whip up Shenandoah waters. Brad had apparently taken the baby that night and Vinnie, suspicious, had followed him.

"I'd never hated anyone before in my life," she told us, "but I hated Brad Elliot. He had a talent for destruction. He'd already hurt Amelia so badly she would never recover. And he'd given poor Ardra a child. I was there when you were born, Caryl. Brad came a week later. He couldn't face the existence of an illegitimate child. He always wanted to play the hero, and he never accepted blame. Ardra had gone away to hide her pregnancy. But she came back to Harpers Ferry for the baby's birth. She wanted to be with her mother, Ida, who was a nurse. Ida delivered Caryl."

Vinnie seemed to gather strength and now she looked at me directly. "Your grandmother Ida tried to hold everything together as long as she could. She would have supported her daughter in spite of you, Daniel, but Brad had other plans. He wanted the baby out of the picture. He claimed that he'd found someone who would take her and raise her in another state."

"Don't tell any more!" Ardra whispered. "I never knew what happened, and I don't want to know!"

Vinnie went on as though Ardra hadn't spoken. "A secret meeting was planned on Virginius Island, and that's where Brad took the baby. I followed him in my car. When he went across the footbridge, I left my car and went after him. I didn't trust him and I was afraid for the baby's life. It was a terrible night, with a high wind blowing, and I could hear the river rushing over rapids. It wasn't raining. Not then."

Vinnie lifted her face to the sun, as though its warmth contrasted with the cold night of her memory.

"Only Brad knew whether he was really going to meet someone. I stumbled after him when he went to the ruins of a factory on the island. The baby was wrapped up well and Brad put her down in a sheltered spot under a stone arch. He seemed to be waiting for someone to come, or perhaps he was only trying to make up his mind about what he would do. It was easy to stay out of sight. All I wanted was to take the baby away from there and carry her home to her mother.

"The ground on the island was strewn with rubble and I must have set a stone rolling. He heard the noise and found me crouching behind a wall. Even in that ragged light I could see his anger. He was out of control."

Vinnie put her hands over her face and a shudder rippled through her. None of us made a sound as we waited, and I didn't dare to look at Ryan. It was as though Vinnie's words had taken us back to that night on the island and it was all happening vividly *now*.

In a moment she raised her head and told us the rest. "He

called me a meddler and flung himself on me in a rage. The next day I had bruises on my throat from his fingers. He might have killed me if I hadn't managed to squirm out of his grasp. I had taken my father's old handgun with me for protection. I threatened him with it and, when he came after me again, I shot him. He fell so heavily. I will always remember the sound of his body striking the ground. I only meant to save myself and save the baby—but he was dead. The baby began to cry and I knew that at any minute the person Brad had come to meet might appear. I couldn't take the chance that there was no such person. And I couldn't take the chance of being found, so I left."

"You ran away after you killed Brad?" Daniel said. "That was a neat solution. What happened next?"

"When I got home, Ida was asleep. I put the baby into her crib and went to see how Ardra was doing. She wasn't in her bed, or anywhere around the house. So I woke Ida up, but she had no idea where Ardra could be. I didn't find her until I went out in the garden—and there she was, huddled on the bench, soaked to the skin. She said she was looking for her baby, but she hadn't seemed quite right since the baby was born. I took her inside and Ida put her to bed. She was bad sick for a week or so and couldn't even talk to the police when they came asking questions about Brad. It seems somebody had reported him missing."

Vinnie stopped, looking off toward the wind chimes that a breeze had touched to musical life.

"Go on," Daniel said.

She shook her head. "There isn't any more."

"What happened to Brad's body?"

"I . . . I never knew. You've got to believe me about that!"

"I don't have to believe you about anything. Not after what you told the police about me."

She still didn't look at him. "It was only the truth. You did have a fight with Brad and you threatened him—I heard you."

"So you managed to save your own neck at my expense. Is that when you started to hate me so much?"

Such anguish rose in the look she turned on her brother that I could only feel sorry for her, no matter what she'd done.

Daniel dropped his arms from their fierce folding and stretched widely. Then he laughed, the sound shocking there in the quiet garden after what we'd just learned.

"A good story, Vinnie," he mocked. "And I don't doubt that you rescued Ardra's baby—the girl's here to vouch for that—but I don't believe the rest of it. I don't think you had the gumption to kill him, Vinnie—not even thirty years ago. But you'd have let me rot in prison for something I didn't do."

Suddenly, startling us, Vinnie shouted at him. "I've told you what happened! I can't help it if you don't believe me."

She held out a shaking hand to Ardra. "Come with me, dear. This has been too much for both of us."

Ardra went with her silently. Daniel didn't speak again until they reached the back door to the house. Then his voice stopped them.

"Who are you protecting, Vinnie?"

She looked at him despairingly. "I wouldn't have let you go to prison. His body was never found, so nothing could be proved."

"But there *was* a body," Daniel said. "There probably still is—somewhere. I couldn't wait around for it to turn up. Not when somebody was trying to frame me."

Ardra pulled away from Vinnie and ran inside. After a moment of staring at her brother without speaking, Vinnie followed. Only four of us were left—Caryl, Ryan, Daniel, and me.

I'd been aware of Ryan all the while, standing apart, listening, watching. Waiting. I still felt stunned by Vinnie's revelations, but after Daniel's further accusations, I didn't know what to think. I still wanted to talk with Ryan, but this wasn't the time.

Caryl was the first to speak, softly and in wonder. "I *am*

here. I'm *alive*. But I might have grown up somewhere else, and there'd be no Egan. Or I might not be alive at all."

She was close to tears, and Ryan went over to her and put his arm around her shoulder. She clung to him, crying helplessly. He held her for a moment, and then took her into the house. I was left alone with my grandfather, who seemed, more than ever, an enigma to me.

"You don't believe any of your sister's story?" I asked.

"What do you think?" Whatever he might be feeling was well hidden behind his masking beard.

My affection for Vinnie, unquestioning until now, had been shaken. "I don't know what to believe. Who do you think Vinnie might be protecting?"

He raised a cynical eyebrow. "There's a choice, isn't there? It even includes your mother."

Startled, I could only stare at him as I felt the shock go through me. "Mother couldn't have been involved in her husband's death," I said, when I found my voice.

"A woman scorned? And she ran away, didn't she?"

I disliked him intensely. My mother had suffered a great deal to protect me, and I believed in her. I turned away and walked toward the door to my room. Were they all lying? Misleading me for their own purposes? Not only Daniel, but those who had spoken against him. Because of fear?

When I reached the low steps, I looked back, but he was gone. The gate to the herb garden stood open and the chimes rang gently in the light breeze.

FOURTEEN

I ESCAPED to my room to breathe deeply again of a scent that belonged to my childhood and to Aunt Vinnie. I wanted to go to her and offer any comfort I could. I wanted to tell her that, no matter what had happened, I wouldn't judge or condemn her. But I knew I mustn't try to do this while I was still upset myself. Besides, how could I be sure of her or anyone else?

Absently I moved about the room, stopping before the stones that had been placed along ledges formed by small square panes of glass. I picked up a smooth pink stone—rose quartz—and held it between my palms. It warmed quickly and felt somehow quieting to my spirit.

All the little stones were interesting—a sandstone "rose" that might have been carved by desert winds; a smooth brown and gold tiger's eye; a brick-red stone that I knew was jasper; the translucent red-orange of a carnelian. I had once done an advertising brochure for a crystal shop in Charlottesville and the owner had given me a small collection of stones very similar to these.

Someone tapped on my door. I hesitated, wondering which one of them I would have to face. Surprisingly, it was Vinnie who opened the door when I called out. I'd have expected her to be upset after what had happened, but she seemed to be herself again, and not the frantic woman who had faced her brother only a little while ago.

She crossed the room to look at the stone I held on my palm as though it were important.

"Rose quartz," she said. "Do you know that's healing for the heart and stands for love?"

I tried to smile as I replaced the glowing little stone on the ledge.

"Are you all right?" Vinnie asked when I turned to her again.

I answered her carefully. This was not the moment to promise allegiance. "I was disturbed by what happened out there, of course, but I'm not as involved as others are. Are *you* all right?"

"You can't help being involved," she said sadly, ignoring my question. "Just as Ardra and Caryl can't. I'm sorry so much ugliness and pain have surfaced. But now, at least, you know what happened."

Did I really? I wondered. "Are you protecting someone?"

"Of course not!" Her indignation seemed real enough, but I wasn't sure of its source. "You can't trust *anything* my brother says. I didn't come to talk about what happened, anyway. I'm afraid even to think about it—I can feel a headache starting. Poor darling Ardra is so badly shaken that Caryl is putting her to bed. I came because there's someone here to see you, Lacey. I tried to put her off, but she's insistent, as only Anne-Marie can be. You'd better talk to her."

Anne-Marie! This could only mean some communication from Miss Lacey, so I thanked Vinnie and went out to the little front parlor that was reserved for the use of guests. Anne-Marie had seated herself stiffly on the edge of a chair, as though relaxing was not something she was accustomed to doing. She stood up when I appeared and looked at me with what seemed a permanent air of disapproval. However, she had been told to deliver a message and she did.

"Miss Lacey wants you to come to her house as soon as you can and she asks that you bring a bag so you can stay for a few days."

There was no question in the invitation, no asking what I might like.

"I don't know—" I began doubtfully.

She continued as though I hadn't said anything. "Miss Lacey wants you to bring Egan with you—to stay for a visit."

The Queen had apparently spoken, and I was supposed to leap dutifully to her bidding. I had other ideas.

"I don't want to do this, Anne-Marie. There are things I need to take care of here, and I haven't begun to work on my book yet."

The woman shrugged. "Shall I tell Miss Lacey that you don't wish to visit her?"

Hearing it put like that, I backed away. "It's just that this is pretty sudden, and—"

"It would seem advisable to do as Miss Lacey wishes, Miss Elliot."

"Why is that?"

"She is making plans for you. Don't you think you ought to know what they are?"

This was the first time I'd heard Anne-Marie put forward an idea of her own. The only time I'd heard her talk freely was when she was showing me Ellen Fenwick's room. Certainly Miss Lacey must be made to understand that I would not allow her to make plans of any kind for me. At the same time, it occurred to me that Miss Lacey might still hold answers to things I wanted to know. Being under the same roof with her would offer endless possibilities.

"I can't come immediately," I said.

She spoke flatly and without expression. "You are expected for dinner."

"Expected—not invited?"

She simply stared back at me, cool and detached.

"All right, I'll come," I said, "but I don't know whether I'll bring Egan. That decision will be up to his mother."

Anne-Marie sniffed. "Egan's mother will not object."

She rose, waiting quietly for my next move. For the first

time I was aware of what a colorless woman she was. Every time I'd seen her she'd worn a plain black dress, without the relief of an accessory to soften the bleak aspect of her appearance. Even her eyes were a pale gray and without expression. She seemed to have barricaded herself against the outside world, and I wondered what unhappiness, what defeats, had made her like this.

"Will you sit down for a minute?" I said more gently. She sat again, reluctantly, and I drew a chair near her, choosing my words carefully.

"I don't understand why you disapprove of me so much, Anne-Marie. Perhaps we really want the same thing. You'd prefer not to have an interloper coming into Miss Lacey's life, but you need to realize that I don't *want* to be an interloper. So perhaps we can make a truce between us."

To my surprise her eyes filled with tears and she fumbled in her pocket for a tissue. Taking this as a good sign, I went on.

"If the things my great-grandmother has been planning worry you, you really needn't be disturbed. I don't want to take your place, you know. I don't want to live in that house at all."

The dam broke before all the emotion that must have been held back for so long. "Last month she told me she was going to let me go! She said she wanted someone more cheerful around her. I try to do everything she wants, and then someone like you—a real relative—comes into her life and she's a new person. She's making plans for you. She won't need me anymore. And where will I go? What will I do?"

Her breakdown distressed me and I didn't know how to deal with it. In her own fearful mind Anne-Marie must have created this make-believe—that she was a member of Miss Lacey's family. Miss Lacey had used her devotion, and she had no right to dismiss it so cruelly. In fact, it was hard to believe that she had.

Again I tried to reassure her. "It may have been a bad day

for her. She may have been upset about something and took it out on you. She'll probably never refer to it again. I can't imagine her running that house without you."

Anne-Marie wiped her eyes and sniffed.

I went on again quickly. "I'm sure everything will be all right. When you go back, tell her that I'll be there for dinner and that I'll bring Egan if I can. This time when I see her I'll make everything clear. I want to go home to Charlottesville soon. My mother needs me. So you needn't worry about my moving in permanently with my great-grandmother. I admire her, but I won't let her run my life."

Anne-Marie stood up and tucked away the bit of damp tissue, probably regretting her unaccustomed outburst. I saw her to the door, and before she turned away, she surprised me again.

"You're a lot like her, Miss Elliot."

She walked out to Miss Lacey's car, got in, and drove away, leaving me to stare after the car in some uncertainty. Then I went in search of Caryl.

Her room was on the second floor across from Vinnie's and next to Ardra's. I ran into her coming out of her mother's room.

She put her fingers to her lips when she saw me. "I've given Momma one of Aunt Vinnie's herbal sleeping capsules and she's drowsing off. Come into my room, so we can talk."

I went through the door she held open for me and stepped into a room that seemed almost like a schoolgirl's. Old posters hung on the walls—one of Nureyev in his glory days, another of the young Bruce Springsteen, and a third an early portrait of Carly Simon and James Taylor. A warm pink seemed to be the predominant color and it suited her. At her invitation I sat down in a chair upholstered in cabbage roses and told her what Miss Lacey wanted.

She shook her head at once. "I don't want Egan going up there any more than I can help it. I know what she's trying to do. And I know how strong she can be. You've got to help me, Lacey. Help me stand up to her."

I had nothing to say to that. I had no desire to be thrown into someone else's adversarial position with my great-grandmother. I had my own battles to fight.

Caryl moved about the room, touching various possessions—books, collections of small wood carvings, articles on her dressing table. She picked up a small, cleverly carved camel and held it up for me to see.

"Grandpa Daniel made this for my mother when she was small. He used to carve wonderful things. You've seen that gryphon's head on Miss Lacey's cane? He made that many years ago."

She dropped the camel, not bothering to set it on its feet, and her face contorted. "That was horrible! I mean, what happened in the garden. He was cruel to Vinnie and I don't want him for a grandfather! Of course my mother was frightened and upset. It's been hard to reassure her. I just wish the past would stay away from us. I don't know what I would have done without Ryan. He helped me with Mother, and he always gives me good advice."

I didn't want to talk about Caryl and Ryan. "What did you mean when you said you knew what Miss Lacey is trying to do?"

"She doesn't think Egan should live with *us*. She hates my mother and she thinks I'm a case of arrested development." Caryl looked ruefully at the three posters. "Maybe I am. I liked everything better when I was a young girl. Having a son like Egan and no husband is scary."

So she was probably looking to Ryan to solve her problem of being alone.

"Miss Lacey's trying to bribe Egan with that drum—and other things," Caryl said. "She's trying to take him away from me and bring him up herself. As if I would allow that! She wants to adopt him, because she doesn't think we can do as much for him as she can."

"There isn't anything she can do legally, is there?"

"I don't think so. But Egan is a special little boy, and I'm not sure I could keep him from going to her if he wanted to."

"What do you mean? You're his mother."

She looked at me sadly. "Sometimes I have the feeling that he's only been loaned to me. Sometimes he says things that are much too wise for his age."

"This will be only a short visit, Caryl."

"Perhaps if I let him go with you, you can watch her with him and see what she does to try to win him over. Keep an eye on him, Lacey. Protect him."

I was going to have my hands full trying to protect myself from whatever Lacey Fenwick Enright had in mind. But I would certainly make an effort.

"All right, I'll try," I promised. "I think Egan likes me."

"Oh, he does! He says you're here to make something good happen."

I didn't care for the sound of that—there was too much responsibility implicit in the remark—and she smiled at my expression.

"Whatever comes, you'll handle it. I know you will! Egan knows something bad has just happened and that his grandma Ardra is sick because of it. So perhaps he'd be better off away with you for a few days."

"I'll be glad to have his company," I said. "What about Shenandoah?"

"Miss Lacey doesn't like cats. And Shenna is comfortable here."

There was one thing I needed to do before I left. I asked where Ryan's room was located and Caryl directed me to a suite of rooms above the guest wing. I went down the hall and found his door open. I could hear music—a deep, resonant voice singing words that had stirred a nation more than a hundred years ago.

John Brown's body lies a'molderin' in the grave,
John Brown's body lies a'molderin' in the grave,
John Brown's body lies a'molderin' in the grave,
His soul is marching on.

And then the rousing "Glory, glory, hallelujah . . ."

The voice was so powerful that I stood in the doorway listening. Ryan sat at a desk near a window, poring over papers that had probably come from Laura Kelly's collection.

I tapped lightly and he looked around. "Come in, Lacey." He got up to turn off the tape player, but I stopped him.

"Please—that's a wonderful voice. Who is the singer?"

"Paul Robeson. It's a collection of his songs and we're lucky to have such a recording. Listen to this—" He stopped the machine and fast-forwarded the tape. Again the mighty voice soared: "O Shenandoah, you rolling river . . ."

I listened entranced. I'd always loved the old folk song, but I'd never heard it sung by a voice like this—a voice that carried the rolling magnificence of the river in every note. I could feel a prickling down my spine. The real Shenandoah was right out there, sweeping past Harpers Ferry, and I knew suddenly that *I* was not "going away" across any "wide Missouri," as the song said. I meant to stay right here where Ryan was. Emotion tingled through me, touched off by a song that spoke to something deep inside me.

When the music ended, Ryan turned off the cassette player and came toward me down the long room. Aware of him in this new way, I watched the easy grace of movement that made him seem so light on his feet. When he stood beside me, I was swept by feelings I didn't know how to deal with.

"Are you all right, Lacey?" he asked, and I knew my face was giving too much away.

I wasn't all right. Part of me needed to be safe inside myself, as I'd always been—where no man could really touch me. Now, without warning, that sense of safety was gone. I was vulnerable to hurt as I'd never been before. Yet I didn't want it any other way.

I tried to answer him. "After what happened in the herb garden, I don't think any of us is entirely all right. I'm upset and confused. And alarmed too. What do you think Daniel Griffin intends?"

"Perhaps no more than what he's doing right now—stirring everyone up, making them remember."

"Poor Vinnie. That was dreadful—the way she told her terrible story."

"If it really happened."

"Do you think Daniel was right in what he said?"

Ryan's look was kind. "Perhaps we'd better let it go for now, Lacey. What will happen will happen, as my mother always says. Maybe the waters are rising."

"That sounds fatalistic."

"We're outside what is happening, Lacey. We can't affect the actions of those who are deeply involved."

"What if I don't choose to be outside? What if everything I'm feeling about those who are my family pulls me into the very center of the maelstrom? You know, Ryan, Miss Lacey doesn't want me to stay outside. I'm going to visit her for a few days so I can find out what she's planning."

"Do you *want* to go to Miss Lacey's?"

"I'd rather stay here, but I *must* persuade her to listen to me. She has a foolish notion that she wants to make me her heir and give me that old house. I don't want any part of it."

"I wish you luck," Ryan said dryly. "At least you won't be far away. And you needn't be tied to the house. There's something we could do tomorrow, if you're willing."

I was willing. More and more, I was ready to do anything that would keep me in Ryan's company. I closed my ears to warning bells that seemed to be sounding inside me.

Ryan went on. "I'm going over to Virginius Island tomorrow morning. Would you like to come along?"

At once I wanted to go, in spite of the lingering horror of Vinnie's story.

"I'd like that," I told him. "Do you have a special purpose in going to the island?"

"Yes—more than ever after hearing Vinnie's story. Besides, I'd like to show you what's there. It's part of your Harpers Ferry heritage. You can even use it in your book. A stranger

in town can often see things that the people who live there are
accustomed to and take for granted. I don't know what you
might notice, but it's a theory I'd like to test."

I'd rather he simply wanted to be with me, but any reason
would do for now.

"I'd love to go," I said, with more warmth in my voice than
I intended.

"Fine! I'll come up to Miss Lacey's tomorrow morning. Say
around ten?"

I agreed, feeling foolishly happy. "Have you found anything interesting in Laura Kelly's papers?"

"It's all interesting, but so far there's nothing to get excited
about. Old letters often deal with what seems like trivia to
anyone but the writer. Nevertheless, I have to be watchful and
look for the unexpected paragraph that proves to be a gold
mine."

"Then I'll leave you to it and go talk to Vinnie," I said. "I'm
supposed to have dinner with Miss Lacey tonight."

He came with me to the door and I was aware of everything
about him. A clean smell of soap and water, and a faint hint
of aftershave. The way his hair curled close to his scalp and
showed flecks of gold in the light. Hair I'd love to touch. His
long-fingered hands—I could imagine what it would feel like
if they caressed me.

I stopped myself sharply. This could lead to nothing but
hurt. It was a long time since I'd been drawn to a man in this
way. Perhaps it had never happened like this before, since my
guard was always up. My mother had frequently told me not
to trust any man too much. So now I didn't dare trust what
was happening.

As I left him and went down the hall to the main part of the
second floor, I heard the music start up again—Paul Robeson
singing "Deep River." I hurried away from the sound and
went to look for Vinnie.

I found her in her bedroom stretched out on the bed,
with a pillow under her knees and a smaller one under her

head. Jasmine was placing a cool damp cloth over her eyes.
"Miss Vinnie's got one of her real bad headaches," Jasmine
told me.

"Then I won't bother her now," I said, and backed toward
the door.

At once Vinnie pushed the cloth away. "It's all right, Jasmine. Let her stay. I'll be all right. You can come back later."

Jasmine gave me a doubtful look and went away.

"I won't stay," I promised. "I just want—"

Vinnie broke in. "Sit down, Lacey."

I pulled a chair over to the bed and did as she wished. She
reached for my hand and held it lovingly. "I'm so glad you're
here. But I'm terribly sorry you had to hear that dreadful
story."

"I'm glad I did. Though I shake inside when I think of what
you must have gone through on that terrible night."

She closed her eyes, speaking softly. "Not all of it was true,
dear. Dan was right about that. I didn't kill your father,
Lacey."

"But then why—?"

"I hoped Dan would be satisfied with my story and stop his
hunting. He *is* dangerous, Lacey. But I don't think he killed
your father. I can see that you're beginning to make friends
with him, and that isn't wise. I just wanted him to believe me
and go away."

"*Are* you protecting someone, Aunt Vinnie?" I asked again.

Her head turned from side to side on the pillow and she
moaned softly. "Just let it be! Don't you go getting involved.
Everything happened so long ago that it doesn't matter anymore. It really doesn't."

I wondered about that. Obviously, Daniel Griffin didn't feel
the same way. As long as Brad's body was unaccounted for,
nothing could be settled—finished. But there was no point in
reminding her of this now. I held her hand and stroked it as
I told her about my planned visit to Miss Lacey's, and that I
would be taking Egan with me.

She didn't object, as I'd thought she might. "If that's what Miss Lacey wants, you'd better go. But what I told you when you first went to see her still holds. Don't let her blow you down. Don't let her run your life."

"As she has run yours in the past?"

"She hasn't really succeeded, though she's certainly tried. I quietly go my own way, because fighting her doesn't do any good—opposition just makes her stronger. Basically she's a good person. You know, don't you, that she provides the money that I still mail to your mother once a year? It devastated her when Amelia left and took you with her. She has so little close family left and Amelia was always her favorite. So, of course, whether she shows it or not, she cares deeply about you. You're Amelia's daughter and her namesake. But that's all the more reason for you to be careful and not let her possess you."

"I'll watch it," I promised. Resistance to Miss Lacey already came easily.

I rose to leave, but Vinnie wasn't ready to let me go. "Tell me about your visit to Laura Kelly's. Once, a long time ago, we were pretty good friends, Laura and I."

This seemed a safe enough subject and I described our visit and told her that I'd seen Henry Elliot there.

That startled her. "Laura's always been an odd one. I can't think why she'd take Henry in. Do you know that Laura and Miss Lacey really detest each other?"

It was my turn to be surprised. "Laura doesn't seem like the sort of person to hate anyone."

"Ordinarily she wouldn't, but Miss Lacey can bring out the worst in people. Then again—that was so long ago that even Laura may have forgotten about it. I don't think Miss Lacey ever forgets anything."

"She wants to leave that old house to me in her will. I'm accepting her invitation and going there for a visit so that I can convince her that I don't want it and won't accept it."

"Poor thing," Vinnie said. "Nobody really loves her. Unless

it's Egan. But I suppose we're all afraid of her. It's hard to love someone you're afraid of. Now she's trying to buy you."

"Caryl says Miss Lacey would like to adopt Egan and raise him as she thinks he should be raised."

"There's not a chance of that!"

But my words had apparently upset her, and she put a hand to her head. "I'm hurting again. Please tell Jasmine I need her. And keep in touch with us while you're gone, Lacey."

I bent to kiss her cheek and she looked up at me, her eyes bright with affection. I went to summon Jasmine and then, as I hurried to my room downstairs, Egan came running along the hall after me.

"Mommy says I can go up to Grandma Lacey's with you. Now I can play my drum all I want! And I can see Grandpa Daniel too."

"I'm glad you're coming with me," I said, though I wished he had been less enthusiastic about his great-great-grand-mother's plan.

"I have to help Mommy pack my bag, but I can leave whenever you're ready."

I told him I'd see him soon and went into my room to take my suitcase from the closet. However, before I left I knew I must call my mother and tell her where I'd be. I sat down beside the phone in my room.

This time she answered herself and her voice sounded stronger. I gave her a carefully edited account of what had happened here, and told her that I was going to stay for a few days with my great-grandmother. I said nothing about Daniel Griffin, since I thought the mention of his presence here might upset her too much.

"You never told me that I had a great-grandmother," I said, "or that she was the one who wrote those checks year after year."

"I couldn't talk about her. I think she never forgave me for leaving. Once I wrote to her, but she never answered. She wasn't kind to my mother and, of course, she detested your father. After all those terrible things happened, she shut herself away in that big house."

"I never knew anything about what happened until I came here," I told her, unable to keep the reproach out of my voice.

"Well, now you know," she said flatly, and then went on in a lighter tone of voice—perhaps to distract me. "Whatever you do, Lacey, don't make friends with Ezekiel. I've never believed that he had any benign feelings toward the family after all that happened."

"Who is Ezekiel?" I asked.

She laughed as though she found my question funny. "Never mind—perhaps you'll find out or perhaps you won't. Please take care of yourself, Lacey dear." She hung up before I could say anything more. At least she sounded more like herself, which made me feel a little easier about being away from her.

FIFTEEN

THIS TIME it was Miss Lacey who met us at the door, while Anne-Marie hovered in the background, looking sour—though she moved quickly enough to do Miss Lacey's bidding.

I had never seen my great-grandmother look so invigorated, and I felt guilty when I realized how much she must have anticipated our coming. I was already braced to oppose whatever she wanted, and I knew that her newfound happiness was misplaced.

She even kissed me on the cheek—a first!—and I caught the fragrance she used. Water lily, its sweetness cut by some spicy scent I couldn't place. She wore sea green today, with a white froth of lace at her throat that reminded me of sea spray. Her cheeks were tinged with a pink that was not artificial—excitement had brought her to life.

When she'd bent to receive a hug from Egan, she told us happily that our rooms were ready for us upstairs. "Anne-Marie will show you the way. With Egan next door, you won't feel alone, Lacey."

She'd known that I wouldn't care to be alone up there so close to Ellen's room. Until now, I hadn't really thought about where I would sleep, and I felt dismayed when I found that my room was the one across from Ellen Fenwick's. That door stood open today, which gave me an uneasy feeling.

As Anne-Marie brought us upstairs, she noticed the direction of my look. "Yes—we are to leave Miss Ellen's door open from now on. Miss Lacey says that you are the one descendant who may make a difference in this house. She wants Ellen Fenwick to know that you are here."

This was a bit more spooky than I liked. By this time my Fenwick blood was pretty diluted, and it didn't descend from Ellen anyway.

Egan skipped about cheerfully, pleased that he would have his own room next to mine. At Vinnie's he shared a room with his mother. Anne-Marie never seemed to alarm him, and she even thawed a little when he spoke to her. Since I'd seen her in tears, I knew that her stern facade could be breached.

She assured Egan that he needn't bother unpacking—she would take care of that and he ran off happily to find his drum.

I went into the room that had been assigned to me and looked around. This time the shades were up and I could glimpse a sky not far from sunset. The window faced the river so I could see Daniel's cottage. He was not in sight, and I wondered if he knew that Egan and I were moving in for a visit.

I hung the few clothes I'd brought in a tall wardrobe, and when I looked into a wavery mirror on its door I found my hair windblown and my mouth smudged. I went in search of a bathroom and made a few repairs.

Back in my room I put on the one dress I'd brought. It was the shade of a dark, glowing ruby with a trim of gilt buttons. My earrings were red carnelians my mother had given me when I was eighteen. Dressing up to look my best gave me more courage. I felt I was ready to meet Miss Lacey again—and perhaps begin the process of standing up to her.

When I went downstairs she was waiting for me in the drawing room. Sitting there on her Victorian sofa with its high carved back, she looked regal and very much in charge. She patted the stiff cushions beside her when I appeared.

"How nice you look. Come and sit by me, Lacey. We can talk a little before dinner."

I sat beside her, but not too close. I didn't mean to be beguiled by this new, open manner. Behind her smooth, un-wrinkled forehead, I could almost see the plans being hatched and I needed to be wary. In the next room—the smaller par-lor—Egan was thumping on his Civil War drum, inventing his own rhythms.

I asked her a question. "If you had lived in the time when this house was built, which side would you have been on—the blue or the gray?"

"Most of the Fenwicks wore blue. But when I read about the war that split us into two states, I sometimes have a stronger sympathy for the South and General Lee than for Mr. Lincoln. By comparison, today seems uneventful."

Considering the state of the world and the frightful events that were happening everywhere, I could hardly feel that life in these United States was uneventful. But of course she was thinking only of this little strip of land that ran down to the meeting of the rivers.

When the front-door knocker sounded, Miss Lacey's eyes sparkled and she smiled at me. "I've invited company for dinner. Ryan Pearce is a young favorite of mine, so I called him about a half hour ago and asked him to join us."

My heart jumped ridiculously, but I managed not to show it.

Anne-Marie invited him in and I heard them talking to-gether as she brought him to the drawing room. By now, she looked almost friendly. Perhaps those tears had been a needed release for her.

He went to Miss Lacey and bowed over her hand like a gallant Southern gentleman—which pleased her enormously. Egan left his drum and came delightedly to greet his friend.

When Anne-Marie summoned us, we went into the long, formal dining room, where Fenwicks must have dined long before the war and ever since.

Miss Lacey sat at one end of the oval table, with Egan placed at the opposite end as the man of the family. He was well propped by phone books and looked suitably dignified. Ryan sat at Miss Lacey's right and I was on her left, across from him.

Again I felt unreasonably happy, though his manner toward me had never been more than friendly.

Apparently there was a cook in the kitchen, whom I hadn't met, but Anne-Marie took on yet another role and served us with as much panache as any butler. Perhaps she was even enjoying herself. Life in this house must be dreadfully dull most of the time. I wondered what sort of private life she led—*if* she even had a private life.

Chicken roasted in olive oil was served with baked yams and fresh spinach from the garden. As Anne-Marie poured the wine, Miss Lacey asked Ryan about Laura Kelly.

"How is she? Daniel tells me you visited her house today."

Ryan spoke easily of our visit to Laura's and told Miss Lacey about the treasure of old papers that had been made available to him. He didn't mention that Henry Elliot was staying with Laura, but apparently Daniel had informed her of this as well. However, Miss Lacey didn't seem to know about the unhappy meeting in the herb garden, when Vinnie told us a story that might not have been entirely true. Nor did anyone mention a man named Ezekiel. My mother's cryptic words had left me curious, and when I found the opportunity I asked about him.

"How did you ever hear about Ezekiel?" Miss Lacey asked in surprise.

I told her what my mother had said—that Ezekiel, whoever he was, had no benign feeling toward the family, and I shouldn't make friends with him.

Miss Lacey sighed. "That sounds like Amelia. She always did have a whimsical streak. You're not likely to make friends with him, since he died in the battle of Shepherdstown, the day after Antietam. He grew up in Harpers Ferry and our families were friends until they moved away, and Ezekiel put on a gray uniform to fight for the South."

"But why would my mother say—?"

Miss Lacey looked at Ryan. "You know the picture well, so tell Lacey."

Ryan explained that in Miss Lacey's searches through old collections being sold at auction, she had come across a crude painting of Ezekiel Montgomery. "His name and rank as captain were written on the back of the canvas. So she bought it and brought it back here many years ago. She knew that Ezekiel had figured in the family history."

Miss Lacey added her own footnote. "The picture is up in Ellen's room, so you can see it when you go upstairs."

"It's a spooky painting," Ryan noted. "Miss Lacey brought it down once so I could examine it."

While we were eating a dessert of fresh strawberry short-cake, the knocker on the front door sounded again. Anne-Marie went to answer and we heard her invite someone into the main parlor. A moment later she came into the dining room to speak to Miss Lacey.

"Mrs. Kelly is here to see you," she said doubtfully. "I've put her in the front parlor."

Miss Lacey frowned. "What on earth can she want? We haven't spoken in years and our last parting was far from friendly. Well, I suppose I'll have to see her."

She rose from the table, and Egan ran to offer her his arm.

"Thank you," she said, "but you stay here with Ryan until I come back. Lacey, why don't you come with me." She slipped her arm through mine.

We crossed the hall to find Laura standing at the piano, looking over the collection of small pictures. She still wore her mocha tweed trousers, though she had changed into a pullover sweater in a pink and brown design. She had wound her long braid around her head, and I thought she looked beautiful, though not entirely serene.

She turned as we reached the door, nodded to me, and spoke to Miss Lacey.

"Good evening. I'm sorry to trouble you, but I'm concerned

about Henry Elliot. He went off this afternoon without saying
where he was going. I haven't seen him since. It occurred to me
that he might have come here. He's not always in control of
his own actions, so I thought I would take him back to my
house—if he's here."

Miss Lacey shook her head. "I haven't seen him. He might
be out back with Daniel, though that doesn't seem likely, if
he's sober. He came up here this morning in an excited state,
but he cooled off and thought better of confronting Daniel."

"If Daniel's staying in your cottage . . ." She hesitated and
then went on: "Do you mind if I go out and talk to him?"

"Do as you like," Miss Lacey said, not altogether approv-
ingly. "Please go with Mrs. Kelly, Lacey, and show her the
way."

I suspected that she wanted a report from me on this meeting, so I started toward the hall door, expecting Laura to
follow. Instead she held back. As I turned to wait for her, she
approached Miss Lacey and held out her hand.

"I've always been sorry about what happened between us.
There was no good reason for us to be angry with each other."

"Perhaps there was," Miss Lacey said. "There was Brad
Elliot and all the trouble he caused. . . ." After a moment's
hesitation she took Laura's hand. "We used to be friends. I
don't see why we can't be again. Let's hope all those dreadful
happenings are water under the bridge."

"I never believed that Daniel had anything to do with
Brad's death, and I still don't, but I shouldn't have been so
insistent about standing up for him."

"That was an unhappy time, and all our emotions were
raw."

Laura nodded without comment, and joined me as I led the
way to the back door. Daniel Griffin was outside, chopping
wood for the cottage stove. When he saw us he raised his ax
in a last chop and left it embedded in the log.

Laura spoke to him warmly as she walked toward him. "I'm
glad you've come home, Daniel. We didn't have much chance

to talk when you came to my house earlier today. Lacey has told me of your wife's death and I'm very sorry."

"Thank you for your concern," Daniel said sincerely.

"You could have stayed at my house, Dan."

"Could I? I don't think so." He sounded gruff, but the look he gave her was almost as kind as the look he gave Egan. "Anyway, I wanted to confront Miss Lacey on her own ground. When she offered to let me stay out here, I took her up on it. This way we have an armed truce, and we can watch each other. Besides, you've got that horse's ass Henry staying with you. We wouldn't mix so well." He paused for a moment and then said, "In the old days you weren't on good terms with Miss Lacey. So why are you here?"

"I was looking for Henry and thought this might be a good opportunity to clear the air with Lacey Enright."

"I haven't seen Henry since I was at your place, and I don't much want to see him. In fact, it might be a good idea if he stays out of my way."

"You do look fierce, Daniel. Did Virginia like your beard?"

"She never saw it like this. I kept it trimmed. But I'm by myself now and it doesn't matter."

"It matters," Laura said. "Anyway, don't waste your anger on poor Henry. He's much too pitiful. I've been trying to sober him up."

"Good luck," Daniel said, shaking his head.

"If he turns up, send him home. And come see me again, Daniel. I'd like that."

He didn't answer, but looked toward the house, listening. "I kept hearing a drum earlier," he said.

I explained about the love affair between Egan and Royal Fenwick's drum.

Daniel nodded gravely. "I can see what she intends with Egan. But what about you, Lacey Elliot? What's she up to with you?"

"Nothing I can't handle."

"You're going back to Charlottesville to your mother?"

"Eventually, Grandfather, but I expect to visit Miss Lacey for a few days. Why don't you come and see us in Charlottesville when I do go back?"

He looked astonished. "I don't think your mother would care to see me."

Laura glanced at her watch. "I must be on my way. Lacey, will you come out to the car with me?"

She held out her hand to Daniel. He seemed more on guard with her as they parted, and she must have sensed this, for she turned away quickly.

We walked around the house to the road, and she went to open the rear door of her car. As I watched, she lifted out a large, wrapped package that could only be a picture.

"I've brought Miss Lacey something as a peace offering," she said and handed it to me.

I could guess what it was. "Royal Fenwick's portrait?"

"Yes. Will you take it to her? I don't want to force her thanks. She isn't very happy about seeing me, though she did put on a good front."

I watched until the car was out of sight, and then I went into the house carrying Laura's package.

S I X T E E N

I TOOK the portrait into the dining room, where Miss Lacey, Egan, and Ryan still sat. "Laura wants you to have this," I told my great-grandmother.

She regarded the package suspiciously. "What is it?"

"I think you'll be pleased. Don't you want to open it?"

"Open it for me," she directed.

I ripped off the paper and held the picture up for her to see.

"Royal Fenwick," she said softly. "I've seen other pictures of him. It was generous of Laura, but I'm not sure I can accept it."

I could hardly believe what she was saying. "But she wants you to have it!"

She waved a hand at me. "Set it down somewhere and I'll think about it. Then come and finish your dessert."

She gave the order as if to a child, but I knew by now that this was her way. I leaned the picture against a wall, and then sat down at the table again. Ryan raised an eyebrow at me, but said nothing.

Miss Lacey seemed not to notice. "What happened between Laura and Daniel just now?"

"Nothing much. Laura asked about Henry, who has gone off somewhere on his own."

When we'd finished our meal, Egan left the table to look more closely at Royal's portrait. "Could I have this up in my room, Grandma? I'd like to look at it. Because of my drum."

When Miss Lacey hesitated, he smiled at her in his own bright way. "I won't let anything happen to it, I promise."

Her smile was fond. "Very well, dear. You may keep the picture in your room for now. Ryan will take it upstairs for you later."

When Egan had gone back to the parlor and his drum, she asked Ryan a direct question. "When are you going to marry Caryl?"

He looked startled. "I didn't know I was marrying anyone."

"Vinnie tells me Caryl is in love with you. And I know you're very fond of Egan. And—"

"Vinnie can be a gossip," he said, stopping her.

I sensed a coiled spring in Ryan, and knew he resented the question. A feeling of tension had come into the room, and, sure enough, Ryan didn't stay long, saying he needed to get back to his work.

"Thank you for dinner, Miss Lacey." He nodded at me. "I'll see you in the morning."

The moment he was gone, Miss Lacey echoed his words. "You are seeing Ryan in the morning?"

I explained that he was taking me to Virginius Island. "He thinks I should know more about what he calls my Harpers Ferry heritage."

Her disapproval was clear, but I couldn't tell whether it was because she disapproved of my going to Virginius Island or because she didn't want Ryan to be interested in me. For one reason or the other she was upset and pleaded weariness. After allowing me to kiss her cheek, she retired to her room.

I looked in on Egan and found him building armies of blue and gray lead soldiers on the rug near the drum.

"Which army do you favor?" I asked when he smiled up at me.

"I'm only playing," he said. "See—here's the boy who carried this drum. He's out ahead of them all, but nobody will shoot him. He wants the armies to be friends."

I knelt to hug him and was touched when he put his arms around my neck. "If you see my mother tomorrow, tell her I'm all right and I love her. And tell Shenandoah that I'll be home soon."

Vinnie didn't need to worry about Egan being "bribed," I thought. He had his own guiding spirit and perhaps everyone should trust in that.

"I'm going upstairs now," I said. "I'll carry the painting of Royal to your room. I think Ryan got distracted and forgot. Will you be coming to bed soon?"

Anne-Marie had entered the room behind us. "I'll see that Egan gets to bed very soon," she assured me.

I felt more emotionally than physically tired. I needed time alone so that I could think about some of the strange events of the day. And so I could think about Ryan—a disturbing road that made me unsure of myself.

When I started up the stairs, Anne-Marie followed me, her eyes alight with an eagerness that made me wary for some reason.

"You wanted to see Ezekiel's picture," she said. "I can show it to you."

I was still puzzled by my mother's whimsical remark, but when Anne-Marie went to Ellen's open door, I hesitated.

She looked back at me. "You won't know this room. Miss Lacey had me clean it up thoroughly. When we came up here yesterday she felt that a change needed to be made. Because of you."

I didn't want to know what she meant by that, but I went into the room and looked around. It had been cleaned and aired, and the ancient draperies had been removed. But while the cobwebs were gone, I could never feel comfortable in this room. I set down Royal's picture, wondering how *he* felt about visiting this room.

Anne-Marie touched a light switch and I saw a framed portrait that hung in a far corner, where I hadn't noticed it before.

Ryan had mentioned that the painting was crude, and this was clear enough in the rather wooden execution. Nevertheless, the painter had managed to present the face of a man handsome enough to break a few hearts. His hair was dark blond, and he was young and beardless. A slight smile knew its own charm. But it was the blue eyes that were remarkable and arrested my attention.

They seemed to look directly at me and did not look away. When I stepped backward to put distance between me and the picture, the eyes followed me intently. Wherever I moved, they watched me, as if in some strange recognition.

I shook off the spell and turned to Anne-Marie, who was watching me as intently as the portrait. "I've seen that sort of trick in paintings before. But why is his picture hanging here in Ellen's room?"

Anne-Marie seemed to know everything connected with this house and she spoke with relish. "Ezekiel was engaged to marry Ellen Fenwick. We have old letters that tell how much in love they were. But when the war started he went into the army as a captain—on the Confederate side, as you can see by his uniform. Ellen Fenwick loved him anyway, but her father was furious. Jud forbade her to ever see him again. So when Ezekiel left to fight with a Virginia regiment, she was forced to break off her engagement. Ezekiel had this picture painted and sent it to her through a friend. She must have hidden it away, so Jud wouldn't destroy it. It wasn't found for a generation or two. He died in the Shepherdstown fighting just after Antietam, so poor little Ellen was already brokenhearted before those marauders took over the house."

A heavy sense of grief seemed to inhabit this room—something no amount of cleaning could sweep away. The eerie way Ezekiel's eyes followed me seemed to ask for something. My mother must have felt this too when she was young.

I picked up Royal's portrait and escaped from both Ezekiel and Anne-Marie by crossing the hall to Egan's room. I hung the picture of my ancestor on a nail that had held a faded print of wildflowers. Satisfied that Egan would like it there, I crossed over to my own room next door. It was too early to go to bed and I was too keyed-up for sleep anyway, so I sat down to read one of the books I had brought with me, a history of Harpers Ferry. After a few pages, I realized that in my present state of mind I couldn't concentrate.

I put the book aside and went to stand at the rear window, where I could look out toward Daniel Griffin's cottage. All was dark out there, and no lights burned in the windows, so he was probably out—roaming about Harpers Ferry on some mysterious search of his own. Moonlight illuminated the yard and touched off sparkles on the river where it flowed far below the steep cliffs.

Whatever I did or thought about, my consciousness of Ellen's room remained. I'd read about "thought forms" in haunted houses. Not ghosts, but something left in another dimension to disquiet those who came within reach.

I knew what I needed to do in this restless state. I changed to warm trousers and a pullover sweater, tied a scarf over my hair, and stole downstairs and out of the house.

The sound of my car starting up in the stillness might rouse the attention of the household, but that couldn't be helped. It took only moments to drive down steep streets to the Lower Town. Parking places were easy to find at this hour and I left my car to walk out to the Point. This was where I'd first come when I reached Harpers Ferry, and it was where I'd met Ryan Pearce.

I watched the river flow over white rapids, its surface dancing with light. Daughter of the Stars, indeed. Clearly I was a romantic at heart, though this was not something I'd realized during my life in Charlottesville. So little had ever touched me there, but now old, blocked-off feelings were beginning to stir.

When Ryan came to stand beside me, as he had done the first time, I didn't feel surprised. It was as though I had come here for an inevitable meeting.

"It seems we've met like this before," he said. I noticed

again the low timbre of his voice and it made me shiver with anticipation. "The river always calls to me when the moon is full. She's lively tonight, but not in one of her tempers."

"I couldn't sleep," I said. "I knew there wasn't any point in going to bed."

"I felt the same way. I kept thinking about you up in that house and I felt concerned. Not that anything could happen to you there. Anne-Marie keeps everything locked up like a fortress at night. And I'm sure your grandfather means *you* no harm. But I felt uneasy just the same."

His concern made me feel warm and happy. I liked his being unable to sleep because he was thinking of me.

"I'm sure no one has a grudge against me," I agreed. "I've come along too late in the scheme of things. All the passions and angers must have claimed their targets by now."

"Are you sure of that?" He stood near me, but not touching me, looking far away toward the Gap. "You're connected at every turn, and you might be a threat without ever knowing it."

"To whom?" I asked.

He let that go. "What did you think about the reunion tonight between Laura and Miss Lacey?"

"I'm not sure my great-grandmother's magnanimous gesture was real."

"I agree. I suspect that deep down Miss Lacey has never forgiven Laura for what happened."

"What did happen?"

"I've only heard stories, but Brad was already married to your mother when he began to look in Laura's direction. Apparently Ardra wasn't the first one to catch his eye. Miss Lacey noticed the warning signs and had it out with Laura, telling her that Brad was off-limits. I doubt that Laura would have ever been attracted to a man so much younger anyway. She was furious with Miss Lacey for doubting her integrity— which was too bad, because Laura had once regarded her as something of a mentor."

The more I learned about my father, the more I pitied my mother. It must have been awful for her, especially if she'd really loved her husband in the beginning, as I was sure she had.

But now, under the spell of the river and the night, I wanted to think only of the man beside me. I knew so little about him. Much of the time he seemed merely an observer or a dreamer, deeply fascinated by the fabric of others' lives. I wished something could happen that would jar him out of his absorption with the past, so that he would spend more time interested in the reality around him.

His next words surprised me. "Lacey, I have a wonderful idea! We don't need to wait until morning. We could visit Virginius Island tonight, while there's bright moonlight. That's the way a ghost town *should* be seen. Are you game?"

"Of course. I'd love that!" I felt suddenly more alive than I'd ever been. I was a dreamer too, in my own way.

"Come along then," he said, taking my arm. We walked down from the Point to Shenandoah Street and past all the darkened windows. Soon the lighted streets lay behind us, and high cliffs of shale rose on our right, clear to Jefferson's Rock.

Two bridges crossed the canal, but one was closed for construction. This one, Ryan told me, had been rebuilt to replicate the original, which had been swept away in a flood.

He took a small flashlight from his pocket, but its beam was too weak to show us very much. The moon did better. The bridge was constructed in four flat-topped arches, two on each side. Between these wooden structures several parallel railings protected one from a tumble into the water. We crossed wooden planks to stand in the center of the bridge, where our view of the canal was unimpeded and we could look down on the water flowing tranquilly beneath us. Moonlight showed the dark boles of trees rising out of water where land had once been. Ryan told me that boats no longer used the canal to bypass the rapids. It had been cleaned out and the banks repaired when the Park took over.

"The island isn't as wild as it once was," Ryan said. "The ruins of what used to be here have been made as safe as possible for visitors, and the walks cleared. There's even a dirt road for work vehicles, though of course no passenger cars are allowed on the island. What used to be factories and homes are only stone foundations—holes in the ground. After the river swept across in a high fury a few times, there wasn't much left to preserve."

When we went on over the bridge, I saw crumbling walls lighted by the moon and clumps of stone that had once been buildings. A ghost town indeed! We moved away from the path and the ground became rough with small stones, so that we had to step carefully. While the moonlight was bright enough, charcoal shadows made every step treacherous. Overhead the black branches of trees formed patterns against a moon-bright sky, striping our faces with shadow.

When we came to a railroad track that cut across our path, Ryan warned me, so I wouldn't stumble over the ties.

"This is the track for the Winchester and Potomac Railroad," he told me. "During the war the railroad carried troops and supplies for Sheridan's Army of the Shenandoah. The rails are still in use."

In only a few moments we had crossed to the other side of the narrow strip of land created by the river. Here we could stand at the edge of the Shenandoah, only a little above water level, and watch the lively white light reflected from the rapids, and the darker gleam where the river flowed more smoothly.

Down a little way from where we stood, a man was fishing at the edge of the river, paying no attention to us. The island was open to the public at night, Ryan told me, since night fishing was popular.

I was sharply aware of night and river and island. And most of all of the man beside me. I stood very still, watching the shimmer of flowing water, wondering if Ryan felt what I felt at this moment—a sense of wonder and something more that caught at my throat. But when he spoke, his thoughts seemed to have turned once more to the past.

"I can't help thinking of all those men and women and children who lived and worked on this island! All the loving and hating, the good and the evil, the human problems that beset them—all gone with the years. Most of them not even remembered. So many died in floods. One woman who escaped wrote about a night when the water rose six feet in four minutes. So many never had a chance. Perhaps what happened here is only a drop in the bucket compared with other disasters, but I wish I could go back to that time. Not to stay, but to record those events and help them be remembered. We forget so quickly."

"That's what you're doing with your book, isn't it—helping people to remember? You'll make Virginius Island come alive for your readers."

"That's why I need to learn so much more. Under the silt that covers the island are still the remnants of human lives. Utensils, toys, jewelry, ornaments—all those possessions that were buried and have been preserved from the water's relentless assault. That's why digging goes on—so that history can be recovered. Since the island was created by the river, its story is special."

I liked the way he felt about his work. He was part of this recovery and re-creation. But it couldn't be his whole life. In my own book I would do just a little of this, and being a writer and an artist gave me some understanding of the absorption that could take over one's life. But not entirely. For me there had to be more, though this was something I was just beginning to realize.

"I want to live *now,*" I said suddenly.

By moonlight his smile was as shadowy as everything else, and as enigmatic. The moon and the river lent so much mystery and romance to what we were doing.

"Then let's talk about the present," he said. "This is your first time on the island—so what do you see?"

I knew he was testing his theory about strangers noticing what had become commonplace and invisible to the natives. I couldn't tell him that at the moment I saw only the man beside me.

"I'll set down my impressions for you on paper sometime when I can look back and think about them," I promised.

He accepted that, and I tried to tell him what the present meant to me. "My life seems to be filled with problems that are alive and not buried under time and silt. I need more wisdom to help me deal with the *present.*"

We walked a little way along the sandy edge of the river, and when I might have stumbled over a root, he caught my arm and steadied me.

"You're right, of course, Lacey. Sometimes I get so caught up in what's gone before that I almost forget about the present. At least, that's what my wife used to say."

He'd mentioned his wife only once before, and I had wondered.

When he spoke again, it was as though I'd asked a question. "We married very young, and after a few years we went in different directions. That time was good for the man I used to be, and I hope it was good for her. But after we broke up, I felt that she was right when she accused me of being too much a dreamer for any woman to tolerate."

"You have to be a dreamer to write books," I said. "In my own way I'm a dreamer too. But at the same time I know I'm here *now.*"

"Perhaps that's what I've let slip away." He turned me to him and kissed me—not gently, not the kiss of a dreamer. "That's for *now,*" he said, with his lips against my cheek.

We started back and he kept my hand in his. I wondered if he could hear my heart racing. The path narrowed and I walked ahead, moving carelessly, as though I floated. But my feet were still earthbound, and when I stepped on a loose bit of shale, only a nearby crumbling wall saved me from pitching into the black hollow at my feet. I clung to the rough wall and found myself looking down into a darkness where moonlight didn't reach. On the other side of the hollow rose a keystone arch, well outlined by the moon.

Ryan pulled me back to safety, but my attention had been caught by something at the bottom of the pit.

"Look, Ryan! What is that down there?"

He leaned on the wall beside me, and the moon, sliding from a thin haze, showed something round and white deep in the hole.

"Stay where you are," Ryan said. "I'll take a closer look." His tone of voice had changed and it added to my own sense that something was wrong.

Our side of the pit was walled with loosening shale, and he went down backward, the stones sliding after him. When he reached the bottom in a clatter, he took out his small flashlight again. In the gloom of the pit, the beam was bright enough to show the upturned face of the man who lay there.

I heard Ryan gasp, and saw his own face, white in the moonlight, as he looked up at me. "It's Henry Elliot. He's dead. He must have been down here for at least an hour. He's cold as ice."

I clung to the wall again, while Ryan scrambled out and stood beside me.

"He was probably drunk and stepped off into space. There's blood all over him, so he must have struck his head on the arch when he fell. The Park's Law Enforcement rangers have their headquarters nearby. Anything that happens on the road is taken care of by the town police. But the rangers have jurisdiction over anything that occurs on grass, or inside a building in the Park District. So Virginius Island is theirs to protect. There'll be someone on duty."

As we crossed the bridge to the road, I no longer found the moonlight mysterious or romantic. I hadn't known that I had an uncle Henry until today, and I hadn't liked what I'd seen of him, but he was my father's brother. Perhaps, on some buried level, kinship spoke to me, for I felt both sorry and sad.

Sorry because a man had died. And sad about all those empty spaces in my life—so much family I hadn't known. Even love that I'd missed. Until now?

In spite of everything, my mind seemed to be replaying those moments beside the river. Was I only dreaming again?

SEVENTEEN

AFTERWARD, as though in a daze, I went through the proper procedures with the ranger in charge. It was necessary to show the officer on duty where Henry had fallen. Other rangers were called in, and there were questions for us to answer. It seemed to puzzle everyone that Ryan and I had been on the island that night. Our reasons didn't sound very sane, but at least Ryan was well known and the research he was doing was a plausible excuse.

When we could finally leave, he drove me to Miss Lacey's house and I was thankful for the lift. I could pick up my car tomorrow. Or today, since by this time it was well after one in the morning.

As might have been expected, Anne-Marie was up and waiting for me. She opened the door as we came up the steps, and burst into words.

"Well, Miss Elliot!" She sounded like a dormitory mistress. "You went off without a word. Miss Lacey has been worried sick, but I finally persuaded her to go back to bed."

Ryan took over quickly and gave Anne-Marie the facts before she could ask questions. "Lacey and I ran into each other in the Lower Town and I wanted her to see Virginius Island by moonlight. Unfortunately, while we were there we discovered that Henry Elliot had fallen into a pit near the river—where there are some old foundations. He was dead when we found him and we've been with the rangers ever since."

For once we seemed to have shocked Anne-Marie speechless. Before she could find words, Ryan told her that I was very tired and her questions would have to wait until morning.

"Everything will work out, Lacey," he told me. "I'll see you tomorrow."

When he'd gone, I went directly up to my room, ignoring Anne-Marie's tendency to mutter. As I got into bed, I felt tired and upset—and elated, all at the same time. I ought to be concerned only with Henry's death, but underneath this very real horror ran a tingling of happiness that wouldn't subside. I still didn't really know how Ryan felt about the future, but I knew how I felt, and, for the moment, that was enough.

When Anne-Marie knocked on the door and came into my room, she surprised me. She turned on a lamp and I saw that she'd brought me a small tray with a glass of milk, a bit of cheese, and some crackers.

"This will help you sleep, Lacey." At least she'd dispensed with the stiffly formal "Miss Elliot."

She stood by while I sipped hot milk, and I knew she still wanted to talk—avidly curious about what had happened. My lack of response finally managed to turn her off, and she left.

I finished the milk, and, for the first time that night, began to feel relaxed and sleepy.

I don't know how long I might have slept in the morning if Miss Lacey hadn't come into my room. She tapped and opened the door before I could rouse myself to answer. When she came to sit beside my bed, I rolled over to look at her in surprise. I'd never seen her so disheveled and, by morning light, she looked as old as her years. She had thrown on an ancient, quilted wrapper, and her white hair was uncombed and wispy. Her small triangle of a face seemed to melt into the folds of her neck.

She had, however, lost none of her peremptory manner. "Tell me about finding Henry," she said at once.

Obviously, Anne-Marie had spread the word. I sat against my pillows and woke up enough to repeat the story.

Listening, she began to relax visibly, as if in relief. "Of course it was bound to happen, with Henry being the drunkard he was. Laura can be glad he didn't fall and break his neck while he was in her house. Anyway, he won't be missed by many. I'm sorry you had the experience of finding him."

As she talked, I began to sense that under her assured manner was a woman badly shaken.

She went on in a rush, though her voice trembled a little now. "You don't know what you've gotten into by coming here. Perhaps old fears have begun to wake up since you came to Harpers Ferry."

Her control had begun to slip, and her hands trembled on her knees. I reached toward her, but she drew her hands away.

"Tell me what you mean, Miss Lacey," I begged.

With an effort, she managed to recover. "Perhaps you've come here as an emissary of your mother. Perhaps you're the one we're all afraid of."

I hoped she wasn't disintegrating mentally. "That's ridiculous! I'm not a threat to anyone, and neither is my mother." But even as I spoke a new uneasiness stirred in me. Was there something more that others knew and I didn't?

She examined me with eyes that had faded to a silvery blue. "I hope you're right," she said. She rose, smoothing back her uncombed hair as though she'd suddenly realized how she must look. When she went out she left my door open, and I saw her cross the hall to Ellen Fenwick's room.

I slipped out of bed and went after her. She, of all people—except perhaps Daniel Griffin—held the key to what had happened in the past. I'd even wondered if it was Miss Lacey whom Vinnie was protecting with her fictional story.

She had stopped before the strange portrait of Ezekiel, and even while the painting's eyes seemed to observe me as I entered the room, I knew those eyes were also watching her.

She spoke to the portrait sadly. "If only *you* had married Ellen, everything might have been different."

I stood just behind her. "How could that be? He would still have gone to war. He could hardly have stayed home to protect her."

She didn't seem startled to find that I had followed her. "He might have taken her safely away from this house, before he went anywhere himself."

"I'm afraid history can't be changed," I said more gently. For the first time since I'd met her, my great-grandmother seemed old and helpless and sad.

"I expect that's true. But the future can always be managed."

She had said "managed" instead of "changed," and her voice had strengthened as though she was trying to pull herself together.

"Do you mean 'manipulated'?" I asked.

She seemed not to hear me as she gazed about the room. "It looks much better, doesn't it, since it's been cleaned up. Though I had a time persuading Anne-Marie to do this. She thinks I've offended Ellen."

When I merely nodded my agreement that it looked better, Miss Lacey raised her chin and gave me her old, daunting stare before she swept out of the room. Her air of new confidence suggested that she was perfectly groomed and fully in charge. But now I had glimpsed the weakness under the pretense of strength.

The portrait's eyes seemed to challenge me, and I smiled at him wryly. "So now everything is your fault, Ezekiel."

He must have been a charmer in life, but perhaps a bit arrogant as well. His look seemed to hint that I knew very little about anything.

There were now three old portraits in this house—though this was hardly unusual for a day when there was no camera in every home, and itinerant painters traveled the countryside, often working for food and lodging. All three were very different—Jud with his arrogant good looks; Royal with a certain nobility about him; and Ezekiel with his endless searching. All three faces haunted me, as though they had something to tell me. But where was I to find the answer?

Back in my room I dressed in jeans and a warm pullover. Spring had not yet turned into summer. When I went downstairs, I found Egan alone at the dining room table eating a good breakfast. His smile of welcome warmed me and I bent to kiss his cheek. This morning he seemed entirely a small boy, with none of that eerie wisdom he sometimes displayed.

I listened to his chatter about young friends and Shenna, smiling at him absently as I drank my coffee. Then he startled me.

"Somebody went across last night—isn't that right?"

"Across? What do you mean?"

"I had a very sad feeling when I woke up this morning. As though it was someone who wasn't ready to go. I hope it's not anyone we know."

"Do you mean that someone died, Egan?"

He shook his head. "Nobody ever dies, but sometimes we go across when we don't mean to."

At times I felt that Egan could see into another dimension that was invisible to the rest of us.

"You remember Henry Elliot?" I asked.

"Sure. Is he the one? Maybe it was time for him to go."

I hoped that was true.

Without my asking, Anne-Marie appeared with a bowl of hot oatmeal and a plate of freshly toasted wheat bread, which she set in front of me. She had nothing to say this morning, and I was just as glad.

This time when I left the house, I let her know and walked out into a fresh spring morning. I breathed flower scents and admired redbud trees as I walked down to the Lower Town. In spite of what had happened to Henry, in spite of the gloom Miss Lacey's house had cast upon me, my spirits lifted. I would see Ryan today.

My car waited where I'd left it, but I wandered past it idly, with no desire to return to Miss Lacey's at once. Perhaps I would drive up to Aunt Vinnie's in a little while and look for Ryan. He was the only one I could talk to about Henry's death. And besides, I wanted to be with him.

Perhaps for now I would try to think about my book and the pictorial map I would make of the Lower Town. Phoning my mother could wait until I got to Vinnie's.

I noticed again the sign for the John Brown exhibit, and decided to explore. The room I stepped into had been well arranged to utilize space. Books, papers, and memorabilia were displayed under glass around the outer rim of the room. In the center were tall, angled screens that displayed old photographs and printed material. One side of the screens showed the faces and histories of John Brown's raiders, while the other showed the faces and the histories of the U.S. Marines who had effected the capture. All looked like ordinary men—yet they had taken part in a stirring historic event.

While I stood reading, I heard again the sound of Paul Robeson's voice raised in those ringing words that had stirred the North from slumber: "John Brown's body lies a'molderin' in the grave."

I walked toward the sound and found myself at the door of a small theater where the story of John Brown had been projected on a screen. Robeson's stirring song was concluding the presentation.

The showing had been well attended and, as the lights came on, the audience filed out slowly. I waited until I thought the theater was empty and then stepped into the space filled with rows of seats to have a look around.

A single member of the audience remained. A man sat in the last row. He was bent forward, his arms on the seat in front of him, as he stared at the empty screen. It was my grandfather, Daniel Griffin.

Perhaps I'd have slipped away without speaking to him, but when he turned and saw me, he gestured to the seat next to him.

"Good morning, Lacey. Have you been watching? Did you hear Sidney Poitier's narration?"

I sat down hesitantly. "I missed the showing," I said. "I was looking at the exhibits outside."

Griffin spoke almost reverently. "I wish I could have known John Brown. I'd have been an abolitionist, of course, and I'd have followed him in his stand against slavery."

"Wasn't it an ill-conceived stand?"

"Things went wrong. He couldn't carry out the plan he envisioned. Yet what he began ended in the freeing of the slaves and the preservation of the Union."

I studied the strong, rugged profile of the man beside me. "You look like some of the pictures I've seen of John Brown. Is that intentional?"

"Accidental," he said, shaking his head. "I'd be proud to look like him, though. How much of the story do you know?"

"Only a little, I'm afraid."

Griffin leaned back in his seat. "He came to this slave state of Virginia meaning to free all its slaves. It wasn't West Virginia then, of course. He believed that the black men would leave their masters and follow him into the mountains around Harpers Ferry, where they would all be safe. The trouble was that he had to keep his plans secret and that very secrecy defeated him. The slaves had no idea that he was coming. His proposal must have seemed frightening to the few who even heard about it. So, of course, there was no mass rising to leave the plantations.

"On the way to Harpers Ferry, Brown picked up several hostages. After he took over the armory, others were added, as employees came to work. In the end, Brown's raiders held perhaps forty hostages crowded into that little engine house."

A bright, intense look shone in Daniel's eyes—those gray eyes I'd thought cold and condemning when I first saw him at the Anvil restaurant. Now a fire burned in them—flames behind gray smoke. Indicating what? I wondered.

"Men died on that terrible night when he held the engine

house against the roused citizenry of the town. Local militia were helpless. But by morning, Washington had sent in a company of United States Marines to free the hostages.

"Brown's resistance was brave, but it didn't last very long. He had been wounded, and he and the raiders who were still alive were taken prisoner. Luckily, no hostages were harmed. The trial—only a matter of form—was held in nearby Charles Town, and Brown was carried into the courtroom on a stretcher. The sentence was death by hanging for all the raiders who had been captured. There were some who had escaped.

"Following Brown's capture, the governor of Virginia interviewed him, and John Brown foretold the coming war between the states and the destruction of Harpers Ferry. When he stood on the scaffold with a hood over his head, the field was surrounded by soldiers, in case there was an attempt to rescue him. The governor warned the citizenry to stay home and arm themselves in order to guard their own property. There wasn't any trouble—perhaps because of the precautions taken. Among the soldiers who witnessed the hanging were cadets from a Virginia military academy that included a professor who would become famous as the Confederate general 'Stonewall' Jackson. And in the ranks of a Richmond company a young actor watched. His name was John Wilkes Booth."

Daniel's words had delivered me to another place and time, but his fierceness was all about the present. The impact of history still mattered in Harpers Ferry, as though past and present were tied together inextricably.

"What happened in the past has never stopped mattering here," he said. "You can feel it, Lacey. Because of the blood strain, you can't help being connected. Nothing is ever lost; not so long as men remember."

I thought of Ryan's words about how much society does *not* remember.

"Perhaps all we can do," I said, "is try not to repeat the mistakes from the past."

His wry look dismissed such a feeble notion. "That's a noble sentiment to which men have paid a great deal of lip service and not much attention."

I couldn't help wondering how much from *his* past was prompting him now. To do what? Take revenge? Extract some payment for his own sufferings?

His look seemed to soften as we regarded each other.

"Do you know where John Brown is buried?" he asked.

"Not exactly."

"His wife was permitted to claim his body after his death, and she took it to their farm in North Elba, New York—near Lake Placid. His tombstone bears inscriptions for his grandfather and his sons lost in battle."

"So far away from Harpers Ferry," I said.

Daniel shook his head sadly. "No man is wise enough to foresee the consequences of his own actions. So we follow some driving emotion to a conclusion that we never expected—and the damage is done. John Brown never meant to contribute to massive bloodshed between the states. He believed that his way could avoid war. Instead, his actions helped to bring on the Civil War. John Wilkes Booth never meant to damage the South—but without Lincoln as a calming influence the damage was enormous."

I spoke softly, drawing him back to the present. "So why are you here, Grandfather? There are already consequences. Can we stop them?"

He stood up and stretched, and I rose with him.

"Do you know about Henry Elliot?" I asked.

His face told me nothing. "What about him?"

I explained how Henry had died, and he heard me through. "So now the score is even," he said, and strode out of the theater, moving so quickly that I knew he didn't want me to follow him.

What score had been evened? And by whom, if anyone?

I walked soberly back to my car, still under the spell cast by Daniel Griffin—and John Brown.

WHEN I went into the house, Vinnie was at the desk talking to guests, and I waited in the small parlor until she was free. Shenandoah wakened from a nap on the sofa and sat up to observe me with wide-eyed interest. I sat down beside her and patted my knee. After some consideration, she accepted the invitation and curled up in my lap to begin her resonant purring. I petted her, and told her that Egan would be coming home soon and she mustn't worry. The sound of my voice, if not my words, seemed to reassure her, and after a moment she went back to sleep. I stroked silky, multicolored fur until Vinnie came to greet me.

"I'm glad you stopped in, Lacey. I don't think you'll want to stay with your great-grandmother now that your mother has come home."

Her news was startling and disturbing. "She has come here? But how? And why?"

Vinnie seemed vague about the *why,* and a bit nervous. "She drove herself up the valley from Charlottesville. She was very tired, so I put her in your room for now. I'll have a free room for her later today."

"Something is wrong, Aunt Vinnie. What aren't you telling me?"

"It's too awful. So sudden. Henry Elliot is dead."

"I know," I said. "Ryan and I were the ones who found him. But how do you know about it?"

She sat down limply. "Ardra told me."

"Ardra?"

"She went up to get Egan this morning, but Miss Lacey wouldn't allow her to bring him home. Everyone up there knew about Henry, but I didn't know *you* found him. What do you think happened to him, Lacey?"

I explained that he had probably been drinking and had fallen into a pit on Virginius Island.

"Why would he go *there?"*

"I don't think anyone has the answer to that yet. Park Service Rangers are investigating. I suppose they'll turn over what they find to the local police. Laura Kelly was looking for him yesterday and couldn't find him."

Vinnie put her hands over her face and began to cry softly.

"Did you care about Henry?" I asked in surprise. So far I hadn't seen anyone cry over his death.

She found a tissue in a pocket and wiped her eyes. "I'm not crying for Henry. He probably deserved whatever happened to him. His death just put me back in that horrible time when your mother left. My tears are for all of us. Me. Poor Ardra. My brother, Daniel. And your mother, of course."

"Not Miss Lacey?"

"She never wanted sympathy from anyone. Not even when her daughter died, and your mother took you away. She held us all off—those who were left."

I didn't want to upset Vinnie any further. I felt there was still something she wasn't telling me, but I let it go.

"I'll see you later," I said, giving her a brief hug before hurrying down the hall to my room.

When I opened the door softly, I found Mother lying awake on the bed with a comforter over her. When she started to sit up, I eased her gently back on the pillows.

"Please rest. It's wonderful to see you, but you should never have made the trip, driving alone. Why did Mrs. Brewster let you go?"

"What could she do? How could she stop me?"

I had to grant her that. This time she sat up against the pillows to face me. The change in her was clear. More color had come into her face, and her eyes were bright with an interest I hadn't seen in them for a long time. Perhaps even a sense of triumph because she'd made the trip? She might be tired from the drive, but she was no frail invalid, and I felt reassured.

"You look as though you're enjoying whatever it is you're up to," I said as I sat down on the side of the bed.

She looked lovingly into my face. "You've changed, dear. Though I hope it's not because of Lacey Fenwick. I'm sorry you've had anything to do with her."

"You named me for her."

"A long time ago I loved her. I thought she was the most wonderful grandmother in the world. When you were born your father and I named you for her. My feelings for her changed very quickly after your father died. She became horrible to all of us. But never mind all that history."

I wanted to know much more and asked her several questions, but she dismissed them all. "Well, at least you can tell me why you've come here," I insisted.

She answered reluctantly. "I don't suppose it's a secret. Vinnie phoned and said I should come and persuade you to go home. She tells me that Henry Elliot is dead—all the more reason for you to be away from here."

"What has his death to do with me—except for finding him?"

Mother closed her eyes. "Vinnie doesn't think it was an accident, and she wants you clear of whatever develops."

I left my place beside her on the bed and sat down in a chair where I could look at her directly. "What did Vinnie mean by that? It's not what the Park rangers seem to think."

"She wouldn't say anything more, but she seems frightened. Anyway, we ought to start back to Charlottesville tomorrow morning at the latest. That will give me time to rest and you time to get your things from Miss Lacey's."

"I don't want to leave now," I said firmly, resisting the pressure I knew she could exert. "I hope you'll stay here for a few days until I can work things out."

She looked alarmed. "What things?"

"I don't know exactly. I have a feeling Miss Lacey may be the one who can tell me what happened to my father. Now that I'm inside her fortress, I'm in a position to find out answers that you've never given me. So much has become clear to me since I came here. I need to finish putting my life together and I can't until I know what really happened. There's a balance wheel that's missing. Perhaps you can't tell me because you don't know."

She closed her eyes. "Maybe it's better if we don't know."

Someone else had said that to me, and I still didn't believe it was true.

"I can't accept that. There's the mystery of my father's disappearance and your running away. From what? Grandfather Daniel was forced to leave to avoid being accused of causing whatever happened to Brad Elliot. What was all that about?"

She focused on one name. "What worries me more than anything else is that my father is here in Harpers Ferry. What does he want?"

"I don't know exactly, but I'm beginning to like him," I said. "Sometimes he frightens me, but there's something strong about him that I respect."

She shook her head sadly. "I know. I once loved him more than I ever loved my mother. By the time I was old enough to value her properly, she was gone. Grandmother Lacey always dismissed her, but I should never have listened to *her*. Perhaps more than anyone else, I'm responsible for my mother's death. I never tried to help her."

"I'm sure your guilt isn't justified," I said. "She was strong enough to manage when Ardra's baby was born."

After a long silence she held out her hand to me and I took it.

"Do what you feel you must, dear, but be very careful. I'll stay here with Vinnie for a few days."

"Thank you." There was still one question she might answer for me. "Why did you and Vinnie quarrel before you left?"

"It doesn't matter anymore. I felt terribly bitter toward my sister, as you might imagine. But Ardra was Vinnie's pet and she defended her. To *me!*"

"You'll see Ardra if you stay. She's living here with Vinnie now."

Mother lay back against her pillows. "Ardra? Here?"

"Yes. And so is my half sister, Caryl, whom I didn't know existed."

I saw the pain in my mother's face, but I wasn't ready to forgive her for all she'd held back from me.

"I tried to protect you," she said faintly.

"From what? From whom?"

"There was such wickedness! My mother knew and she died because she wasn't strong enough to face all that happened."

"Ardra seems faded and helpless. It's hard to imagine her doing what she did—having an affair with my father. She's aged much more than you have, even with your illness. I don't know if she's strong enough to face you."

"Don't count on that. She always had a knack for making herself seem helpless. I grew up with her and did a lot of protecting of my younger sister. She could flutter about, but when she wanted something her will turned to steel."

"I don't really like Ardra, but I'm growing fond of Caryl. And I love her little boy Egan. He's so bright—and somehow *good.*"

"I do want to see *him.* Vinnie never mentioned Caryl or Egan in her letters."

"You could have asked for information."

"I suppose I didn't want to know. I tried to cut us off from everyone in this place."

"Which you certainly did," I said flatly, and was immediately sorry when tears came into her eyes. I put my arms around her and kissed her cheek. "Never mind. It's opening up the past that's important. So *I* can understand the present. What does Henry have to do with what's going on now?"

"Henry was never much good, Lacey. I'm sorry about his death, but he always tried to interfere. He never wanted Brad to marry me."

"Because he had a thing for you himself? Laura Kelly told me he did."

"Laura? Is she still around? She used to be honey among the bees when she was young. Even my father—"

"Yes—she told me."

"She would!"

Someone tapped on the door, and when I opened it Ryan was standing there. My heart did its new sort of somersault at the sight of him.

"Vinnie tells me your mother is here," he said.

I was hardly calm and collected, but I invited him in. He went over to the bed at once and took her hand. "I'm glad you've come, Mrs. Elliot," he said, smiling down at her. "I'm Ryan Pearce, a sort of resident friend of the family."

She roused herself in response to his smile. "Oh, yes. Vinnie tells me you and Caryl—"

"Don't believe everything Vinnie says, Mrs. Elliot. I'm afraid she has a romantic streak."

He chatted with my mother for a few minutes and then turned to me. "There's something I'd like to show you, Lacey. If you can come up to my workroom. May I borrow her for a little while, Mrs. Elliot?"

"Of course," I said. Mother was already nodding.

"I'll rest," she assured me. "Then we'll visit some more."

When I'd closed the door and we were walking along the hall, Ryan said, "I've been talking to the Park rangers who took over last night. The local police are in on the investigation now."

His tone was so grave that I had a dark feeling about what was to come.

"It's pretty clear that Henry's fall didn't cause his death. The blow to his head was in front, but when we found him he was lying on his back. They think someone struck him straight-on with a heavy object. There will be an autopsy to decide the cause of death, but the police are already considering this a murder case."

So Vinnie had been right. Suddenly I felt shaky.

Ryan put an arm around me as we walked. "Are you all right, Lacey?"

I leaned into his arm. Too much was crowding in on me and my mother's arrival didn't help.

When we reached his work area, he pulled a second chair over to his desk, and I sat down beside him. The diary Laura had given him was open on the desk and I saw again the lines in faded brown ink slanting across the page.

He picked up the book. "This is surprising. I'd like you to read it for yourself. I didn't recognize who the writer was right away. Her name is Sarah Lang."

"Lang?" I jogged my memory. "Wasn't one of the deserters who broke into the Fenwick house named Orin Lang? Was this woman his wife?"

"Not his wife."

"His daughter, then?"

"As Miss Lacey probably told you, Ellen Fenwick had a baby that Jud refused to keep after his daughter died in childbirth. She wasn't even named when she was given away to a family in Charles Town that was paid for taking her.

"Orin seems to have developed a conscience when he recovered from his wound and found that his friends were dead. He learned where the baby was and he and his wife adopted her and gave her the name she would carry for the rest of her life."

I took the closed book he held out to me and traced a finger over faded violets. "What a wonderful story! I'm glad Sarah didn't have to suffer for a tragedy that wasn't her fault. Does this diary tell us what happened to her? If she married and had children, perhaps there are Fenwick and Lang descendants somewhere."

"I've thought of that. I haven't read the whole book carefully, but at the end of the diary she writes about leaving Virginia. Living was hard after the war, and when her adoptive mother died, Orin decided to go North to find work. She writes movingly about the upheaval in their lives."

"How did the book turn up in a Charles Town collection if she and Orin went North?"

"Who knows? But I think you should take it now. Perhaps you'll find something I missed that will give us a lead as to what happened to some of the family. There are nearly a hundred years unaccounted for since Sarah wrote in this book."

I was eager to read Sarah's words. "I'd better get back to Miss Lacey's soon. My mother wants me to go home with her, but I've persuaded her that I need to stay until I know what Miss Lacey can tell me about my father."

"I'm glad you're staying, but I don't think you *could* leave. There's the matter of Henry's death. The local police will want to ask us more questions now. I wouldn't be surprised if the State Police are called in as well. Henry was dead for some hours before we found him, so there's no question of our being under suspicion. Besides, we didn't have a motive."

I stood up, still feeling uncertain. "I have to be going now, but I'll be back to see my mother. Will you keep an eye out for her in the meantime, Ryan?"

There was no moonlight now, so the spell was gone. Nevertheless, his look was as warm as a caress. He reached out to trace a finger gently down my cheek. "Dear Lacey. Take care while you're with your great-grandmother. Henry's death seems unrelated to your family's tangled past, but until we know what happened—just take care. Of course I'll see your mother. Perhaps we can get better acquainted."

When I left him, I stopped in to let Mother know I was leaving, but would see her soon. I knew that she regretted my returning to my great-grandmother's, but she let me go without objecting.

On my way out of the house, however, Vinnie stopped me. "I don't know what's going on," she said. "But I must talk to you. Come up to my room for a moment."

She sounded so urgent that I went with her unquestioningly. We sat before an empty grate, the door closed against chance visitors.

"I must talk to someone or I'll go mad! I want to tell you what really happened the night Brad died. Henry tipped me off that Brad meant to give the baby away secretly. He didn't care how Ardra felt. He had this crazy idea that no one must know. Of course this is a small town, and everyone knows what's happening. So his secret wasn't really a secret, except for this Virginius Island part. But he was a remarkably stubborn man, and you couldn't tell him that. He claimed to be meeting someone on Virginius Island who would take the baby away, keep her identity a secret, and give her a home. When Henry called me, I found that Brad must have slipped into the house and taken Caryl. When I looked, the baby was gone." She broke off, more distraught than I'd ever seen her.

"So you did go to Virginius Island that night?"

"Yes. I crossed the bridge and went only a little way. A storm was blowing up, and the island seemed a frightening place. I'd brought a flashlight, so I saw the body in my path before I stumbled over it. It was Brad, and he was dead. There was no sign of the baby, though I searched all around for her. I went home, planning to call the rangers' headquarters. But when I got there, Caryl was in her crib sleeping soundly, and Ardra's bed was empty. That frightened me more than anything on the island, and I didn't call anyone. I couldn't find Ardra anywhere in the house. I was afraid that, weak as she was, she had followed Brad to the island and brought Caryl home. Who else could have done that? And if she'd gone there, had she killed Brad? I didn't look in the herb garden until an hour or so later. I don't know how long she'd been there, sitting in the rain. I brought her into the house, got her into a dry, warm nightgown, and put her to bed with hot water bottles."

"Did she tell you what happened?"

"She was in no state to explain anything. She just kept saying that Brad had never loved her and she didn't want to live. She was sick—delirious for several days before I pulled her through. I took care of the baby—you see, I loved Caryl from the beginning. When Ardra recovered she didn't remember anything that happened that night. I couldn't let her be accused—and she would have been if I'd told anyone about what had happened."

So now I knew. Someone had seen my father's body. The faint hope that had always stayed alive in me that my father and I would someday meet was quietly extinguished.

My immediate concern was for Vinnie. She had been lying and keeping tragic secrets for all these years. Now that she had finally confided in someone, the dam had broken and she'd dissolved into tears.

I knelt beside her and put my arms around her. However foolish she'd been, my affection for her didn't waver. "I'm glad you've told me this, but I have to ask you another question. What happened to my father's body?"

She turned her head wretchedly from side to side. "I don't know. He was simply reported missing and then his jacket was found and it was assumed that he'd drowned in the river until the police discovered the bullet hole. I knew that he hadn't drowned, but I couldn't speak out. Ardra has a strong, resilient core, and even the mildest people are capable of violent action, once the anger they've been suppressing surfaces. Apparently she wiped out all memory of that night, so not even Ardra knows what happened." Vinnie looked at me with teary eyes. "Lacey, what if it was your mother who killed him? She was far stronger mentally and physically than Ardra. And she did run away."

I couldn't accept that for a moment and I tried to harden

myself against Vinnie. "So you let your brother be blamed in order to save Ardra?"

She covered her face with her hands. "Ardra had always been like a daughter to me and I loved her baby. I knew Daniel could take care of himself."

This wasn't an attitude I found commendable, but I loved and pitied Vinnie. Since there was nothing I could do to save her from the past, I kissed her cheek and pressed my face against hers. When I left, she was still crying.

I went out to my car, and on the drive up to Miss Lacey's I tried to put all the unanswered questions out of my mind. There was still the present to deal with—and for me that included Ryan. We hadn't had time to get to know each other, but something was happening that I'd never experienced before. Perhaps it was happening to him too. My cheek still tingled from the touch of his fingers.

By the time I reached Miss Lacey's, I hadn't worked out anything in my mind. The diary lay on the seat beside me and I slipped it into my handbag. I knew I'd better read it before I showed it to Miss Lacey.

For once, no one was waiting for me when I reached the unlocked door. I let myself into the hall and stood quietly, listening. No small boy was playing Royal Fenwick's drum. No television or radio had been turned on. No voices spoke anywhere. The silence was unsettling.

As I walked past the door of the front parlor I looked in, but the room was empty. So was the rear parlor. The drum sat on the floor, its sticks nearby. I didn't want to call out, but where was everybody?

"Are you home, Lacey?" The sound of my great-grandmother's voice was actually welcome. After what had happened last night, I was more than a little jittery.

The voice had come from what had once been a library, but had been turned into a downstairs bedroom for Miss Lacey. I went to the doorway and looked into her well-appointed sitting room and bedroom. The graceful furniture belonged to an early American period: probably Duncan Phyfe.

The fire had burned to coals in a generous fireplace and it created a focus for Miss Lacey as she sat staring into glowing red and black, her hands clasped in her lap. She wore a long wool robe of a dark wine color and every lock of her hair was neatly combed. Only her face looked oddly disarranged, as though something was coming apart inside her.

"You've been a long time away, Lacey." The words were more pleading than critical. "I'm glad you're back. I was afraid you might have gone away with your mother."

I stared at her, startled. "How did you know she was here? Did Vinnie call you?"

"Amelia came to see me yesterday afternoon. You weren't here."

"But how could she? I spoke with her in the early afternoon and Vinnie said she drove up from Charlottesville this morning and came right to her house."

"Perhaps that was the impression your mother wanted to give. Remember it's only a two-hour drive from Charlottesville. She came to Harpers Ferry late yesterday afternoon and stayed at the Hilltop House last night. I told her I could put her up here, but she didn't want that, for some reason."

I dropped onto a chair opposite Miss Lacey. "I don't understand. I've just been with her and she didn't say anything about seeing you, or about arriving yesterday."

"Amelia could always be devious." Miss Lacey's smile was not amused. "Perhaps she takes after me. *You* think I'm devious, don't you, young Lacey?"

"I don't know what to think about anybody or anything." That, at least, was true. I knew Mother must have had a reason for what she'd done, and I assumed she would tell me soon.

"Why did she come here to see you first?"

"She didn't. She came to see you. Apparently you'd told her you were planning to stay with me for a few days. She wanted to take you back to Charlottesville right away. When I told her you were out, she said she'd come back. I haven't seen her since."

Miss Lacey's account sounded cool and impersonal, considering the fact that these two were grandmother and granddaughter.

"How did you feel about seeing her again?" I asked.

"How should I feel about someone who went away without even a goodbye?"

"The money we received from Vinnie for all those years came from you, so you must have felt something for her."

Miss Lacey had stared into the embers as we talked, but now she raised her head and looked directly at me. "The money was meant to take care of *you* while you were in your mother's charge. I always knew you would come back to Harpers Ferry someday."

Her eyes seemed to glow with a light that might be triumph. For the first time I felt sorry for her. She had lived—reigned—alone here on her hilltop, shutting out friends and relatives. Making up her own scenario for a future that would never happen.

"Now that you're here," she went on, "we must talk about plans."

I spoke as firmly as I could. "I hope we can talk, but not about what you call plans."

"What else is there to talk about?"

I put the question before her that I'd been longing to ask. "I'm sure you know more about what happened to my father than anyone else, if only you would tell me."

Lowered eyelids warned me that she was on guard. "How should I know anything?"

"I think you make it your business to know about everything that happens in Harpers Ferry. Perhaps you weren't so isolated in those days."

"That may be true, but there's nothing I can tell you about your father's disappearance."

"Why not? I can't believe you don't know anything," I challenged.

"Don't ask me. Ask Laura Kelly."

"What has Laura to do with this?"

"She knew Henry, didn't she?"

Suddenly, she sounded old and plaintive. "Can you see my cane anywhere, Lacey? I'm always misplacing things these days."

I suspected that she was creating a smoke screen to distract me, but I looked around and saw a cane propped against the end of the sofa across the room. As I picked it up, I saw that it was a walking stick and not her usual handsome cane.

"Where is your beautiful gryphon?" I asked as I handed it to her.

"I seem to have lost my favorite cane. Did you know that Daniel carved that gryphon's head for me a long time ago? He used to have a special gift for creating beautiful wood carvings."

She used the stick and one hand to push herself up from her chair. "Come into the dining room, Lacey. I'm using it as an office this morning, and I want to show you what I've done."

I followed her down the hall past Jud Fenwick's glowering portrait, and saw with misgivings the papers she had spread out on the dining room table. It was as though she'd never heard my rejection of her "plans."

"Sit down, Lacey. I want you to read this new draft of my will. I haven't consulted anyone about it yet because I wanted to show it to you first."

I sat down, but I didn't touch the papers. "If you go ahead with your idea of leaving this house to me, I will refuse to accept it," I told her.

"Of course you'll accept it. I'm sure your mother will advise you to. It will be a wonderful place for you to live when I'm gone. There will be money to keep it up, of course. And I'm sure Anne-Marie will want to continue as housekeeper as long as she is able."

My great-grandmother was as impossible to reason with as anyone I'd ever met. The thought of living for years in this mausoleum, with Anne-Marie watching me out of the shadows, was appalling.

"What if I should marry and want a house of my own?"

"My husband came gladly into this house, and he enjoyed living here."

"Miss Lacey"— I couldn't yet call her Great-grandmother—"do you ever listen to anything anyone says to you?"

Her direct look fixed itself on me, but she didn't seem displeased. "Not if I can help it. I know what I want and I usually manage to get it. So why should I listen to such nonsense from you?"

There was nothing to do but pack up and leave this house. I left her sitting there and walked to the door.

"I'm not going to look through those papers. I want nothing to do with them. I'll leave for Aunt Vinnie's as soon as I can get packed. My mother is waiting for me there."

Miss Lacey seemed to shrivel a little. Even her voice was smaller when she spoke. "Perhaps I *might* tell you something more about your father."

This was a bribe, obviously, and I turned my back on it. In spite of all I still wanted to know, I was tired of playing games. I would need to look somewhere else and expect nothing more from Lacey Fenwick Enright.

Just then Egan came running down the hall to join us. "Look what I found for you!" he cried and waved the cane with the gryphon's head at Miss Lacey.

She took it from him calmly. "Thank you, Egan. Tell me where you found it."

He smiled angelically. "Shenandoah found it."

"Perhaps you'd better explain how that happened," she said.

For once Egan avoided her gaze and looked at me pleadingly.

"What have you been up to, Egan?" Miss Lacey asked, a stern note creeping into her voice.

"I didn't think anybody would care if I went down to visit Shenandoah."

"*I* care. You are not supposed to leave this house without telling Anne-Marie or me."

"I'm sorry, Grandma, but Shenandoah needed me. I could *feel* that—so I had to go. When I got to Aunt Vinnie's, I went out to the herb garden and Shenandoah was there waiting to show me something. She was scratching in the tarragon and I saw the head of your cane sticking out. So I picked it up. It wasn't buried or anything—it was just there. So I played with Shenna and then I brought it right up here to you."

Miss Lacey was examining the cane. She held it out to me. "You have young eyes, Lacey—tell me what you see."

I took it from her and saw a deep crack that marred the beak and ran up across the gryphon's head. A dark, sticky stain followed the crack and spread out. Something that resembled dried blood. My hand began to shake.

"It's cracked, and there's blood on it," I said. "When did you lose this, Miss Lacey?"

The lines of her face had deepened. "It's hard to remember. Sometimes I get along quite well without a stick. I think I missed it yesterday. So how could it possibly turn up in Vinnie's herb garden?"

"Shenandoah didn't know it was yours," Egan explained.

She smiled at him. "Thank you for bringing it to me, dear. Now run along and play. I want to talk with Lacey."

When he'd gone she asked a direct question. "Do you think my cane killed Henry?"

"It's possible. You had better turn it over to the police. They can check it for fingerprints, if Egan hasn't spoiled what may have been there."

"I will. But not yet. I need to think about this. There was only one person who was in my house yesterday afternoon and at Vinnie's this morning and that's your mother."

"I won't stay and listen to such nonsense. How could you say this about your own granddaughter?"

She held the cane tightly, studying the carving. "That is not something I care to discuss."

"My mother had nothing to do with the disappearance of your cane or the condition it's in now," I said firmly, hoping she wouldn't notice that I was trembling, as though from a chill.

"As you please, Lacey. I'm sorry you're leaving, but I'm going to keep Egan here with me for a few days."

As another blood heir? I wondered. But that was for Egan's mother to decide.

She sat with her hands folded on the cane, covering the crack, not looking at anything. I left her and went up to my room.

NINETEEN

BACK IN my room I was tempted to sit down with the diary and find out what Ryan had discovered in its pages, but I was too upset to sit still. I decided I must see Laura Kelly at once and find out why Miss Lacey had told me to talk to her.

It took only a few minutes to pack. As I went downstairs with my bag, I could hear Egan playing Royal's drum. I stopped in to tell him that I was going back to Vinnie's because my mother had arrived, and that I was sure he would be brought home soon. He seemed to accept this change of plans, though his look was grave.

Miss Lacey was nowhere in sight when I went to the front door, but before I could go outside, Anne-Marie came from a room down the hall, looking as dark and glowering as Jud Fenwick's portrait.

"How can you leave like this?" she asked abruptly. "You've upset Miss Lacey. I'm afraid she's going to be ill."

"I don't think she will be. That's one tough lady!"

The glower was supplanted by a look of unhappiness, and I knew it had been only a defense. The woman was close to tears again. I'd never have suspected that Anne-Marie was such a sensitive soul.

"I'm sorry," I said. "Miss Lacey has upset me too. I should think you'd be pleased to know that I won't have anything to do with the will she wants to make."

"I only want to see her happy." Anne-Marie took a deep breath and seemed to get her emotions under control. "She isn't going to send me away. She was out of sorts that day and she's said she's sorry."

This was probably because Miss Lacey knew very well how much she needed Anne-Marie. I hoped the woman's devotion would pay off. Though I wouldn't put it past my great-grandmother to leave her nothing at all in her will. I wondered if there'd been many clashes between them over the years.

Before I could go out the door that Anne-Marie held open for me, Miss Lacey came into the hall and thumped the floor with her damaged cane. Apparently, she had recovered from dejection.

"You weren't going to say goodbye?" she demanded.

I reassured her quietly. "It isn't really goodbye. I will see you again very soon, I'm sure."

She dismissed me with a look and spoke to her housekeeper. "Come into the dining room and help me, please. I have decided to change the plans for my will." She looked past Anne-Marie to where I stood in the doorway and spoke cuttingly. "I have decided to leave everything I have to Anne-Marie." She turned regally and walked into the dining room.

Anne-Marie looked after her, stunned and disbelieving. I didn't want to be part of this drama anymore, and I hurried down the steps to my car. For once it seemed my great-grandmother might do the right and generous thing. Now Anne-Marie would be taken care of, and not cast adrift because of some whim of Miss Lacey's.

I was preoccupied and didn't notice until I slid into the driver's seat that someone waited for me in my unlocked car.

"I thought you might give me a lift," Daniel Griffin said, his grin a little cocky.

"Of course," I said, trying not to appear startled. "Where to?"

"Laura Kelly's house. She just phoned and said she wants to talk to me about Henry."

"Fine," I said. "I want to see Laura myself, so we can go together."

He accepted this without comment. During the trip he was silent, looking straight ahead through the windshield.

Laura's house on Bolivar Heights was not more than a ten-minute drive, and by the time I drew up in front of the beautiful white and gray structure, I had collected myself to some extent. This time the upper window where Henry Elliot had stood peering down at me on my last visit was empty. I felt again a sense of shock at the thought of what had happened to him. It was frightening to think that Miss Lacey's cane might have been used to kill him.

Laura greeted us in her usual friendly fashion, and, since the early afternoon was sunny and warm, she led us to the far, open corner that looked out over fields where an army had once set its tents. Daniel and I sat down in wicker chairs. Laura leaned against the white railing. I could see the distant roofs of Harpers Ferry scattered among budding trees before the land dropped out of sight. Only the Potomac was visible from where I sat. The air was still, the view peaceful, and I began to relax.

Laura started without preliminaries. "I've been thinking about Henry's last day here, Daniel—though I haven't said anything about this until now. He told me he knew what had happened to his brother—that he knew how Brad had died. Something that had happened on Virginius Island. I tried to get him to tell me more, but he wouldn't. I've wondered if Brad's body might be buried there."

I gasped, and Laura gave me a sympathetic look and went on.

"I've wondered if your father's body was what Henry was looking for on the island, Lacey. He was talking wildly, his thoughts shooting off in all directions. He refused to say any more and rushed upstairs. That was just before you arrived yesterday and then, of course, that was the last time I saw him."

"He was drunk," Daniel said decisively.

"No more than usual, Dan. Just enough to go spreading a story around town that was *asking* for trouble."

"Why at this late date?" Daniel wondered.

Laura glanced at him. "Because you're here, perhaps. Some sort of conscience must have been weighing on him over the years."

"Do you think *Henry* might have killed his brother?" Daniel asked. "They didn't like each other. They often fought."

"They were very different, and Henry was jealous of Brad, but I don't think he had enough passion in him to kill anyone."

Daniel's eyes were bright with amusement. "I remember that Henry had a passion for *you* at one time."

"And for a few other women," Laura said dryly. "Including Ardra. He was like Brad in that way. And he always wanted Brad's women."

"When I saw Miss Lacey just now, she told me to ask you what happened to my father. What did she mean?" I asked.

Laura shook her head at me. "I've already told you what I know. Maybe she was just trying to divert you."

Daniel returned to the subject of Henry. "Sometimes I've wondered if being drunk was part of an act for him. What if he only suspected what had happened to Brad, and was trying to smoke out his killer?"

"If that's true, he may have succeeded."

Daniel looked off toward the rooftops of Harpers Ferry, seeming to speak his thoughts aloud. "Maybe I could try the same tactic. That is, spread the word that I know who killed Henry."

"I don't like that idea at all," Laura said firmly. "Now that you've come home—"

"*Home!* I have no home. I came here to find out the truth and clear up the lies that were told about me. All that fake evidence that was used against me ruined my life."

"What was the evidence?" I asked. "I know that people

believed what they wanted to believe, but was there anything else?"

"Talk! Just plenty of useless, malicious talk. I left under a cloud, but I left to save myself from being arrested."

Laura moved from the railing and sat down in a chair beside Daniel. "There's something more I should tell you. It's something I've kept silent about because there was no point in telling anyone. But perhaps you'll make something of it now."

"Go on," Daniel said, suddenly alert.

"This goes back to when Caryl was born. Brad came to see me almost a week later. He wanted to give the baby away. He asked me to keep her secretly until he found a family that would adopt her. Of course I refused. Brad had an obsession about keeping what had happened quiet. He was trying desperately to move beyond the disgrace of having seduced his wife's sister and gotten her pregnant. Unrealistic, of course. The very next day after he came to see me, he disappeared and I never saw him again. I have a strong feeling that something happened on Virginius Island—and now Henry has been killed on the island. But the baby was never given away, and Caryl grew up in a loving family."

I said nothing about what Vinnie had revealed to me, and instead told them about Miss Lacey's cane and how it had been found in Vinnie's garden. "It isn't likely that Vinnie put it there—but do you think someone is trying to involve her?" I carefully avoided Miss Lacey's outrageous comment about my mother.

"We're getting close," Daniel said. "History has begun to repeat itself."

When the telephone rang inside the house, Laura went to answer it, and I spoke to Daniel.

"It could be dangerous for you if you do what you suggested and tell people you know who killed Henry."

"I'm not all that excited about staying alive, and besides, I'm not Henry. I'd keep looking over my shoulder and I wouldn't get drunk."

"Please take care of yourself. Egan needs you," I said. "And I do too."

He had a wonderful smile that I'd never seen before. "Thank you, Granddaughter."

"That's Ryan," Laura said, returning. "He has been trying to track you down, Lacey. Will you take the call inside?"

When I picked up the phone, Ryan spoke quickly. "You'd better come back to Vinnie's, Lacey. There's trouble brewing with your mother. I think you should be here."

I didn't ask any questions. I just told him I'd come at once. After I'd explained to Laura and Daniel that Ryan needed to see me, I hurried out to my car.

When I reached Vinnie's, I was relieved to find Ryan waiting for me on the front porch.

"I wanted to prepare you," he said. "Your mother is very upset. She wants to do something Vinnie thinks she shouldn't. She wants to talk to her sister."

"That doesn't sound unreasonable. Why shouldn't she talk to Ardra? After all these years, surely—"

Ryan took my hand, quieting me. "When someone has held anger and resentment in for years, as your mother has, all that negative emotion can begin to fester. So Vinnie's trying to keep your mother from confronting her sister. Vinnie thinks Ardra shouldn't be forced to face Amelia because of mistakes Ardra made when she was so much younger."

I could guess why Vinnie was trying to protect Ardra. She believed she knew what Ardra had done—and if my mother turned on her sister, who could anticipate what might happen? But I couldn't say this to anyone. Not yet.

"What about Caryl?" I asked. "Can't she help?"

"She's the only one working at the shop, so she's out of it right now. Vinnie and I hoped you might talk to your mother before things get out of hand."

"I'm not sure Mother will listen to anything I say. I've begun to realize how little I really know her. But I'll try anyway."

"What about you, Lacey? Are you all right?"

"I'm frightened. I feel as if there's someone out there watching us."

"I know that feeling." He held me and I put my head against his shoulder. His arms were strong, and I actually felt safe for just a moment. Knowing I had to go to my mother, I reluctantly pulled away, but not before kissing his mouth softly.

Ryan came with me down the hall and left me at the door of my room. I tapped and went in. Mother was standing at the side door looking out into the sunny garden. The rigid set of her shoulders told me how tense she was.

"Come and sit down," I said, and drew her toward the comfortable armchair. She had picked up the rose quartz pebble and was tossing it angrily back and forth between her hands. If rose quartz had a calming effect, she wasn't allowing it to work!

I pulled the desk chair over and sat before her, knee to knee. Then I took one of her hands in mine. "Ryan says you want to have something out with your sister. Can you tell me about it?"

She pulled away, tossing the pink stone again, perhaps unaware of what she was doing. "Listen to me, Lacey! You've never known what I went through before we left Harpers Ferry. When your father and my sister had an affair, I held back everything I was feeling. I was in love with Brad then and I thought his fling with my seductive, giddy little sister was a travesty, but I still wanted him to come back to me. I used to be jealous of the love Vinnie gave Ardra, but I know now that Ardra needed her, because our mother had so little outward love to give."

She was silent for a moment, then quieted her hands and breathed deeply. The effort didn't help—I watched as her anger surged up again.

"Now I want everything in the open! It's time for me to confront Ardra and see to it that she understands just what she did. She's never faced up to that. Not even when Caryl was born."

I tried to distract her. "What about you and Ida? When people talk about my grandmother, they always sound vague. And what about my grandfather—did he love Ida?"

"She was his wife, and I think she was good for him. She knew he'd been in love with Laura before he married her. He was a restless, passionate man and quick to anger. Perhaps he thought he would find peace with my mother."

"He's probably calmed down by this time," I said, though I actually wasn't too sure. "I like him. I'm glad I came here and am beginning to know and understand all these things about our past. Now that we're finally talking about all this, can you tell me what happened before you left Harpers Ferry?"

She didn't want her own anger to be diluted, but perhaps she knew that by this time she owed me the truth.

"Ardra's interest in Brad didn't last. I never thought it would, but I didn't realize how much she'd begun to hate him. Of course my mother was under my father's thumb, and she wasn't any help. He was playing the outraged father. Sometimes I've thought that he really did kill Brad. It was a terrible mess, and I couldn't speak my mind to Ardra then. She was my little sister and I somehow felt guilty, as though I could have prevented all this from happening if I'd only been a better wife or a more exciting companion. Now therapists and psychologists write books to help women turn self-blame into healthy anger, but I had no such tools then. I was alone with my shame and my doubt."

Carefully, as though it mattered, Mother set the rose quartz on the table, and folded her hands more calmly. I waited for what would come next.

"What I did," she said after a pause, "was to suppress my desire to tell Ardra what I thought of her behavior. I never tried to confront Brad, either. Then, suddenly, he was dead and it was too late."

"Vinnie told me you left after Caryl was born?"

"That's right, everything seemed to be happening so fast. I still loved your father, I suppose, and I had you to think about. I didn't know what to do. My father was outraged by all this and Vinnie, for once in her life, was equally stirred up. My father wanted to see Brad punished, but Vinnie's only desire was to protect her wayward young niece. Vinnie thinks Ardra killed Brad. She hasn't said so, but I know she does."

"What do *you* think?"

She didn't answer directly. "People were saying that my father killed Brad. And then *he* disappeared too. Less than a week later, my mother killed herself. After that, all I wanted was to get as far away from here as I could and take you with me. Everyone had acted so badly, including my grandmother. I couldn't bear to face anything. So I took you to Charlottesville and erased the past. In some ways I've never regretted that. Though my mother's death added to my feeling of desperate grief. At the time I blamed myself for that too. But now I know the responsibility for all this unhappiness rests with Ardra."

Her eyes looked a little wild and her mouth twisted into a grimace. This time I took both her hands and held them tightly. "Stop it! There's no use in venting all your years of suppressed anger on poor Ardra now. I don't think she's as culpable as you've suspected."

I wasn't sure I believed my own words, but I had to keep my mother away from Ardra until she was calm again and more like the reasonable woman I knew.

This began to happen more quickly than I expected it to, or perhaps she'd just become so practiced in wearing a mask that she could put it on at will. Quietly, she drew her hands away and began to talk about the past two days.

"I haven't told you everything, Lacey. I didn't arrive in Harpers Ferry this morning. After you phoned me at home yesterday, I packed my suitcase and drove up here. I stayed last night at Hilltop House."

"Miss Lacey told me. She said that you'd come to see her late yesterday afternoon. But why?"

"I knew you were staying with her and it was you I was coming to get. But the person I wanted to find was Henry. I needed to see him before I talked to anyone else. I thought he might be there."

"Henry! But why would you want to see him?" A feeling of new anxiety swept through me, as I watched her pull a sweater around her shoulders.

"After you left for Harpers Ferry, I phoned Vinnie and asked her to fill me in on what was happening. I didn't tell her that you were on your way. Among other things, she said that Henry was in town and behaving in a strange manner that didn't seem entirely due to liquor. I'd always suspected that Henry knew more about Brad's disappearance than he let on. So I decided to confront him too and get him to talk to me."

"Did you see him yesterday?"

"No. Grandmother told me he was staying at Laura's, but when I got there he'd apparently gone out. Laura wasn't home either."

"Miss Lacey didn't mention that you were looking for Henry when I spoke with her earlier."

"I asked her not to. I wanted to finish what I had to do before anyone knew I was here. But I had no luck in finding Henry."

"And now he's dead. You've heard about that?"

"Vinnie told me this morning. Then I was frightened all over again. Lacey, I want you to come back to Charlottesville with me right away. Neither of us must stay here any longer."

"I don't want to leave," I said.

She studied me thoughtfully. "It's this young man, Ryan, isn't it?"

I wasn't ready for confidences. "Ryan and I found Henry's body. And now that they suspect that it was murder, the police will want me around for more questioning. But if you'd rather not stay—"

"I'll stay until we can leave here together." She looked startled as someone knocked on the door, but it was only Vinnie.

"Are you all right, Amelia?" she asked, coming into the room.

My mother avoided her eyes. "I don't suppose I'll be all right until I've talked to Ardra. It won't be pleasant, but it must be done."

So she hadn't been deflected from her purpose, after all.

Vinnie prickled. "What good will that do? I'm sure she's suffered enough over all that happened. Now she has Caryl for consolation, and she's made a good life for herself. I don't want you to upset her. Ardra's health is frail, and she hasn't the strength to face the storm you might let loose. So I've asked Caryl to close the shop for a few days and take her mother away."

"No! I *must* see her."

"I don't think Ardra wants to see you, Amelia. I'll ask Jasmine to bring a tray so that you and Lacey can have your lunch in here."

Before my mother could answer, there was a tap at the door. When I went to open it, I found Ardra standing there. She looked white and uncertain as she walked past me into the room to face her sister.

"Amelia," she said—just her name. Then, "I'm sorry you've been so ill."

Mother didn't move from her chair, and her eyes never left Ardra's face, though she didn't speak. As I watched, I could see her anger fading. In her resentful memories, she must never have imagined that her once attractive, flirtatious sister would look like this.

Trembling, Ardra dropped down on the edge of the bed, unable to meet her sister's level gaze. When she spoke, her voice was far from steady.

"There's nothing you can say to me that I haven't said to myself, Amelia. I haven't any excuses. I was young and self-centered and very foolish."

Mother nodded gravely. "You were all of those things. You thought Brad considerate and kind—understanding. And, of course, not understood by me. *I* remember. He liked women, and he liked women to like him. But then he always needed someone new to build up the excitement again and to reassure him of his own charm and worth."

Ardra's eyes misted, and given another moment, I think she would have gone to put her arm around Amelia. But my mother wanted none of that.

"I expected to have a great deal of anger to vent when I saw you again, Ardra. But now I only feel sorry for you. We still have our relationships with Brad in common. Only our feelings for him have turned to bitterness and regret. Am I right?"

Ardra covered her face with her hands and didn't answer.

Vinnie had stood apart, listening anxiously. Now she went to Ardra. "Come along, dear. It's nearly time for lunch."

They went out together, and I put my arms around my mother. "I'm proud of you. You must have resented her terribly over the years—perhaps hated her. But you handled yourself well just now."

"I handled nothing. I've done nothing for you to be proud of. I could see that she'd be too easy to demolish. She's punished herself enough in her thoughts, and she's done all the harm she will ever do."

How little I'd known my mother. A child takes a parent for granted, and I'd never dreamed of the life of suffering that had been held away from me. There had always been a barrier I couldn't cross, but now perhaps we could be friends on a more mature and equal level.

She was still thinking about Ardra, and she mused aloud. "When I was young, I was jealous of the way Vinnie always sided with my sister and protected her. She was more like Vinnie's child than like our mother's. Since I've come here nothing has changed. I suppose Vinnie needs someone to depend on her, to need *her*. That's something she never had from me."

Ryan brought our lunch on a tray and stayed to eat with us. I wanted to tell him what had just happened, but that would have to wait. We chatted with my mother as we ate and then left her to rest.

One of the things I liked about Ryan was his enthusiasm. Much of the time he was a quiet man, but he could light up when action was needed. Something had sparked this quality in him now.

"I've been tracking down everyone who knew Henry Elliot," he said as we walked down the hall, "and I have an interesting lead. I may be onto something—so will you come with me, Lacey?"

His excitement touched me and of course I would go with him anytime, anywhere.

TWENTY

★ ★
★ ★ ★ ★
★ ★ ★ ★ ★
★ ★ ★ ★ ★
★ ★ ★ ★

CHARLES TOWN was another old community in West Virginia, and only a few miles west of Harpers Ferry. It had long been famous for its racetrack and its fine old houses, many of which had been built in the previous century. And, of course, John Brown's trial had been held there—and his execution. The building Ryan drove us to was recent and modern—a large single-story white structure with aluminum siding and big glass windows all around. It belonged to the National Park Service and housed the Division of Conservation. Its special function was to preserve historical artifacts that were on exhibit in Park sites around the country.

This was where Henry had worked for several years as a custodian. The building was divided into spacious labs that handled various parts of the preservation process. Valuable artifacts were sent here to be worked on, and the division also provided information to anyone who needed it on the mounting of historic objects for display, on pest control, and on how to best exhibit such treasures. Royal Fenwick's drum was to be repaired here for Miss Lacey, who was a special patron. Eventually, the drum would go to a museum in Shepherdstown.

The men and women who worked here were devoted to repairing and preserving the remarkable objects that came to them out of history. Ryan, apparently, was a frequent visitor, since there were always bits of information to be picked up when local artifacts arrived.

On the drive to Charles Town, he'd told me that one of the lab heads, Stan Wallace, had been especially kind to Henry Elliot. Henry had counted on him as a friend, and, upon hearing of Henry's death, Stan had called Laura right away. What had come out of the conversation had caused Laura to call Ryan and suggest that he have a talk with Stan. What she'd reported had stirred Ryan's curiosity.

The building was more than twenty thousand square feet in size, and we walked down a long corridor to the lab where Stan worked. It was a big white room, brightly lighted, though without glare, offering clear light for the fine work that might be required. The walls were covered with useful shelves and cupboards, with framed posters interspersed here and there. Several long tables held artifacts that were being worked on.

Stan was a tall, dark-haired man with a friendly manner. Clearly he had been fond of Henry and willing to listen to his occasional outpourings. Not that Henry had revealed many details, Stan told us. "I think he must have carried something on his conscience for years. Secrets, perhaps, that contributed to his drinking."

Stan found chairs for us near a table where two large elephant's feet showed evidence of crumbling. They were trophies from Theodore Roosevelt's house on Long Island, Stan told us, and then returned to the subject of Henry, while I thought about the poor elephant.

Henry had been obsessed by a desire to recover something from Virginius Island that had been long buried there. He talked to Stan about a crime that he believed had been committed, though he never explained what it was. "I thought he was fantasizing some of the time and I didn't press him for details," Stan said. "I guess I thought he'd tell me if he wanted me to know."

He pushed one of the hollow feet out of the way and sat on a corner of the table as he talked.

"Henry told me he was going to the island to do some digging—so that he would have something to show the police. He wasn't secretive about what he meant to do, so someone might have heard about his plan and followed him. This morning I told the local Park rangers all that he'd said and they're off on a digging expedition of their own around the place where Henry was found. I doubt that they'll turn up anything of interest, since I couldn't tell them what to look for."

Ryan explained that Henry was my uncle—Brad Elliot's brother.

"Do you think it's possible that Henry might have been looking for my father's body?" I asked.

Stan looked startled. "He never indicated what he was digging for, as I said, and with all the work that has been done on the island in recent years, I should think anything as large as a body would have been found."

I felt increasingly uncomfortable as I listened. It was hard to believe that we were sitting here talking calmly about a buried body. I had no real feelings for my father, but what had happened to Henry had made death seem close and very real.

"It seems more likely," Ryan said, "that Henry was searching for something else—some smaller object that he knew was buried on the island in a certain place."

None of this helped very much, though we agreed it might provide the motive behind Henry's killing. We thanked Stan, who walked us out. On the way he stopped beside a dressmaker's form on which a man's coat from another century had been placed. The material was a fine, dark blue wool, made with the short shoulder cape that had once been the fashion.

"You might be interested in this, Miss Elliot," Stan said. "It was a gift from Mrs. Lacey Enright to a local museum. We're working on some fraying and mending a few moth holes. The coat belonged to Royal Fenwick—a member of your family, I believe."

More than once since I'd come to Harpers Ferry I'd felt a

pull toward those who'd lived more than a hundred years
before my time. I touched the coat lightly before we walked on
past other objects that were here for repair. A handsome
Georgian mirror lay on a table, its varnish being restored. A
pair of men's dress slippers had been worn by George Washington. A beautiful pictorial hand-weaving of a Blue Ridge
Mountain scene was being worked on by a young woman
intent upon her needle.

When we walked out to Ryan's car, I could sense his disap-
pointment. On the drive back to Harpers Ferry, he put this
feeling into words.

"I'd hoped for more. Henry evidently had something on his
mind, but he didn't give Stan enough information. I have a
feeling that there's a lead there that we're missing, but I don't
know what it is. What are you planning to do now, Lacey?"

"I have the diary you gave me. I don't want to postpone
reading it any longer."

Ryan had an errand to do in the Lower Town, and when
he'd dropped me off at Vinnie's, I went straight to my room.
There I found a note from Vinnie. She had a room for Amelia
now, and she had moved her into it. "Let her rest for a while,"
the note ended, "she's very tired."

I was glad to be alone. I sat down near a window where the
light was good, and held the small volume with its violets and
four-leaf clovers in my hands for a few moments before I
began to read. Long ago Sarah Lang had held this book as I
was doing, and had written down her feelings and thoughts. It
was hard to believe that she'd been the baby born to Ellen
Fenwick.

Sarah had apparently led a happy life with Orin Lang and
his wife. I couldn't tell by reading her words whether she had
ever been told the story of her real mother's ordeal or of her
adopted father's part in the tragedy. It was clear that she loved
her adoptive parents.

I skimmed through some of the description of her younger
years. When she was twelve Orin had moved the two of them

to a Pennsylvania town where he'd opened a small grocery store. Sarah enjoyed new friends, parties, a beau or two. She seemed a happy, bright young girl who savored her life and enjoyed writing about its small happenings. Though he did well, Orin was homesick for Jefferson County, and at the end of the diary Sarah wrote that her father was returning to live in Charles Town, while she was to be married and would be moving north with her husband to Winnipeg, Canada. There she promised to start a new diary that would record her married life as Mrs. Philip St. Pol. She was leaving this book behind with her father. Perhaps there were bits in the diary that she hadn't wanted her new husband to read.

I came to the end, regretful that I must let Sarah go and never know what became of her. The book seemed light in my hands to carry all those hours of a young life. As I sat holding it and wondering about her, two things echoed in my mind: Winnipeg, Canada, and the name St. Pol. Hadn't Anne-Marie St. Pol come here from Winnipeg? Someone had mentioned that once. Was it possible that there was a connection of some sort? Could Anne-Marie have learned the story of her family's connection with the Fenwicks and come here deliberately to seek out Miss Lacey and establish her own ties with the past? I wondered. She was fairly young when she came here thirty-five years ago.

If Miss Lacey knew this, why had she never mentioned it?

I needed to see her at once. I told Vinnie where I was going and drove up to my great-grandmother's house.

The door was unlocked when I arrived, and since no one answered my knock, I let myself in. When I looked into the formal parlor, I found my great-grandmother sitting on the sofa holding a framed photograph in her hands. After the way we had parted this morning, I wasn't sure she would be pleased to see me, and I hesitated in the doorway.

"May I talk with you a moment?" I asked.

Wordlessly, she held the picture out to me. I took it, but I didn't recognize the face of the woman who sat, back erect, staring into the camera's lens.

"That's your grandmother," she said. "My daughter, Ida Enright Griffin. I've been thinking about how we all failed her. If I'd been more sensitive to what she was going through, she might be alive now."

For the first time I recognized in Lacey Enright a woman totally alone. She had never involved herself with others to any great extent—it was obvious that Vinnie and Ardra and Caryl had no real relationship with her. I doubted that generosity and compassion had ever been part of her character. Perhaps in these later years she was realizing how much she had lost. I wondered if that was the reason she was trying to coax Egan into loving her and even trying to bribe me into staying close.

"Sit down," she said, taking back the picture.

For once she was not dressed in one of her long, colorful gowns, but wore brown pants with a creamy turtleneck that helped hide the folds of her neck. "I've been working in the garden this afternoon. With spring already here, I have a great deal of catching up to do." She spoke in an almost absent manner, as though something in her had given up.

I sat beside her on the sofa and held out the diary. "This is a diary that Sarah Lang kept—Ellen Fenwick's daughter. It has just surfaced in a collection of papers that were left to Laura Kelly. She showed it to Ryan and he gave it to me."

Miss Lacey took the book from me. "No, I didn't know about this one."

"At the end, Sarah talks about moving to Winnipeg, Canada, with her new husband, Philip St. Pol."

"You've made the connection, haven't you? I'm not surprised."

"It seemed obvious as soon as I read what Sarah had written. Did you know she was adopted by Orin Lang, one of the deserters who attacked Ellen?"

Miss Lacey took the book from me calmly. "I know. But I didn't know that this diary still existed. Sarah was Anne-Marie's mother's great-grandmother. When her mother died,

Anne-Marie found the diaries Sarah had kept during her life in Winnipeg, and she came to Harpers Ferry to find anyone who might be left of her family. She brought one of the diaries to show me when she first came to see me all those years ago. She no longer had any family left, and I felt sorry for her, and curious about all that past history. In the diary I read, Sarah had set down the story of her mother's rape and death, as it had been told to her by her guilt-ridden father when he was dying. How do you like sharing a common bloodline with Anne-Marie?"

I was intrigued and interested. Now I could better understand Anne-Marie's obsession with Ellen's room upstairs and her air of proprietorship toward Miss Lacey. I could even understand what I'd thought was jealousy toward me and my family.

"It's only right that you leave this house to Anne-Marie, as you intend to do," I said. "She'll value it and appreciate it more than anyone else."

"Oh, that!" Miss Lacey spoke carelessly. "I made out a new will to spite you, but Anne-Marie knows I'd never let it stand. Sarah was born a bastard, the daughter of a criminal. This historic house is not going to anyone of that bloodline!"

Her words shocked me, and a new sympathy for Anne-Marie began to stir.

But before I could speak, Miss Lacey looked toward the door to the hall. "Come in, Anne-Marie. You've been listening, haven't you? Lacey has brought me something that may interest you."

Anne-Marie came into the room boldly and took the book Miss Lacey held out. She had, indeed, heard every word, and I could sense the anger welling up in her.

Like Miss Lacey, she wore slacks and had put on a navy blue windbreaker. Out of her familiar black clothes, she looked stronger, somehow, and more formidable than ever. Anne-Marie could take care of herself, and for just a moment I felt a little afraid for Miss Lacey. Anger that had festered for so many years might be dangerous.

When she spoke, her voice rose to a pitch I'd never heard in her before. For her, there was no one else in the room but Miss Lacey.

"I served you faithfully, loyally for thirty-five years. I've listened to you when I shouldn't have. I didn't marry Henry Elliot when we were in love because you insisted that it would be a mistake."

I gasped. This I had never expected—Anne-Marie and Henry!

Miss Lacey thumped her cane on the floor indignantly. "You should thank me. Look how he turned out."

Anger was growing into rage. For a moment I thought she would strike Miss Lacey, and I made a move to prevent this. But she turned violently away and stormed out of the room— out of the house. I ran after her and watched her climb into Miss Lacey's car.

My great-grandmother had followed me, and I saw by her face that she knew she had gone too far.

"We must go after her!" Miss Lacey cried. "Whatever she intends, we must stop her. She may harm herself."

So my great-grandmother cared something about Anne-Marie, after all. Or did she only need her to make her own life comfortable?

Miss Lacey took my arm and we went down the steps and out to my car together. As I turned the key in the ignition, I looked back at the house. Egan stood at the gallery railing, watching.

"Tell Grandpa Daniel that we need him!" I called. But he only watched solemnly as I pulled the car away from the curb and set out after Anne-Marie.

I KEPT a discreet distance behind the other car, and hoped that Anne-Marie wouldn't notice us. She drove down to the Lower Town and out Shenandoah Street to where Virginius Island stretched along the shore, separated from land by the narrow canal.

When she was across, we left my car and went after her on foot. She didn't go far—only to the pit in the ground, once the foundation of a factory, where Ryan and I had found Henry. I knew we were about to learn why Henry had come here, and I felt a chill that had nothing to do with the air around me and the darkening evening.

Anne-Marie seemed to be searching for something on the ground. After a few moments she pulled a garden trowel from her coat pocket, knelt beside a part of the old brick foundation, and began to dig into the silt-covered bricks at the base of the structure.

Miss Lacey and I had crouched behind some tall bushes, and she gripped my arm so tightly that I winced. After several moments of digging, a brick came loose, and Anne-Marie reached into the hollow. When she stood up, she held in her hand what appeared to be a rotting leather pouch. She held it away from her clothes and shook dirt loose from its sides. Then she gingerly slid her hand into the pouch and drew out an ancient pistol.

Miss Lacey cried out and stepped from behind the bushes. I followed her, and Anne-Marie stared at us in angry surprise.

"Where did *you* come from?"

Miss Lacey spoke with as much dignity as she would have assumed at home. "That gun belonged to Royal Fenwick. It's been missing for thirty years."

"You shouldn't have followed me." The anger was gone and something cold and deadly had taken its place. She spoke directly to Miss Lacey. "You've made your last mistake."

I put an arm protectively around my great-grandmother's shoulders and tried to speak as calmly as I could to Anne-Marie.

"You weren't yourself back at the house. Miss Lacey was worried about you."

"Do you know why this pistol was here?" Anne-Marie went on, ignoring my feeble words. "It's the gun I used to kill Brad Elliot. Henry buried it here so it wouldn't be found. I wanted him to throw it into the canal, but Henry could be cunning. He took my handbag to protect the gun. I suspect that he thought there might be some identifying traces of me on it—and perhaps he'd need to produce it sometime in order to save his own neck. I think that's what he meant to do yesterday. But I followed him here."

"*You* killed both Brad and Henry?" Miss Lacey said softly. She sagged a little in the circle of my arm and I sensed her growing weakness.

"He was going to talk, so I had to stop him. I killed him with your cane, Miss Lacey—a sort of poetic justice. Then I added the touch of leaving it in Vinnie's herb garden. I could imagine them all trying to figure that out! Only Egan found it first."

Perhaps the worst part of what was happening was that Anne-Marie was enjoying herself, and that very fact frightened me. I didn't know what wild move she might make next, and I had to keep her talking.

"What happened when my father died?" I asked, grateful that my voice managed not to tremble.

Now she seemed to enjoy her revelations all the more. "The night Brad died, he brought Ardra's baby to the island. He told Henry he was meeting someone who would take her away and adopt her. All he cared about was keeping his ugly secret from being revealed. Henry and I were in love in those days, and Henry was a lot better man than his brother was. Henry knew that what Brad was doing was wrong, and we came here together to stop him. Those two had a terrible fight. Brad was out-of-his-head crazy, and I think he might have killed Henry, who wasn't nearly as strong—except for me. I'd brought that old Civil War pistol along—it was the only weapon I could think of, and I knew Miss Lacey was proud of it and had kept it in firing condition.

"When Brad knocked Henry down and then picked up a heavy branch to use as a club to finish him off, I shot him." She waved the ancient gun at us wildly. "It was so easy. I don't know how I did it—one shot and he was dead. Henry got his wind back and we dragged Brad's body across the island and rolled it into the river. The Shenandoah was wild that night and the body disappeared from sight in minutes. I guess the river tore his coat from him and that's how it came to be found on that rock downriver a couple of days later. Nothing else was ever seen of him again.

"Henry said we must get the baby and take it home. But I knew from the way he spoke that everything was over between us. I'd saved his life by killing his brother—and in some twisted way he could never forgive me for that. So it wasn't just you, Miss Lacey, who kept me from marrying Henry."

This time I had heard the true story, and now I was more afraid than ever of what Anne-Marie might do. "Let's go home," I said to Miss Lacey.

Anne-Marie seemed not to hear me, and Miss Lacey didn't move.

"Henry buried the gun right down there, and I thought it would be safe enough behind a brick in the wall. Maybe better than throwing it into the canal, which could be dragged. I brought the baby out from under the stone arch where Brad had placed her, and we took her back to Vinnie's. We left her inside the back door, and Ardra must have found her and put her into her crib."

"What about whoever it was that was supposed to meet Brad on the island?" I asked quietly.

"Who knows if there was such a person? Who knows what Brad meant to do? I think he was a little crazy that night. Anyway, everything stayed quiet for the next thirty years. Daniel was being blamed, and that was fine with me. Until Henry began to talk about opening it all up and telling the truth, so Daniel wouldn't be blamed anymore. Now Henry won't tell and I have the gun that might have incriminated me. I also have a big debt to pay off with you, Miss Lacey."

Miss Lacey roused herself and stepped away from my arm. "I took you in. I gave you a home for all these years."

"And you treated me like a servant! There's Fenwick blood in my veins too. I'm sorry you're in the middle of this, Lacey, but I don't have a choice now."

She still had the old gun in her hands, and she moved so quickly that I couldn't escape the blow when it came. The butt of the pistol struck my head, and I went down, half-stunned. I sensed everything in a kind of fog—my throbbing head, the wetness on my cheek. I was vaguely aware that Anne-Marie had Miss Lacey by the arm and was pulling her across the island toward the river. I was also aware of a rising moon lighting the sky, but I couldn't move, couldn't even cry out.

When I heard feet pounding across the bridge, I tried to sit up. Ryan and Daniel Griffin were running—Ryan toward me, and Daniel to where Anne-Marie had dragged Miss Lacey halfway across the island. Ryan knelt beside me and all I wanted was the safety of his arms around me, holding me in love and concern.

Somehow I heard enough to know that Daniel had caught Anne-Marie, and that Miss Lacey was returning with them to where Ryan knelt beside me. She seemed to have recovered her strength and courage, and she came to me at once.

"Dear Lacey!" she cried. "You're hurt. We must take care of you—"

"Listen!" I said. I didn't want to miss what Daniel was saying. His words cut through my foggy brain.

"Anne-Marie St. Pol, we're holding you for the murders of Brad Elliot and his brother, Henry."

He was making a citizen's arrest! My brain cleared and I tried to stand up, but Ryan pushed me down gently.

Anne-Marie's sudden movement startled us all. She twisted away from Daniel and ran—not toward the bridge, but across the island to the river. The same course she had been forcing Miss Lacey to take. When she reached the bank she kicked off her shoes and plunged into the water, swimming with strong, sure strokes toward the rapids. A wind had come up and I could hear the rushing of the water in its ready response.

Daniel started after her, but Ryan called out to him. "Wait, Dan! The current out there can be wild. She'll drown before she can break free of it. She knows what she's doing. She's made her choice."

From where I was I couldn't see the water, but as I listened intently I heard a cry that rose above the river sounds—a human voice. And after that only the river spoke.

Miss Lacey began to cry and Daniel put an arm about her, steadying her. "We must get you home. We'll call the police from there." He held her gently as she dropped against him, and he gave us a look as he took her over the bridge—a look that was somehow filled with sadness, with triumph, with hope.

Ryan was still holding me. "A visit to the hospital comes next for you," he said.

But I was already feeling better—just shaky. "If you'll drive me to Vinnie's, she'll take care of my cut, and I promise I'll see a doctor tomorrow."

He wiped my cheek with a clean handkerchief. The bleeding had stopped, so I probably wasn't seriously hurt. After he'd kissed me—very gently this time—we too went back across the bridge to Ryan's car.

AFTERWORD

IN HER new will Miss Lacey left everything to her grand-daughter Amelia Elliot. My mother decided that she didn't want to live in Charlottesville without me, and she has moved in with Miss Lacey. My mother looks after her now, not as Anne-Marie had done, but in a way that has brought a new caring into Miss Lacey's life.

My dreams have become real. Ryan and I are building our home on Bolivar Heights, not far from Laura Kelly's. I was worried at first about telling Caryl our plans, but she took the news that we would be married with a generosity that is typical of my sister. She had been in love with Ryan, she confessed to me, but she'd known he didn't feel the same way. So I must be happy and not worry about her.

Daniel has stayed on in the cabin behind Miss Lacey's house, and he's doing some wonderful wood carving again, including a new head for Miss Lacey's cane. Not a gryphon—this time he has chosen a phoenix. Egan visits him often and is learning to whittle. Sometimes Daniel calls on Laura Kelly, though he says I must think nothing of that.

My children's book is nearly finished and I've loved telling the story of Harpers Ferry. Ryan thinks my pictorial maps are beautiful. He's especially fond of little houses that seem to be three-dimensional, set along High Street and Potomac and Shenandoah. Once more we are out on the point where the rivers meet and three states touch. Tonight the rivers are quiet, and the Daughter of the Stars glints with light as she flows toward her endless meeting with the Potomac.

Ryan and I are silent, listening to the night and the movement of the water around us. Silent, but very close. I think we are sensing the past and the present as they come together like the rivers and flow into the future.

Not far from here, but long ago in time, there had been a mingling of mist and gunsmoke that drifted across a field, hiding the evidence of a terrible deed. Perhaps only now has that smoke blown away—dispersed at last by the truth. Both the wronged and the guilty can sleep, since the present has paid for the past.

Ryan senses that my thoughts are growing long, and his arm tightens about me. I turn to him, and when he kisses me a promise is made all over again between us. Our closeness and trust are sweet as we two dreamers walk back to Shenandoah and climb the High Street of Harpers Ferry.

About the Author

PHYLLIS A. WHITNEY was born in Yokohama, Japan, of American parents, and has also lived in the Philippines and China. After the death of her father in China, she and her mother returned to the United States, which she saw for the first time when she was fifteen. This early travel has exerted a strong influence on her work; many of her novels are set in areas she has visited in Europe, Africa, and the Orient, as well as in the places she has lived.

Phyllis A. Whitney is the author's maiden name. (The *A* stands for Ayame, which is the Japanese word for "iris.") She is a widow and lives near her daughter in Virginia. In 1975, she was elected president of the Mystery Writers of America, and in 1988 received the organization's Grand Master Award for lifetime achievement. She is also the recipient of the Agatha Award for lifetime achievement given by Malice Domestic.

In 1994, Sisters in Crime awarded her a plaque for "A Woman Who's Made a Difference." This refers to her efforts on behalf of women mystery writers.

Since 1941, when she attained her first hardcover publication, she has become an international success. More than forty million copies of her novels are in print in American paperback editions. Her novels for adults now number thirty-eight, and her devoted following has made best-sellers of these titles, including *Star Flight, The Ebony Swan, Woman Without a Past, The Singing Stones, Rainbow in the Mist, Feather on the Moon, Silversword,* and *Dream of Orchids.*